D1360631

Dreaming in Irish

Sarah-Jane McKenna

Sarah-Jane McKenna

2022

This is a work of fiction. All of the names, characters, organizations, places, and events portrayed in this novel are either products of the author's imagination or are used fictitiously. Any resemblance to real or actual events, locales, or persons, living or dead, is entirely coincidental.

ISBN: 1717248829
ISBN-13: 978-1717248824

PART ONE: JUST LIKE THAT

CHAPTER 1

"I got a message from some hospital in Vermont. Eileen was in an accident, and I was listed as an Emergency Contact. It came in last night; I don't know how I missed it."

"I got the same message, Sean. I'm leaving for the airport in a few minutes; I should be in Vermont by 3:30. Have you tried calling the hospital?"

"No, I called you first. But I'll try there next. Call me from the airport, and I'll let you know what I've found out. Do you think I should tell Mom?"

"She's going to be furious with us, but, no. I think we should wait until we know more. Only if you can avoid her until then, of course. You know she'll read on your face that something's wrong."

"That's true enough. I can be on the road this morning. I just need to sort a few things out. I hope we know something before then though, because Mom should be in that car with me. Kevin too."

"I know. I know. Look, I've got to get going. I'll call you from the airport. Keep trying the hospital."

Kate took a quick shower, packed a suitcase, grabbed her laptop, and headed to Miami International Airport.

✦ ✦ ✦

Sean hung up wishing Margot were home with him. She had crawled out of bed before dawn to make it to some big breakfast meeting downtown. The meetings were all big lately. It was the Mayor's last year in office, and he had a lot of loose ends he wanted tied up before he handed over the keys to City Hall. This meant that all of his senior staff, including Margot, were working triple time.

He swiped through the hundreds of photos that lived on his phone, searching for the last one Eileen had sent him. It was a selfie of her and Molly, taken when they were decorating their Christmas tree. Remnants of hot chocolate and whipped cream adorned their upper lips: matching mustaches atop matching grins. He tapped Molly's nose through the screen, and then Eileen's for good measure. They looked so alike.

Sean was pushing nineteen when Eileen was born and had clear memories of her childhood. Like the Doyles before him, he chose Fordham for college. The summer before his freshman year, he moved into what was then a make-shift garden-floor apartment on Pineapple Street. It was barebones, but afforded a degree of independence for him and a little less chaos for his parents. Busy studying, playing rugby, and running off to whatever part-time job he had at the moment, he still made time to dote on Eileen. Not like Kevin—those two were inseparable—but he and Eileen were tight.

Kevin. His little brother, Eileen's protector, Molly's godfather, and housemate to Sean and Margot. The Kevin zone, on the third floor of 22 Pineapple Street, included a bedroom and bath to the rear, and his version of a man cave—equal parts office, library, and gym—toward the front. On his way down to the shared kitchen and living room on the second floor, Sean had noticed Kevin's door was open and the bed made. Probably out for what had lately become a regular morning walk. Margot was sure Kevin was sneaking out after she and Sean turned in upstairs and enjoying a secret romance. Sean was just as certain Margot was wrong. Daydreaming his way down to the ferry landing and back was more like it.

Sean gazed at the photo, smiling at a memory of trying to teach Eileen how to throw a Frisbee. She was a klutz then and had never really grown out of it. He kissed the screen.

"Please let them be okay."

Sean turned his attention to a hot shower. There was a lot to do, if he wanted to get on the road quickly.

Kevin raised Anya's perfectly manicured hand to his lips and kissed it gallantly. Then he slipped her hand into the pocket of his jacket, and they sat side-by-side on the promenade bench that had become their favorite meeting place. Since running into each other on a slightly drunken Fourth of July, they enjoyed risking discovery by hiding in plain sight.

"So what's on your agenda today?"

"Sean and I are doing a walk-through with the Court Street client. Thanks again for that referral. If everything goes smoothly, we'll be starting the job in two weeks."

"Big bucks?"

"Very big bucks. What we have here is the best of circumstances: a clear calendar at Doyle Contracting meets the deep pockets of a co-op board that wants a new lobby in six weeks. Six weeks…that's premium rates. I love a client in a hurry."

She brushed away the clump of hair that had fallen to the bridge of his glasses. "Smug is not an attractive look on you."

He blushed. "No, I don't suppose it is."

They teased and flirted until Kevin's phone sprang to life.

"We've been found out," he said, winking at Anya. He took the call to the promenade railing. When he turned back to face Anya, the morning's joy was gone from his face.

Kevin shoved his phone in his pocket, and held Anya's hand once more. He filled her in on what little he knew, as they walked together in the direction of Pineapple Street. They said their goodbyes at the corner, and he made a beeline for Number 22.

CHAPTER 2

After making her way through security, Kate wandered around the airport waiting for her flight, watching others waiting for their flights. She had been living in Miami for six years, but she still felt a little out of her element. Flats fishing in the Florida Keys, a hobby pursued at every semester break and more than a few weekends, was the extent of her acclamation to South Florida. Mostly, she counted the days until she could return to civilization, which for her meant New York. A life slightly on hold, but hardly unlived.

She had joined the academic ranks over a decade ago, and done everything possible to position herself for a job back in New York. But those jobs were hard to come by. She was still biding her time teaching in Miami, giving talks at conferences around the globe, and publishing, publishing, publishing. She ran at a pace that was envied by many, and, it had to be said, resented by some. She had hoped for years that something would open up in the City, so she could get back to the place that made the most sense to her. But here it was, another new year recently begun—she couldn't believe January was already over, even if just barely—and a New York return was no closer to being a possibility than it had been the year before, or the one before that.

She found a payphone—unbelievably—and dug a phone card out of her tote. This was one of those rare moments she wished she hadn't ditched her cell phone: the last in a long line of things she had been told she needed, but decided she didn't. It wound up in the kitchen junk drawer with a bunch of stuff that cut her fingers whenever she reached in there. Sean picked up on the first ring: "Kate, I got through to the hospital, but they wouldn't say more than that Eileen and Eric had been in a car accident. Rules about what they can and can't say on a phone, I guess." He paused, and Kate could hear him exhale. "They didn't say anything about Molly being admitted though."

"We are now pre-boarding the nine o'clock flight to Burlington at Gate 7" was her cue to follow the sunburned visitors heading to the snowy north. "Sean, I have to go, they just called my flight. I'll call you from Vermont." She walked down the tunnel, entered the plane, and found her seat.

Kate stayed awake the entire flight. This was a first, and she flew a lot. A friend once dubbed her a 'commuting narcoleptic,' and truer words were seldom spoken. If she wasn't driving, and the vehicle moved, Kate slept. Subways, busses, planes, it didn't matter. But not knowing what awaited her in Vermont had her brain and heart short-circuiting. She couldn't sleep. One minute she thought things would be serious, but recoverable; the next, she thought the worst. Kate's entire *modus operandi* was one of aesthetics and order; making her uniquely suited to research in the arts, but not a lot else.

She admired beauty and could find it as readily in a pattern of schooling fish as at an amateur production of *Our Town*. And, like most professional researchers, she was driven to assembling order from chaos and inclined toward maintaining an emotional distance. Her propensity for logic bordered on the ridiculous, and it was a useless quality under the circumstances. If anything, it made her imagine the worst. The only logical explanation for her being asked to come to the hospital, while being told nothing about Eileen's condition, was the one thing she was absolutely incapable of comprehending. She looked through the window, into a loose line of clouds, and saw Eileen there.

Eileen was, in many ways, the love of Kate's life and the thought of her in pain pushed the limits of what Kate could handle. Born when Kate was already thirteen-years old, she sometimes thought Eileen was the reason she decided not to have children of her own. No kids: a choice that ended more than one relationship, but one she had never regretted. She felt she already was a mother. To Eileen. Eileen had been a beautiful child and an opinionated, stubborn, and brash teenager. She was every bit a Doyle. But by the time Eileen was seven, Kate was out of the house for good. Eileen's teen years were spent with Kate largely absent. They stayed in touch by phone and with summer visits, but Kate was immersed in graduate school by the time Eileen was in high school, and living in Florida by the time Eileen married Eric and moved to Vermont in search of a life closer to the earth than New York City afforded. Kate became a frequent visitor to Vermont, even more so since the birth of her goddaughter, Molly. Eric and Eileen seemed to have a nice life up there and never gave any indication of wanting to head back to the big city. Molly was born early in their marriage, but they settled into parenthood as easily as they did married life. The little girl was now a sweet, huggy, two-year old, filled with curiosity and energy, and beginning to talk more every day. She looked a lot like her mother at that age too, Kate thought. She stared out the window, her mind racing a mile a minute. Tears fell, as the flight attendants announced that passengers should prepare for landing.

The plane drifted downward, and Kate was soon walking through Burlington Airport for the first time. She usually flew into Boston and drove over. Stretching out the kinks from her 5' 10" frame with every step, Kate looked around the little airport, and put her ever-present tote on the floor. She hoped that touching her toes a few times and reaching for the ceiling might help her focus on the physical rather than mental. She wished for a quiet mind, shook out her hands and feet, grabbed her tote and carry-on, and headed outside to the taxi stand. She was at the hospital in twenty minutes.

"I'm looking for my sister, Eileen Johnson. I got a message that she was admitted after an accident."

The woman at the Information Desk hit her keyboard a few times and directed Kate to the fifth floor, where a nurse there hit a few buttons on his computer and then, Kate thought—but couldn't be 100% sure—averted eye contact.

"Somebody will be with you in just a few minutes. Can I offer you a cup of coffee or a water?," he asked the center of her face. Kate passed on the offer, but then asked if she could have any information on Eileen's condition. "I can only tell you that she was admitted with her husband last night after a car accident. Dr. Bhatnagar will be out soon. Take a seat. And help yourself," he said, pointing to a counter in the waiting room, "if you change your mind."

"Can you tell me where her daughter is? Was Molly in the car too?"

"I really don't know anything more than what I told you. Please take a seat. You can leave your bag behind the desk, if you like. My shift just started, so I'll be here a while."

Kate held onto her carry-on, and wheeled it to the lounge. She took a seat, with her radar on full alert. She had no idea who to call to ask about Molly and felt entirely alone. She had met one of Eileen and Eric's neighbors during her last trip up—what was her name? Kelly? Carrie? Kerry?—and they seemed to be pretty close, but Kate had no idea how to contact her. As her thoughts raced, the neighbor appeared. She was red-eyed and holding Molly, who was sound asleep. Kate's heart raced at the sight of her niece. She stood up, and ran her hand gently over Molly's head, tears pooling in relief at the sight of her niece safe and sound.

"Kate, I'm Casey Graf. We met when you were up for Christmas. Has Dr. Bhatnagar come to see you?" She spoke softly and slowly, and was clearly struggling to maintain her composure.

"No, I just got here. I haven't spoken with anybody yet.

What happened? How are they? Do you know their room number?"

She reached toward Kate, and rested a hand on her shoulder. "There is no room number. They were hit by an SUV on their way to my house to pick up Molly. I was watching her while they went to do some shopping. I'm so sorry, Kate."

Kate stared at Casey, keeping her eyes glued to the older woman while she pulled Molly gently into her arms. She settled with her niece into a plastic chair. The smell of Molly's hair regulated Kate's breathing, but still no words formed. So this is what shock is. Casey offered information and soothing words in a soft voice. Something about dead on arrival, nothing the doctors could do, they hadn't suffered, she went on.

Kate wondered if they saw the SUV heading toward them. If there was so much as a second of awareness, then they had suffered the knowledge of leaving Molly. There was no doubt that they would both have faced a lifetime of physical pain recovering from an accident to prevent Molly enduring the loss of her parents.

Kate's nose rested on Molly's head, smelling her hair, while she rubbed her back. Her senses though were muted by the questions running through her head. How to tell Kitty? How to tell the boys? How to tell Eric's parents? Where to find his parents? What to do? Am I breathing?

Dr. Bhatnagar arrived. He said all the correct things, but none of the right ones.

Kate wondered how Molly continued to sleep and how the planet could continue spinning under the circumstances. But spin it did. Faster and faster, until Casey, sensing the inevitable, took Molly from Kate's arms, just before Kate slid to the floor.

Kate's forehead bumped against the side of the chair she had tumbled out of. Pulling herself up to the seat, she asked the doctor to take her to Eileen.

"Of course. She's downstairs. Eric is too. Come with me."

As they entered the elevator, Kate asked for the details of the crash. It turned out that a man was driving to the Parks

Department with his kids to recycle their Christmas tree, and he ran a stop sign.

"He told the police that he reached back to break up his kids bickering and between that and bad vision from the tree, he missed the sign. He's new to the area and doesn't know the roads very well. This truly was an accident. A horrible, tragic accident."

The elevator doors opened on to a disarmingly benign floor. Kate had never been to a morgue before, but she expected a space that reflected the finality of its temporary occupants. This was a bit businesslike. Staff at desks, others pushing carts silently over tiled floors, and a woman on a stepstool changing a light bulb. Ordinary people going about what to them was, she supposed, an ordinary day.

They passed through a set of automatic doors. She was cold, and gripped her jacket tightly: at least that followed the expected script. There was an attendant standing between two gurneys. She could tell which was which by the shapes of the bodies, their outlines clear beneath the sheets. Dr. Bhatnagar nodded to the attendant, a young man with kind eyes.

"Can I say goodbye to Eric first?"

"Of course," he replied, lifting back the sheet with care and folding it just below Eric's shoulders.

Kate gasped at the sight of him, and her hand reflexively covered her mouth.

"Is that from the steering wheel?"

"No. The airbag deployed. His injuries are from the impact of the roof, I believe. Their car flipped over the guardrail."

Kate kissed her fingertips and touched Eric's right cheek, which was miraculously free of bruising. It was the only part of his face that was.

"Goodbye," she whispered. "And thank you for loving Eileen." She took a deep breath, then quickly looked away as the sheet was put back in its place.

"Do you want to take a few minutes?"

Kate shook her head. "No. But tell me first, did Eileen suffer the same sort of injuries as Eric? Will her face be bruised too?"

"No." He looked at Kate waiting for some indication that he should proceed. But Kate was staring down at Eileen's immobile, sheet-covered body. She touched the side closest to her, and traced its hem. The attendant pulled the sheet back to reveal Eileen's face. Her hair was damp and her face was a little swollen. Kate brushed the hair from her sister's forehead and kissed her on the nose. Then something caught her eye, or, rather, the absence of something did. She had given a simple Trinity Knot to Eileen on her sixteenth birthday, and Eileen never took it off. Kate wanted it for Molly. Dr. Bhatnagar retrieved two small bags from a nearby trolley. One contained items Eric had on his person at the time of the crash, and the other Eileen's belongings. Kate held Eileen's up to the light and could see the necklace through the plastic. She slipped both bags into her tote.

"Can I sit with her for a little while?," she asked Dr. Bhatnagar. "Just for a few minutes?"

"Of course." He slid a chair beside Kate, and she sat down. "Hey, you." She touched Eileen's hand. It was cold. Kate took it between her own and tried to rub it warm. Kate kissed Eileen's fingers and placed her arm back by her side, tucking it under the sheet just a little. She looked closely at Eileen's face. It was clear that Eileen was truly gone, and that took some of the sting out of leaving her here in this cold place. But just a little. She took a picture of Molly out of her wallet and tucked it under Eileen's hand.

"I love you," she whispered in Eileen's ear. She placed the sheet over her little sister's face herself, waving off both the attendant and Dr. Bhatnagar, who were standing by to help. In turn, she looked into each of their kind eyes, "will you stay with her?"

Both nodded, and Dr. Bhatnagar assured Kate that he would stay until his shift ended.

"She won't be alone, I promise. Neither will Eric."

"Thank you."

As she walked to the exit, Dr. Bhatnagar said that Eric and

Eileen would be released in the morning.

"And then what happens?"

"There's only one funeral home in the area. We can contact them for you. And then they'll get in touch with you tomorrow. Will you be staying at the cabin?"

Kate nodded. "I'll be bringing Molly home."

She took the elevator back upstairs.

Molly and Casey were where she had left them, but Molly was now awake. She reached out for Kate with the great speed and weight of well-loved toddlers the world over: it never dawns on them that the person they are reaching for won't catch them. And catch her, Kate did.

"Big hug for me, Molly?"

"Big hug. Kiss nose."

Kate kissed her niece's nose then rubbed it with her own. This was their big greeting on Kate's recent Christmas visit.

"Mommy and Daddy have to stay here, sweetie. So, I'm going to go home with you. Is that okay?"

Molly's big blue eyes looked at her blankly. "Mama and Dada have boo-boos."

"Yes, that's right. So, they will stay here with the doctor. Come on, sweetie, let's go home." She looked to Casey, who took Kate's bag to lead the way to her car.

"You have boo-boo," Molly said, gently touching a spot just above Kate's left eye. "Boo-boo."

Kate caught her reflection in a framed print in the waiting room. She brushed aside the auburn mess falling across her forehead and saw that the chair had done a bit of damage. She wiped it with the back of her sleeve, and they headed out the door.

It was already starting to get dark—the nature of a Vermont winter—when Casey dropped them off at the cabin. The door was unlocked. After getting Molly fed, washed up and into her pajamas, they snuggled in for a bedtime reading of *Curious George Makes Pancakes*. It was only six o'clock, but Molly was asleep in the turn of a page. Kate tucked the little girl in and went to the kitchen to call Sean and tell him the horrible news. But with Molly now safely tucked in, and in her own company for the first time since arriving in Vermont, the façade of holding herself together crumbled.

She made it as far as the kitchen sink when the morning coffee, last night's dinner, and the food she shared with Molly came rushing out of her amidst heaving sobs. She turned the cold tap and splashed water on her face. When it fell back into the sink, it was mixed with bile that chased after tears. The second time she scooped the cold water in her hands, they were shaking so much, it landed back in the sink. She threw the switch on the garbage disposal and watched the liquid pain get sucked down along with shreds of lettuce from what must have been Eric and Eileen's last family meal. She took a glass from the cabinet over the sink, filled it with ice and water, and sat at the table.

Then she got back up and opened a cabinet in the living room, knowing what she would find there. She opened the top of the Jameson's, took a mouthful and forced herself to keep it down. Then she returned to the kitchen and picked up the phone. She called Sean's cell, but the voice that answered on the first ring did not belong to her brother.

"Kate, it's Mom."

Mom. Catherine—Kitty to everybody—had been through a lot in recent years. But she was still a force of nature. Her spare time since retiring as a school nurse was spent tracing her ancestry—she was fourth-generation Irish-American—and sharing the photos and documents she unearthed with everybody else in the family. The only break she took from that hobby was two years tending her husband, Bill, through Alzheimer's. There was no time for hobbies then.

Kitty and Bill gifted their Brooklyn brownstone to Kate's brothers—Sean and Kevin—before heading down to North Carolina for what was supposed to be a sun-filled retirement of golf for him and gardening for her. They could easily have gotten over $1 million for the three-bedroom house on Pineapple Street, which had doubled in value several times since they bought it in the 1970s. But they agreed they didn't need $1 million for the retirement they planned. They also wanted the house to remain in the family, and Kate's life was in Florida for the foreseeable future, and Eileen was settled in Vermont. Sean and Kevin were successful contractors, with no interest in leaving the Heights, but neither one wanted to live at the mercy of an enormous mortgage. It was Bill who came up with a solution that everybody jumped at: Sean and Kevin would annually gift their parents the maximum allowed before the I.R.S. would be involved, and their parents would use that to supplement their retirement savings (him) and pension (her). The boys also agreed that if Bill and Kitty ever chose or had to move back to Brooklyn, that they would properly renovate the parlor-floor apartment for them. It was a win-win for both generations, and an insurance policy for the next.

They were only in North Carolina for six months when Kitty began to notice that Bill was getting forgetful. He was also becoming increasingly short-tempered, which she initially took to his being out of sorts from the move. Until this retirement, he—like Kitty—had spent his entire life in Brooklyn. A series of tests revealed the early onset of what had been named dementia. Within a year it was re-named Alzheimer's, and not long after, Kitty was a widow.

After a few months on her own, she looked around North Carolina and didn't like what she saw. Kitty had phoned Sean with the firm message that she "wanted out. The old men are circling like vultures and the widowed club women are looking at me sideways. Please get down here with your brother, and take me and your father's ashes home. We never should have left Brooklyn. Be here next Saturday. I'll be packed and ready."

The boys carved a proper apartment within the lower part of the brownstone in record time, and it was waiting for her by the time they arrived at 22 Pineapple Street dragging Mom's things along in a U-Haul. In the year since she'd been back, she was reinstated as the block's official granny-in-residence and was once again contributing to the Brooklyn Dodgers "Love the Bums" blog (she practically owned the Pee Wee Reese section), tending to geraniums on her window sill, and harvesting vegetables in the back garden. All was right with her world, until the phone call from Vermont.

"Tell me, Kate."

"I can't, Mom. I can't tell you." Kate closed her eyes. "Can I talk to Sean?"

Kitty didn't reply. She handed the phone to her son.

"It's me."

"Where are you?"

"We're halfway through Massachusetts. I just stopped for gas. Margot's grabbing a coffee, and then we'll be on our way again."

"And Kevin?"

"He's not far behind us. Maybe an hour or so."

"So you're still off the highway then?"

"Yeah, Katie. Tell me."

"She's gone. Eric too," she spoke in a whisper, trying desperately to hold herself together. "Molly wasn't in the car. She's here with me at the cabin. She's sleeping."

"Jesus, Kate."

Kate could hear Kitty in the background. She wanted to know everything. Sean held the phone between them, and Kate told them all she knew.

CHAPTER 3

Kate woke up on the couch, nose-to-nose with Molly.

"Potty, Auntie Katie, potty."

"Okay, sweetie. Let's go to the potty." She hurled herself off the couch and staggered after Molly. She looked at her watch. It was 5am. Where were Mom and Sean?

Molly sat on the potty with her *Curious George* book, while Kate sat on the edge of the tub rubbing sleep from her eyes. Kate was thinking of when and what to tell Molly, when the little girl interrupted asking for a wipe.

Washing up and getting dressed kept them occupied until they sat down for breakfast; and halfway through their cereal, Casey and her husband, Joe, arrived at the door carrying two bags of groceries, a casserole, and a bunch of flowers.

"We thought you could do with these," Joe said as he set everything on the counter and Casey grabbed a vase from atop the fridge. "Our granddaughters arrived last night for a visit, and they'd love to see Molly. We thought it might be a good idea for Casey to stay with you this morning. Help you with things." He pulled off his gloves and set a calloused hand reassuringly on Kate's shoulder. "We're here for whatever you need," he said, looking her square in the eyes. "Just name it."

Kate's bias against small town life was challenged, as it

often was in this old New England town. The couple standing before her were kind, knowing, and practical. "Thank you, Joe. Let me gather some of Molly's things."

Once Molly was packed and out the door with Joe, Kate and Casey sat down over coffee. "Casey, I don't have the slightest idea what I'm supposed to do here. My brothers and mother are on their way up. They'll know what to do. I just...I need to breathe."

The kitchen phone rang. Kate looked toward it, and then back at Casey.

"Should I answer it?"

Casey grabbed it on the third ring.

"Hello, the Johnson residence...just a minute."

She handed it to Kate. "It's your brother. It's Kevin."

Kate snatched the phone away from Casey, mouthing *sorry*, which Casey waived off before getting to work in the kitchen.

"Kev, where are you guys?"

"We're at the hospital. Mom insisted we come here first. And then—Kate, she's okay—Mom had what the doctor called 'an episode.' The doctor checked her in just for the night. He wants to keep an eye on her. He gave her something to sleep too."

"Oh, Kevin."

"I know, I know. But, really, the doctor thinks she'll be alright. It's the shock, and the drive...I'm actually glad we spent the night here."

"Should I head over?"

"No. Stay put. We'll be to you when Mom gets discharged."

"Can I talk to her?"

"No. She's still sleeping."

"Love you."

"Love you back."

She looked to Casey. "They'll be here later."

"Go take a shower, Kate, and get yourself together. It's going to be a busy day. I'll just putter around here and make a few things so you don't have to bother with cooking later. They'll be hungry."

Kate unpacked, undressed, and stepped into the shower. She stood beneath the hot water for an hour, letting it pour over her while she stared at the tiled wall, her mind filled with thoughts of her father. She wanted his calm ways desperately to help navigate this situation, but knew it was a blessing he wasn't alive to hear of Eileen's death. Dad and Eileen were thick as thieves. Co-conspirators of the most memorable Doyle family hijinks, leaders of every outing, and now, together, the faces that would be forever absent in every future family photo. Casey knocked on the bathroom door.

"You okay, Kate? You've been in there a long time."

"Yeah, I'm all right. Be out in a minute." And she was. Dressed and tired, but as ready to face things as she could manage to be.

The rest of the morning was spent at Eileen's kitchen table dealing with the business of death. Phone calls to the hospital, Casey calling Eileen's and Eric's friends to break the news. The funeral parlor sent somebody over to discuss details for a wake and to take notes for an obituary in the local newspaper.

Kitty called from the hospital. "The boys and I talked, Kate. We agreed that I should be the one to call Eric's parents. Eileen kept a phone list on the side of the fridge. Their number should be there." As she looked for the list, Kate remembered that Eric's parents lived in upstate New York with their daughter. It wasn't very far. Maybe they could be here as soon as today. She gave her mother the number.

"I can't believe they're gone, Kate."

"I know, Mom." Kate heard her mother's intake of breath and heard the reassuring words of her brothers in the background.

"I'm hanging up now. I love you. We'll be there soon enough." Kitty hung up the phone. And Kate cried at her mother's strength and grace, and at her own loss. The tears fell for an hour, with Casey alternately fussing over her and leaving her alone. Finally, Casey parked herself in a chair and directed Kate to the couch.

"Stretch out there. Let's share all the reasons we loved

them. It'll be good for us. Me first."

The two women spent the rest of the afternoon sharing Eileen stories. Eileen the city-girl-turned-organic gardener, the former no-kids-for-me-turned-perfect-mother, the "I-hate-computers" gal turned champion blogger, and the keeper of lyrics to all silly songs, including "Smelly Cat." They even managed to smile, sitting there talking as the rain began to fall outside. It was becoming, as Kate's friends in Ireland would say, "a soft day." The kind of rain that Kate had taken to calling "sneaky rain" during her years in Dublin: you looked out your window and saw nothing discernable falling from the sky, but you stepped outdoors and were soggy in just a few steps. In the time she lived there for her PhD studies and post-doctoral fellowship, Kate had fallen in love with the city. At some point, she was determined to go back to Ireland for part-time residency. A vacation home out on the Aran Islands was part of her "when I grow up" fantasy project. In the light of this day, she realized her sister's death was an immediate call-to-action for an adulthood postponed. That she was turning forty this year was also a factor. Her thoughts were interrupted by the return of Joe and Molly.

Casey and Joe started to make a salad and sandwiches and heated up Casey's casserole, while Kate got Molly into the tub. This kid just loved the water and making a game of getting her hair washed. She wanted to "poo" Auntie Katie's hair too. Kate dunked her head into the warm suds and let Molly have at it. No sooner had they begun making horns with their soapy hair when familiar voices could be heard out in the living room.

"Who's that, Molly? Who could that be? Is that Grammy Kitty out there?"

"Gammy Kitty!" Molly shouted, raising her arms in the air.

The kid wanted out. Kate pulled Molly from the tub and wrapped a towel around her. Molly wiggled out of the towel, and ran bare-assed and soapy-headed into the living room toward the waiting arms of her doting grandmother.

Kate's brown eyes filled up at the sight of her mother's face as she grabbed on to her granddaughter in a hug so tight it made her knuckles shine. Standing behind Kitty and Molly were Sean and Kevin. The faces of both men showed every anxious moment of the past day. Sean, forty-five-years old and a partner with his brother in Doyle Contracting, was 6' 5" of pure charm. His green eyes were lined and set off by deep, dark bags of sadness and his height was diminished by shoulders that told the story of trying to carry the burden of a big brother now less one little sister. Kevin was not much better. The smaller of the two men, he took after Mom, and appeared to Kate as having shrunk under the weight of Eileen's death. He looked crushed, and Kate ran to him for a hug.

Behind them stood Sean's partner, Margot: Auntie Gogo to Molly. Margot was the anti-Doyle in many ways, but nonetheless a perfect addition to the family. She and Sean had only been dating for two months when Sean announced to the family that he had met "the one" and intended to propose. Dad spoke first: "Margot? The politics girl? You barely know her."

There was much bickering and telling Dad to shush, but Sean made his intentions—and Margot's qualities—clear: "I love her. That's really all I need to know." And that was that. Six years and one New York City mayoral administration later, they remained very much in love and together, but unmarried. Margot said no. She loved Sean to pieces. She simply did not believe in marriage, and Sean had learned to live with that.

In addition to being direct, smart, and a major player in City politics, Margot was a perfect physical complement to Sean's beauty. At 6', she stood nearly as tall as him, and shared his jet-black hair and green eyes. If you didn't notice their always touching each other, you'd have thought they were brother and sister. They were a perfect match in looks and temperament.

Kevin was altogether Sean's opposite. Handsome, like his brother, but in a way that grew on you rather than being overtly obvious. Kevin's naturally down-turned mouth and brown eyes were just like Kate's. But he was tall and dark-haired like his brother. His eyes were hidden behind glasses that did little to conceal his deep crow's feet. "He smiles with his eyes," their mother was fond of saying, so the lines of joy showed atop his face rather than at the mouth. It did, however, tend to lend him a rather serious look, another trait he shared with Kate. But he was a keen listener, and more than one woman had fallen for that great trait. Lots of girlfriends, but still single; that was their Kevin. He said once, when pressed about his singledom, that he rather liked his own company: "I'm usually having too good a time doing whatever I'm doing at home to go out." Fair enough. He spent a lot of time with Anya, a long-time family friend and local real estate maven, but it didn't appear to be very serious. Sometimes they appeared to be a couple, and other times it seemed platonic. Kate could never tell if they were just friends or something more; not even Anya's visit to Miami on Kate's last birthday with Kevin cleared that up.

But here the boys were now, with Kitty, in Eileen's house. And Kate couldn't let go of Kevin.

"What are we going to do?" Kate whispered to her brother.

"We'll get through this, Katie. We'll get through this." But both were in such pain and determined to hide it from Molly. "Let's go outside," he said, pushing his glasses up his nose. "I've got cigarettes."

They left the others in the living room with a naked Molly and ventured out to the porch to share the teenage vice they now reserved for what they came to refer to as life's "too-much" moments—any major deviations from their shared preference for order.

"Does Molly know that they're gone?"

"No. She just knows they have boo-boos and are with the doctor at the hospital. She's distracted with people coming and going, but that's going to end soon. I guess I hoped one of you would be able to find the right words. This is way out of my skill-set, Kevin."

"Look. You're her godmother, I'm her godfather, and Mom is getting on. Her incident at the hospital made that crystal clear. We can't put this on her. I know she's a tough cookie, but Dad's death took a toll on her. I see it with her back in Brooklyn. You're not around enough to notice it maybe—and that's not a shot at you—but it's true. She's slowing down. I think we need to take this on ourselves." He put out his half-smoked cigarette. "But you see more of Molly than I do. What's your take? When should we talk about it with her?"

"Maybe that's where Mom comes in. Let's ask her how to deal with this, but—you're right—we need to make it clear to her that we'll take care of Molly. Let's have her tell us the best approach to take."

No sooner had Kate spoken those words than Kitty appeared on the porch.

"I knew I'd find you out here doing that. Give one to your mother now."

Kevin handed Kitty a cigarette and lit it for her.

"Mom, Kate and I were just trying to get a handle on telling Molly."

"Let Molly tell you in her own way when she wants to know things. She'll ask questions when she has them. You can be sure she'll have them, and I expect they'll come soon. Have you thought about which of you will take care of her? You're her godparents. It's up to the two of you, I think. Is there a will? Did Eileen and Eric talk to either of you about being guardians?"

Kitty's speech was getting faster, and her breath labored; Mom was starting to come undone. It wasn't something Kate saw often, and it freaked her out a little. She took the cigarette out of Kitty's hand.

"Eileen asked me about it once, and I said yes. But I don't know if they ever put it in writing. Casey gave me this," she pulled a business card from her back pocket. "It's the lawyer who most of their friends use. I'll phone him later."

Kate watched her mother sit on the step. She looked so fragile. Kevin was right; this was too much even for the toughest of cookies.

Kate thought of how many times she had read accounts

about the death of a child being entirely unnatural, and for the first time she understood what that meant. Her mother was clearly in the depths of the most profound turmoil; trying to keep things together without her husband to share in such a horrifying grief. It was as though without Bill she lacked the ability to articulate the well of sorrow she was experiencing. For the first time in her life, Kate was witness to an unspeakable trauma. She had lectured often on the impact of 'bearing witness', and she understood now what that truly meant. For the second time in as many days, she questioned the substance of her academic life. Or its lack of substance. She entered the profession full of steam, dedicated to the importance of literature; an advocate for its healing properties and role in giving order to a chaotic world. Today, she wasn't so sure that it mattered very much. It hadn't helped prepare her for this at all. She was gutted. Maybe, she thought, it would help her heal at some point. But she was skeptical.

"Kate, go inside. I need to sit out here with Kevin for a while. We'll be in soon."

Kate scraped her cigarette against the side of the porch and stuck it in an empty flower pot. She got up, and reached for the door. Kevin sat beside Kitty, and Kate heard their shared sobs as she went inside. And just like that she knew her brother would take care of Kitty. As she entered the house, she knew somehow that she would be taking care of Molly. But she also knew that Kevin, Kitty, Sean, and Margot would be there to help her make things as right as they could possibly be.

CHAPTER 4

The arrival of Eric's family, the Catholic funeral mass (at Kitty's insistence) and more secular memorial service (at Sean, Kevin, and Kate's insistence) all gave the next week a sense of order. Eric's parents and Kitty were given authority to determine where Eric and Eileen's ashes should be interred. Somehow, this had been overlooked in their will: a circumstance that left the lawyers apologetic and embarrassed. The three agreed this should be determined by where Molly would be living. So the ashes were kept with the lawyers until the reading of the will. Sean thought they should look for bills that might need attention, but nobody could bring themselves to invade the privacy of Eric and Eileen's home office. The services distracted both families from addressing the big question: Who would look after Molly? But that answer came on the morning when Casey joined the Doyles and Johnsons in the offices of Klein, Kennedy and Smith for the reading of Eileen and Eric's will, dated just six months earlier.

Eileen and Eric's assets stunned everybody except the lawyers in the room. Eric had patented three software applications that were in wide use on tablets and smartphones the world over, and there was no indication that the royalties would end any time soon. Before reading the distribution of assets, John Smith, Esq. produced a copy of the paperwork Eric and Eileen had signed that left the business decisions with him or his designates. Then he turned his attention to the will.

The sum of $50,000 was bequeathed to a charity where both Eric and Eileen volunteered.

The same sum was also given to the local public library.

Casey and Joe were left $10,000 "to take that trip to Australia you've been talking about for as long as we've been so fortunate to be neighbors."

Sean received $25,000 and was given a letter left to him by Eileen.

Eric's parents were left $100,000, and Eric's sister, $25,000. All three were also given letters from Eric.

$100,000 was left to Kitty, along with a letter from Eileen.

Then Mr. Smith addressed the godparents. "To Kevin and Kate Doyle, godparents of Molly and siblings of Eileen, we leave $25,000 each and the remainder of our assets upon the settlement of all outstanding debts. These and future assets are to be held in trust for Molly's upbringing and the remaining funds shall be held in trust for her until she reaches the age of eighteen. These fund are to be managed and allocated as Kevin and Kate deem appropriate. We furthermore appoint Kate Doyle the guardian of our beloved daughter, Molly. It is our sincere request that Molly be known and loved by her paternal family members, even though Kate will be her guardian." And there was a letter from Eileen for each of the Doyles.

All eyes were on Kate as she sat facing the lawyer. "Yes," she whispered. She turned to Kevin, who nodded and put a reassuring hand on her arm. "And not in Florida. I can't do this alone. And I don't think Eric and Eileen would have wanted me to."

Papers were signed, and hugs given and received. On the way out of the office, Kate stood with Eric's parents and sister: "I want you to know that I will follow their wishes to the letter. I have a lot of things to figure out, but we will stay a family. I give you my word on that. And I'll include you in everything. I'll keep you in the loop of every decision I make. I promise."

"We know, Kate," replied Eric's father. "Just keep her in our life."

In the car on the way back to Eileen's house, it was decided that Kitty, Sean, and Margot would take Molly to Brooklyn while Kate returned to Florida and Kevin dealt with more lawyering and possibly listing the house. Anya would help long distance, but was on-call to drive up if needed.

Joe had been looking after Molly at the house, and he let it be known immediately upon their arrival that Molly had spent the better part of the afternoon pleading to go see parents at the boo-boo hospital. All eyes were on the grandparents, and they faced the heart-breaking task with a stoicism that would later be recalled by the assembled aunts and uncles as the embodiment of elegant courage.

Kitty and Eric's parents took Molly to her bedroom, while the rest of the sad group sat out on the porch. Eric's sister huddled together with Sean, and they shared with each other the letters they had been given by the lawyer. Margot kept the tea coming as smiles, hugs, and tears accompanied sharing of the letters. Kate took her letter and her laptop into the spare bedroom to find a flight to Miami.

As the printer dispensed her boarding pass, Kate removed Eileen's letter from her tote and placed it on the desk. This would contain the last words she would hear from Eileen, and Kate was simultaneously eager and afraid. Her tea grew cold while she stroked the envelope. It was linen—the real deal—and felt soft and silky. Finally, she slit the top and unfolded the pages. Eileen's beautiful stationery had her initials embossed on top and the paper matched the envelope. The girl loved good paper. The letter was handwritten:

> Dear Katie,
> If you are reading this, I have moved on. I write this
> with Eric snoring beside me and Molly dreaming
> away between us. I am the happiest woman in the
> world. But we meet with our lawyers tomorrow to
> sign our wills. We didn't deliberately keep things

from you. The truth is, we became a little embarrassed about the money once it passed the million dollar mark.

Let's face it, neither Eric nor I were raised with quite so many zeros. Live well with it...I mean it! Find a nice home for you and Molly. One where she can grow and you can unpack all your lovely books. I wanted to be sure to tell you how much you mean to me just one more time. I love you, love you, love you.

I have spent my entire life connected to you and faced each day knowing, without a doubt, that you had my back. This is a sister's greatest gift.

Now I leave the future of my greatest gift and joy in your care. Molly and Eric are my world. If you are reading this, Eric is with me, but Molly is with you. Teach her as you taught me. Love her as you loved me. Help this little girl navigate the bumpy world without cynicism. Help her be as happy as her mother.

Your loving sister, Eileen

Kate scanned the letter and emailed it to herself. It was a bittersweet addition to the family archives that she would one day share with Molly. She took the original out to the porch to show the boys, who, in turn, shared theirs.

Sean lost it completely as he read his letter aloud:

Dear Big Brother #1,
What can I say? You were there for me for every hug that a little sister could ever need. When I think of Pineapple Street, yours is the first face that I see. Isn't that funny?

My biggest thanks is that you and Margot showed me what a true partnership was all about. Without you and Margot, there would be no me and Eric. Your example gave me the greatest joy of my life.

Thank you, my dear #1.
    Go Giants,
    Stay with Margot,
    Your loving sister, Eileen

Kate put her arms around her sobbing brother and wished that she could ease his pain. But her own anguish kept her from saying anything beyond, "I second her, big guy. You're the best." Sean wiped his eyes and managed a little smile when Kate added, "go Giants" under her breath.

Kevin removed his glasses, stood up, and passed his letter to Kate. She read it to herself while Kevin paced the front yard:

Dear #2,
Second in line for the throne, as you like to say, but never second in my heart. You and Sean share top billing with me—always have, always will. I miss you both already. I know Kate is a tough independent girl, but you'll need to look after her now. She'll need your help raising Molly, but she'll also need you to show her what a wonderful auntie-mommy she has been since Molly was born.

    Above everybody else, Eric and I trusted you to be godfather to our precious daughter. And you've been the best. Do you know how much Molly loves you? So much, she trembles whenever your car pulls up or she knows you're on the phone. It's the sweetest thing. Keep her safe from this crazy world, Kevin. And thank you from the bottom of my heart for looking out for me, and, in your own quiet way, shouting "I love you" to me—and my little girl—with each and every glance. You are our little shared secret: we both know, every day of our lives, that we come first with you. That has been your gift to me.

    I love you back,
    Your devoted #2

Kate blew her nose on her sleeve, folded the letter and slipped it into the pocket of her jeans. How in the world will we ever get past this?, she wondered. Her thoughts were interrupted by Margot's hand, resting on her shoulder.

"Were you able to find a flight?"

"I booked one for Sunday morning. I can't say how long it will take me to wrap things up there, but I hope to be in Brooklyn in two or three weeks."

"Don't worry," Margot said, "take as much time as you need. Molly will have the full run of Pineapple Street for as long as you need. That goes for you too after you wrap things up in Miami." She paused. "Do you know what this will mean for you work-wise? Will you have to find a replacement for the semester or do they do that for you?"

Ah, Margot. She adored Eileen and Eric and had taken their deaths hard. But she was a rock for Sean. And now, showing her political instincts, it was clear she would have Kate's back too. She had read Kate's mind, and the nagging thoughts of the career-minded everywhere when life threw them a curveball: is there a Plan B?

Margot often teased Kate that she took herself way too seriously, but when it came to career concerns, the women were equally pragmatic.

"I have no idea how this works, to tell you the truth. The closest example I have is when people leave for illness, but that's never been permanent. And right now it's only three weeks into the spring semester...shit, Margot, I don't have a clue."

What Kate didn't say is that nobody she knew had ever walked away from a tenure-track job before actually going up for their tenure review. Unless they had decided to leave academia permanently or were aware they fell short of the requirements for promotion.

Kate was in unchartered territory. She had already published a book and numerous journal articles, had excellent teaching reviews, and served on university committees. Her case, although a year away, was considered a slam-dunk. She was already working on a second book, putting her on a fast-track from which she was about to step off. She thought of the research sitting in a heap atop her desk in Miami: only partially read and totally unorganized. She also thought about the enormity of the risk she was considering. Best keep it to herself for now. Universities were frequently cutting tenured positions in favor of Visiting Professors and adjuncts. She had been down that road herself once at a college in Philly, and it was a nightmare. She thought it unlikely that all universities were like the one she toiled at as a non-tenured faculty member before landing in Miami, but some had to be. She shivered at the memory of those years, but there was a strong possibility that Kate would not find another full-time position, let alone one on a tenure track. She would need time to get settled with Molly. Money would not be a pressing concern, but Kate was a worker. And she took pride in that.

The state of her career was a fear, but it didn't hold a candle to her worry over Molly. Kate had no idea what to expect, but Margot said she would look into family therapists to be sure the best advice would be available. Everybody was in agreement: whatever was needed to help Molly through this was the priority. Kitty had been the first to broach the need for a therapist, much to everybody's amazement. She was the queen of playing it close to the vest. But, as she said, "if I can adjust, so can all of you." A woman of surprises.

Kitty and Eric's parents came out on the porch. Molly had been in with her grannies and grampy for two hours. All Kitty said about what transpired was that Molly was told Mommy and Daddy were in heaven. That they loved Molly very much and didn't want to leave her, but she would be living with Auntie Katie now in a new home near Pineapple Street. Kitty also said that they showed Molly pictures of her with her parents and told the little girl stories about them. That was all Kitty or Eric's parents shared. They stayed with Molly until she drifted off to sleep. The nap was brief, and when the little girl joined her family on the porch, she was distracted, but functioning. That was more than could be said of the adults gathered around her with eager hugs or of the grandparents who appeared much older than they had when they entered that room.

Eric's parents and sister said their goodbyes and headed home. Margot made an early supper, got Molly bathed and into her jammies before tucking her in with the promise that Grammy Kitty would be in soon for a night-night story. Kitty, Kate, and the boys went back to the porch to admire the stars that were just starting to fill the night sky.

Settling into the porch swing, Kitty asked Kate and the boys to stay nearby: "I need to read the letter Eileen left me, but I'm afraid to do it alone. Will you stay out here with me for a while?"

"Of course, Mom," said Sean. "We'll just sit here on the steps."

Kitty slipped the envelope out of her purse and stared at it for a while. What, Kate wondered, could possibly be going through Kitty's mind at this moment? She must be missing Dad terribly. They had known each other since they were teenagers growing up in Brooklyn. Mom used to joke about the fact that Dad, six years her senior and the brother of one of Kitty's friends, had known her for her entire life. They'd been through fifty years of marriage, the loss of their parents, the raising of four kids, breast cancer...so very much. But here Kitty was without him as she faced the final words of their youngest child.

When they turned back, Kitty was looking down at the letter with tears streaming down her face. She handed it over to Kevin, who went to hug her, but she waved him off.

"Keep this. I'm going to bed now." And she went inside, got changed, washed up, brushed her teeth, and climbed into bed beside her granddaughter.

Kevin read the letter to Sean and Kate.

Dear Mom,
Eric and I are going to the lawyers tomorrow to sign

our wills, and I hope you never actually read this letter. You know I love you, and I know you love me. You've been the best Mom a girl could ever hope to have. And the best granny too. Know that Molly loves you just as much as I do. If Eric were awake right now, he would tell me to add that you are the best mother-in-law too. He was so afraid of you and Dad! Not to mention the rest of the Doyles. But you all won him over by trusting in his love for me. Thank you for that.

You know how I used to tease you that your glasses had rose lenses? Well, I get it now. When we love, we see everything in a happy hue because we have to. It's the only way to get by in the world and have faith that things will be better for those we love. I couldn't understand it when I was younger, but I see now how it is a matter of survival. You taught me that by example. Sorry it took me so long to figure it all out. Sorrier still to be thanking you for your lessons in this letter.

Thank you too for teaching me the joy of quiet. I can't count the hours I watched you slowly going back and forth in your rocking chair with a book in your lap and a cup of tea nearby. Kids running in and out, Dad screaming at the television…nothing broke the trance. It was a wonder, and it taught me the beauty of 'getting away from it all' without being away from the ones you love. It was a life lesson in the grace of solitude.

Thank you for your family archives. Molly loves seeing the old photographs. Who's this one? Who's that one? Where am I? It goes on for hours. Of course, the ones she loves best are of you. Particularly that one from your honeymoon. You know the one I mean. Dad must have taken the picture, and there you are all of twenty-one, wiping the hair out of your eyes and staring into the sunshine. Molly's right, "soooo pretty." I'm sorry I never looked into the Doyle archives like you encouraged me to. I hope Molly will when she's bigger.

Most of all, thank you for always pretending that you have no idea how funny you are. You really do have the best sense of humor of anybody I know. When I think of you, I think of you smiling. And Molly has your smile, so I have you with me every day. And I always will.

Love,
The runt

Kevin folded the letter and tucked it into his pocket. One by one, they said their goodnights and filed off to bed.

CHAPTER 5

The whole crew took Kate to the airport early Sunday morning. The goodbyes were different than usual. No rushing today, she said goodbye to each one separately, and they all hugged and kissed at the curb: a first for the usually undemonstrative family. Molly held her tightly.

"Big hug?"

"Big hug, kiss nose."

Kate slept through the entire flight, waking up only at landing. That was a first. She got off the plane and walked through Miami airport in a daze, hopped in a taxi and sailed through mostly empty Sunday streets with the window down. The air was warm and heavy and felt good on her face. She looked around at the passing roller-bladers and joggers, appreciating the rhythms of Miami and the beauty of the pastels shared by the buildings and the shirts of the late-morning exercisers. The people and the architecture were displaying a lovely unity. As usual, her appreciation came a bit late in the game. She had mostly complained about this city by the sea in the years she'd called it home. It never failed. As soon as she knew she was moving along, the present place suddenly seemed to scrub up pretty well. Even Philly, although that took some effort.

Brian was waiting at her apartment with bagels, fruit, coffee, juice and the most perfectly rolled joint she had ever seen.

"Are you kidding?"

"Trust me. This is the perfect appetizer today. Take a few hits and these bagels will taste like you got them in Brooklyn."

Brian. Kate's neighbor and colleague. Born-and-raised in Miami: from kindergarten to graduate school and now teaching at his *alma mater*. A great teacher, prolific writer, and purveyor of the finest grass east of the Mississippi.

"Tell me everything."

Kate threw her bag on the living room floor and herself onto her ratty, old sofa. She smoked, ate everything Brian offered, and she talked. From the funeral to the will to her decision to move back to Brooklyn to live with Molly.

"Now I need a shower."

She left Brian sitting on the floor in a bit of a stupor, as she shut the bathroom door behind her. Before the shower, she filled the tub with hot water and took a soak. The buzz she felt from the few hits off that tidy joint were doing her good, and Brian was right: those bagels were *good*. A full belly and the tingle of mental numbness put the troubles of the past days just out of her reach. But the sorrow remained, and it was exhausting. She expected tomorrow to make her even worse for wear, but it would also bring diversions: her first day back at work and more catching up than she wanted to face. And there was the book. She had to pull it together before heading north. The thought of it cleared her head. She pulled the tub stopper, took a shower, and went into battle mode.

Showered and dressed, Kate realized that being in her own surroundings was helping to reclaim the equilibrium she had been without for the ten days in Vermont. She looked carefully into the mirror, and pulled the few white strands that crawled through her auburn hair at the temples. Brian was right: she looked awful. For the first time, she thought she was starting to look her age, but there was something else staring back at her too. It was the face of her mother and her grandmother.

Something in the eyes that made the face look wise. That was a first, and she would accept it even if lines and dark circles were part of the deal.

Brian had tidied up the kitchen and left a note telling her he would be home in an hour or so. And to call her if she needed anything.

She checked her landline for messages. There were several from Paul. Where was she? What was going on? Was everything all right? She dialed his number, but it went to voicemail: "I'm home, Eileen and Eric were in a car accident. No, I'm not all right, but I will be. Where are you?" In transit no doubt. Paul was on sabbatical and busy making the conference rounds.

Kate entered her tiny excuse for a home office, turned on the light, and looked around. Everything was just as she'd left it: a mess. Overflowing bookshelves, with a secret order known only to Kate, had always provided comfort when she entered the room. Now, they seemed to reflect the implosion of her life, the unwritten book, and how much packing needed to be done.

Thank goodness for Anya, who assured Kate that she would have at least two movers at her place late Monday afternoon to start making lists and getting things organized. If all went according to plan, Kate would soon be in an empty apartment and a storage pod of her worldly possessions would show up in Brooklyn once she found an apartment there. By the end of March, Miami would be history for her. Metaphorically speaking, she liked the notion of her life fitting into a tidy pod. It would give the appearance of order. Maybe even that she actually knew what she was doing when, for the first time in her life, she was terrified at starting over.

She had occasionally wondered when 'starting over' would stop. Her family joked about her somewhat vagabond life, but she often sensed an underlying current of worry when they did. Kate believed that what attracted her to the academic life was based, in part, on the certainty that every fifteen-week semester would have a beginning, a midterm, and an end, and every journal article or conference paper would have a tidy finality, concluding in a bound volume or an end-of-conference cocktail party. No dragging on, and a guaranteed start-over when the next semester or project got underway. It carried over into her personal life too.

Somewhere around her thirtieth birthday, the Doyles stopped asking Kate if she was seeing anybody. There had been plenty of diversions over the years, but mostly Kate preferred long-distance relationships. She had never placed *Get Married* on her to-do list and was usually friends with the men in her life long before they became lovers. No particularly messy break-ups either, and she expected former lovers to go back to being friends. It was always a kick in the teeth when one got married and stopped calling or returning her calls, until it was explained to her—more than a little late in the game—that new wives transformed a *Former Lovers* list into a *Do Not Contact* list. This nugget of information had baffled her. When she shared it with Brian, he informed her that the entire world knew the Rule of the New Wife.

"Really, Kate," he chastised her, "how have you gotten this far in life with so little information on how the world operates? It's not by your rules, honey, it's by the rules of the neurotically competitive. Get with the program."

Relaying this conversation to her happily married best friend, Gillian, was met with annoyance. Gillian argued that it wasn't the wife who cut off the ex-girlfriends, it was the newly husbanded.

"Honestly, do you really think I would cut off Glen's exes? Do you know any women with enough hours in the day to even think about that? Men just say that because they don't want to change the relationship rules, if they can avoid it. Do you blame them? It's exhausting to keep score. Easier to cut the connection."

Either way, Kate felt like an idiot. But it served as a wake-up call to just how inept her social skills were from years of living in books.

She looked at the two mountains of paper, which

represented her second monograph, stacked on her desk. Two publishers wanted to see the manuscript when it was done, but Kate had lately thought that perhaps they were more interested in it than she was. The profession being what is was, she was expected to keep the machine moving. So she was writing about a group of playwrights who had a fair amount in common with those she discussed in her first book. And she was finding it hard to get motivated. It felt like recycling, but switching gears was neither encouraged nor expected. She sat at her desk and began sifting through the mess, with NPR calmly chatting away in the background.

An author was being interviewed for his new book about a failed climbing expedition up K2. This group of climbers had spent weeks on the mountain waiting for the perfect weather to ascend to the peak, but they encountered problems on the final ascent and subsequent descent that resulted in eleven deaths.

"Why," the host asked, "were these climbers so fixed on K2? Isn't Kilimanjaro the premier climb?"

"Kilimanjaro," the author replied, "is the climb you mention to neighbors. K2 is the one you brag about to fellow climbers. It's the more difficult one: steeper and more challenging."

Inspired, Kate scribbled K2 on one sticky note and Kilimanjaro on another. The mountain of research that she had already read and annotated became Kilimanjaro, the other K2. Her K2 was indeed steeper, but it was also—in direct opposition to the radio geography lesson—a lot higher. The challenge was on: she had to complete a full draft of this book and get a proposal out within two weeks, before her resignation made its way around the gossip mill and she was professionally fucked. Nobody left a tenure-track position a year shy of tenure, unless it was clear tenure would be denied. Since department chairs and other mentors were just as invested in seeing a hire reach the holy grail, even borderline cases made it through. She was about to set herself up for a storm of professional trouble. The book might be her best way to salvage things. A quick trip to the kitchen for provisions, and she was ready. Armed with coffee and a sandwich, Kate faced K2 hoping she wouldn't fall out of her chair.

Five hours later and still a few inches from the promised land, her phone rang. It was Paul.

"Kate, I just got back to Atlanta. How are you?"

"I'm in the middle of climbing K2 and having some oxygen problems."

"Come again?"

"I have a lot to tell you. Did you get my message about Eileen and Eric?"

"Yes, and I'm so sorry. How are you holding up?"

Paul was an only child and his parents had died years ago. Except for a few distant cousins, family ties were not a part of his life. But he was a sweet man with no shortage of compassion for Kate's family tragedy.

"Pretty well, I think. Brian was by, and he stocked the fridge, so I'm being well looked after. But I could use you here to help me figure out how to resign. I'm moving up to Brooklyn to live with Molly."

"That's a lot of news. Are you sure about resigning? Maybe you should approach it as a leave-of-absence until you get settled in New York. Have you spoken with anybody in your department yet?"

"No, just Brian. But he won't say anything until I do." At least she didn't think so. But he was a notorious gossip. "Leave-of-absence is a great idea. Any other thoughts?"

"Only that I miss you, and I wish I could be there. I can't get to Miami until Friday night and then only for the weekend. I have to be in Chicago that Sunday night for my next conference. This week is New York. Do you want me to check on anything for you in Brooklyn while I'm there?"

A bold offer. Paul had never met her family, except for Kevin, when he came down for a little vacation with Anya. The foursome spent a lazy weekend together that coincided with Kate's birthday. The plan had been to go to Key West, but they stopped in Islamorada for lunch and never made it any further. Three days of flats fishing, grouper sandwiches and too many beers: a bonding session to be sure, but it still made Kate a little uncomfortable to ask Paul to check in on Pineapple Street. She seldom mixed her worlds during the best of times; and it was out of the question now that her life was undergoing a seismic shift.

"No, that's okay. They'll all have their hands full with Molly. It will be her first week there. I think it's best that she just have family around for now. But I really appreciate it. I do."

There was a brief silence. But it spoke volumes, just as Kate's turning down his offer had done. He was reaching over a line that Kate did not want crossed.

"I'm working on the book," Kate filled the void, "I need to have a draft done in about ten days. Think I can turn the piles of research and my scraps of half-thoughts into something by then?"

"Of course; you can do anything. Get back to it. I'll see you Friday night."

It felt to Kate that Friday night would be the start of a goodbye weekend. She didn't want to bring Miami with her to Brooklyn. Paul was a great guy, but maintaining that connection was a complication she had no room in her head to comprehend. Well, two years was a pretty good run.

Monday morning was a caffeine-fueled race of replying to emails, and the afternoon's classes spent making up lost lectures. Kate felt like she was digging in sand. But she pressed on, determined to be at least partly caught up on things before asking Ray, her department chair, for a meeting to fill him in on her plans. Ray was as compassionate, smart, and fair a boss as ever there could be, but she knew that any compassion he felt for her would have to go on a back-burner while he processed the administrative mess she would be handing him. She had been in touch about Eileen, and a handful of canceled classes were certainly not a problem under the circumstances. But he had no idea about Kate's moving to Brooklyn. She planned to talk through her need to step down from the department committees she was on and then see how he took that news before broaching the leave-of-absence request that Paul had suggested. She went right to his office after her last class, and lingered in the doorway while he fed a few files to the shredder.

"Kate, I'm so glad to see you back. How are you holding up? Come in, come in."

"I'm okay, but Ray, my sister named me executor of her estate, and I'll need to spend some time on that. Is there any chance you can find a replacement for my committee work for the rest of the semester?"

"Of course. What about your classes though?"

An opening. "I'm only teaching the two—one undergrad and one graduate seminar—do you think there's a chance I can bring somebody in to share them with me? So that if I do have to go back north for a while, there will be some continuity?"

"We have an advanced graduate student that will jump at the chance to share Modern Drama with you. You know him: Charley Allen. Smart kid. And we have a few junior faculty that need to get over their fear of teaching a graduate course."

They put together a list of likely candidates for the graduate seminar, narrowed things down, and Ray was already phoning their first-choice when Kate left for her office to email Charley. Kate had a reply from one happy grad student in short order. She printed out the course materials, left them in his mailbox and headed out the door.

Climbing into her car, she discovered she had left the window open just enough for that afternoon's rain to have dripped inside. Her car smelled like feet. She covered the driver's seat in paper towels in an attempt to keep her ass dry and headed to the car wash. There weren't a lot of things she could count on living in South Florida, but an afternoon rain followed by 90-degree heat was one of them. Another was that getting your car cleaned on a Monday night was not a problem.

A third was that a drive-through liquor store was never too far away. Within an hour, she was home with a bottle of red wine.

Brian was pacing in her hallway.

"There you are! I ran into your movers downstairs hours ago. They said you were supposed to meet them here at five o'clock. They put me on the phone with your brother's friend, Anya—who's all business, by the way—and then showed me a bunch of emails. I finally let them into your place. They're all business too. They're making lists and labeling things."

"I completely forgot they were coming. Was Anya pissed?"

"Well, I don't think she's throwing you a party any time soon."

Kate handed him the bottle, and he followed her into the apartment, fumbling for the corkscrew on his keychain all the while.

"Classy guy. Pour me a glass too."

"Will do. Good luck with the movers. Wait till you get a load of them."

A tall, broad-shouldered woman, hands on hips, in a T-shirt with *Back Up, or I'll Use My Opera Voice* stretched across the front of it was standing in the middle of the office. She introduced herself, in a voice that suggested more than a passing acquaintance with scotch and cigarettes, as Pearl, before turning to a young man with a shy smile, "and this is my son, Phil."

They said their hellos, Kate made her apologies and just as she was about to ask them where things stood, her eyes fell on her bookshelves. Her books and DVDs were no longer double- and triple-stacked on the shelves. There was just a single row on the floor, spines out, crawling along the walls and circling in like a conch shell. Kate gasped.

Pearl was a quick study.

"Don't worry. We actually removed them in order. Phil's been inputting all the titles into his tablet, so you can sort them all either by title or author. He already did the same with your DVDs. Nice movie collection by the way. Phil, show her your list, while I put some boxes together."

Pearl left the room, and Phil showed Kate the DVD inventory.

"Do I really own 239 movies?"

"You sure do. And you have a lot of Mom's favorites, so she was real particular about how I set up the file. She even dusted the cases as we went along. All you have to do is tell me whether you want them sorted by director, title, or genre, and then we'll know which ones to box together."

"Genre? You cross-listed them by genre?"

"I was an English major," he said with more than a hint of pride. "And Anya said you were an English professor, so I figured genre was a possibility. I plan to teach high school, but the district had cutbacks. Until something opens up, I substitute to stay on the radar and work for Mom."

"Well, I love the genre option, but let's just sort them by director. You already have boxes too?"

"We do," Pearl said, as she walked into the office with two glasses of wine. "Hope you don't mind that I helped myself. Here, you look like you could use this," she handed a glass to Kate. "It'll take the edge off the books-on-the-floor situation. The boxes are stacked up in the bedroom, but I have four ready in the living room for the DVDs. By director it is. This is great wine, by the way." She tossed Phil a marker, and lowered herself into the desk chair: "oh, a wheelie chair. I love these things."

"Me too. But watch out for the rug there, it's easy to…"

Too late. The wheel got caught and Pearl was stuck in mid-spin.

"Hey, look at that. I didn't spill a drop. Now, Anya tells me you want to be ready to go a week from Friday. That's fine, but you'll need to stay on top of the schedule. I've gone ahead and drafted one, but you have to fill in some blanks for me. Once we have it figured out, I'll schedule the pod. I have three movers to get things downstairs, and I'll be delivering your things myself. I've never been to New York, and I need an excuse to visit my ex. He lives in Jersey. He was a disaster of a husband, but he's a lot of fun. I want to go up and torture him a little."

If she read the twinkle in Pearl's eye right, and she was pretty sure she did, Pearl was looking for some ex-husband nookie. She and Pearl would get along just fine.

"Pearl, can we talk about the cost for your services?"

"Sure, but there's not much to discuss. Anya has sent me some major jobs just when I needed them—New Yorkers buying winter places here—and I've wanted to repay the favor for a long time. There won't be any charge for my time or Phil's for that matter. Figure $1000 or so for expenses, $200 for my nephews, and then the cube. It will all come in under $3000. Can you handle $500 now and the rest when I deliver to Brooklyn? All cash, if you don't mind."

"I don't mind. And, yes, I can," Kate said, relieved. Eileen had mentioned in her letter to Kate about being embarrassed about the wealth she and Eric had accumulated. Kate wondered how she would adjust to it as Molly's trustee. Slowly, and probably not without clumsiness, she thought.

They made up a room-by-room schedule while Phil packed the DVDs out in the living room, and Kate knew that Anya had sent her an A-Team. Before they left, Phil assembled a big cardboard wardrobe and left Kate with four boxes for, as Pearl put it, "the crap you know you won't need now and probably haven't touched in years. We all have about four boxes of that, don't you think?" The boxes were labeled *Kitchen Stuff I Will Probably Throw Away*, *Bedroom Stuff I Will Probably Throw Away*, *Clothing I Will Probably Donate*, and *Miscellaneous Crap*.

Pearl and Phil said their good-byes, and Kate, with Brian's help, had the four boxes filled within an hour. Brian took a few things for himself before padding off to his place.

Kate returned to the office to tackle a bit more mountain climbing. By the time she got to bed, the mountains were fully scaled. A lot got thrown away, and she now had a reasonably organized and practical amount of research at her fingertips, so she could start a rough outline at light of day.

As she crawled into bed, she reached for the phone, channeling Bogie: "if it's three o'clock in the morning in

Casablanca, what time is it in New York? Or is it…," she dialed Gillian's number. Gillian was her Sam. Friends forever, and they had certainly been through the wars. Kids or not, middle-of-the-night phone calls remained their standard mode of communication.

"Hi sweetie. Thank you for sending flowers to the funeral. They were beautiful. Listen, I'm moving back to Brooklyn, and I'll be there in about two weeks. Call me. We need to make a list."

Kate and Gillian had been making lists since grammar school. They began with *Greatest Bands*, *Favorite Movies*, and *Places We'll Visit When We're Older*. Those were topped by Dire Straits, *The Maltese Falcon*, and Ireland. Over the years, they graduated to Gillian's *Names That No Child of Mine Will Ever Have*, *Women We Must Fix Kevin Up With*, and their ongoing *List of Assholes*. Xavier, Kathy (who used to babysit Eileen sometimes), and Gabe (from their senior year homeroom) topped those honors. The *List of Assholes* remained an ongoing preoccupation. Gabe still topped it. Funny how the ones who crap on you at key times in your life never fade from the memory entirely.

Gillian lived in an enormous Tribeca loft that her late father had the guts and smarts to purchase back when Tribeca was so barren the city was giving tax abatements to anybody willing to call the outpost home. She had inherited it mortgage-free at the ripe old age of twenty-five, affording her the wonderful luxury of living an artist's life without significant money worries. Along the way, she married Glen and had four children. Even with a family of six, there was plenty of room. She had been an in-demand character actress, but when she turned thirty things slowed down, and she bought an old theater in the village, renaming it Vanguard Arts. It became a magnet for Hollywood types looking to retain credibility as "real" actors. They often returned the favor by recommending her for film roles, and, in the past few years, she had become a household name. Nobody was more delighted than Kate, who loved emailing paparazzi snaps with obnoxious captions to her old friend.

Gillian was, without a doubt, the busiest person Kate knew. This was the only reason she had decided to delay before talking to her about her plans. Kate couldn't wait to see Gillian and for Molly to meet Gillian's kids: two sets of Irish twins, each one sharper and sweeter than the next.

Gillian's oldest daughter, ten-year old Sarah, was Kate's goddaughter, and they were thick-as-thieves. The bubbly redhead had spent a week every summer with Kate since she was two, and it was always a series of adventures combined with 'stay-at-home' days of pajamas, movies, and quiet. The adventures were somewhat predictable, depending on where they were for their summer vacation. Miami? Searching for hidden treasures with an old metal detector on the beach, fishing in Biscayne Bay, or a drive down to the Keys to the dolphin center. Sarah loved baseball—big Mets fan much to her father's relief—so a game was always factored in. But the summer she turned eight was special: they took a road trip to Fenway and Wrigley. Her request for this trip earned her a moniker of 'budding historian' that stuck. The big trip, in planning ever since seeing *Ratatouille* together, would be to Paris when she turned thirteen.

Kate's phone rang just as she was about to drift off to sleep.

"What? What?? What???"

"Are you in the City?"

"Yes, yes, I'm home. But I leave soon for Los Angeles—just for two days and then I'm back here for a show—Kate, what's going on?"

"Molly is on her way to Brooklyn with Mom and the boys, and she's going to live there with me. I'm so going to need your help."

Kate barely got the last words out before she began to cry. The enormity of her situation was painful 24/7, but the pain was particularly unbearable in the quiet of the night.

Gillian let Kate have her cry before saying softly, "Whatever I can do. You know that. How's Kitty? I'll go over with the kids before I leave for L.A."

Kate dried her eyes and filled Gillian in on all the details. Hanging up the phone, she looked at the clock. It was almost 4am, and she was exhausted. Setting the alarm for eleven o'clock, she thanked her stars that she didn't have to teach in a few hours. She fell asleep grateful for her dear friend and happy at the prospect of Gillian's kids, especially Sarah, helping her spoil Molly silly.

CHAPTER 6

Kate woke up before her alarm, made some coffee and headed into her office. She had the outline finished by noon, dealt with emails, and threw on her bathing suit. A swim would clear her head. She grabbed a towel and headed out. Walking through the lobby, she ran into Pearl.

"Phil's outside setting up the pod. We'd like to start loading it up with a few heavy items, so we can move the boxes in as you fill them up. Any furniture you can live without until you move?"

"Pearl, I hadn't thought about that yet. Can you give me an hour to figure it out? I'm just heading to the pool."

"No problem. I'll get some more boxes together. Can I have a key?"

Kate gave Pearl her keys and flip-flopped to the parking lot, where Phil was busy tapping away on his inventory of Kate's worldly possessions.

"Hi, Kate. Did you see Mom? We need a few big pieces to anchor the front of the pod before we start loading boxes in. These are my cousins, Sam and Dave."

"Sam and Dave? Seriously?," Kate asked, shaking hands with the cousins. They definitely shared the family gene that gave Pearl her stature. They looked like they could carry her sofa down on their backs. They must have tortured Phil mercilessly when they were kids. Poor Phil.

"Yup," the taller one answered. "Mom and dad love their Memphis Soul."

"Pearl's upstairs. Go ahead and pack up the bed, I can sleep on the sofa until I leave. I'll tell you what else can go as soon as I get back. I just need an hour."

She walked up the steps and through the gate, peeled off her shirt, pulled her hair up into a bun, and looked down. Eileen had been right: Kate had one ugly pair of feet. It was the first time a memory of Eileen didn't take her breath away. She smiled and looked a bit closer: the flip-flops were even uglier than her goofy toes. She tossed them into the garbage can and dove into the deep end of the pool.

She took her first lap, content that she had thrown something out, but worried that Pearl might be disappointed to see one less thing in a *Crap* box. Kate was certain that Pearl was up there now assembling at least two more boxes with labels that would put *Crap* to shame. By her fourth lap, she had decided the whole bedroom could be packed up. She just needed clothes for a week and those could live in her closet. By the mile mark, she decided that the kitchen table and chairs could go too: she could make do with her two bar stools at the counter. One mile later, she was out of the pool and heading upstairs.

The boys had already dismantled her queen-sized bed, and the DVD and *Crap* boxes were in the hallway. Empty boxes and rolls of bubble-wrap filled her living room.

"Wow, you guys move fast. Can you give me a box big enough to hold five drawers of clothes? I'll have the dresser and nightstand emptied in fifteen minutes. You can go ahead and start taking apart the kitchen table. That can go in the pod with the chairs. All the lamps can go too, except the one on my desk."

Kate sifted through her dresser and nightstand, making a little stack of the things she needed to see her through the drive up to Brooklyn. With everybody on the same page, she got changed and left Pearl and company behind to drive to campus. Ray was hanging out near her office.

"How goes the book?"

"It's coming along. I have the outline done, and I'm starting Chapter One tonight. How goes the graduate course co-teaching?"

"Karyn's going to join you for that. It's all settled. Can I come in for a few minutes?"

Kate unlocked her office and Ray followed her inside.

"I know this is a hard time for you, but, well, it's just that I need to know how much time you think you might need off. Do you think a semester leave is a good idea? I can arrange that. You have a sabbatical due too; you can start that now, if you want. It would keep you on full pay through the summer and then half pay in the fall. What do you think?"

Kate's eyes filled with tears, and the stress of the past few weeks came gushing out. She told Ray that Molly was moving to Brooklyn and that she would like to be there to help her get settled. A half-truth, to be sure, but this was still a full step above what she had said to him Monday. She felt a little less guilty, but thought it best to let this play out with Ray leading the way.

"The sabbatical would take a lot of pressure off me. Are you sure you can arrange it?"

"Just fill out the forms, they're all on the Faculty webpage. I'll start drafting an email to the Dean explaining things, but you should make an appointment with her yourself. How soon do you want to be up north?"

"A week from Friday would be best. Molly is getting there tomorrow, and I want to be there as soon as possible to help out. Do you think this can all be arranged that quickly?"

"Of course. Under the circumstances, Kate, I can't imagine the Dean turning it down. And we've got your classes covered. Get in touch with her. I'll go start the wheels in motion from my end."

Ray left. Kate closed her office door, got herself together, and emailed the Dean. The grapevine moved fast in this college, but even so, Kate was shocked to hear back before she even finished finding the Sabbatical Request Form.

Dear Kate, I heard about the accident. I am so sorry for your loss. Of course I'm free to meet with you. Stop up any time after four o'clock.

So Kate spent the rest of the afternoon organizing files to hand over to Charley and Karyn. As she was filling out the request for her sabbatical, her office phone rang. This happened so infrequently—everybody emailed, even if their office was just down the hall—that she didn't know what the noise was at first.

"Hello?"

"Kate, it's Sean. Sorry to bother you at work, but I wanted to let you know I'm back at Pineapple Street with Mom and Molly. We got in last night. Any word on when you'll be heading up?"

"I'm meeting with my Dean this afternoon to submit a sabbatical request. I'll know more by dinner. But I already told my boss that I hope to be on the road next Friday. If everything goes okay, I'll be pulling up in front of the house in less than two weeks. How's Mom?"

"She's doing alright. We're all sort of waiting for her to crack a bit, but I'm starting to think that's not going to happen. She's running rings around all of us. And Gillian came over this afternoon with her kids, so she's having fun catching up with all of them. Sarah's been amazing. She's mother henning up a storm. And Alice seems to have decided Molly is her own doll. She's pretty jazzed not to be the smallest one for a change. They've been playing in the living room all day. Her sons have commandeered Kevin's X-Box."

"That's all good news. I hope to have some to add later today. Where can I reach you at six-ish?"

"On my cell phone, Kate. Remember those? You used to have one and, by the way, you better plan on getting another one before you leave Miami. The only thing Mom has been complaining about is the fact that you'll be driving up without a phone. Will you please get a phone?"

"Yes, okay. Tell her I'm getting a phone. Do they still make them without internet access? I just want a plain phone, not a smartphone."

"Sure. There's one left in America. Go to any chain store. Look for the aisle covered in dust. You'll find it between an abacus and a pencil sharpener."

"No need to get snarky. Can I say hi to Molly?"

He called her to the phone. "Katie?"

"Yes, Molly, it's me. How are you sweetie? Are you having fun with Auntie Gillian and Alice and Sarah?"

Judging from the sounds on the other end, Molly was shaking her head up and down in a yes.

"I'm in Florida. Remember coming here and swimming in the pool?"

"Mmmm."

"I miss you."

"Miss you," she replied, in her little sing-song voice. She gave the phone back to Sean.

"Get here soon, Kate."

"Will do."

Kate got back to the business at hand, packing and emailing until heading up to the Dean's office. Unlike the faculty offices—which could best be described as cells with windows—the Dean worked in a carpeted corner office with views of the bay bridge. There was music on low in the background, plants everywhere, magazines on the coffee table. While Dean Anderson poured them each a cold glass of water, Kate took a seat on the sofa thinking it was like being in the waiting room of a dermatology office.

"Nice digs, aren't they?"

"Your office is gorgeous. And thank you for seeing me on such short notice, Dean Anderson."

"Susan. Call me Susan."

"Susan, I have the paperwork here, and I hope you can consider my request quickly. My brother called this afternoon asking when I would be up north, and I didn't know what to tell him. Our niece is there now, and the sooner I can join her the better. How long do these things take to be processed?"

"They take as long as it takes me to read and sign them. And I'm a fast reader."

Susan signed the forms, handed them out to her assistant, and wished Kate well.

"You'll be with us through next week. If there's anything you need, let me know."

Kate was driving through the Big Wave liquor store within an hour. Remembering that Pearl was probably still at her place, she picked up an extra bottle of wine. Paul was due Friday, so she got a bottle of whiskey too. She drove away with bottles clinking in their bag on the passenger seat and heard a siren behind her when she was just two blocks from her apartment. She pulled over.

She opened the window and reached over for her registration.

"License, registration, and insurance card."

Kate handed them over. "What's the trouble?"

The officer looked over at the bags, with their bright red Big Wave Liquors logo, sitting on her passenger seat.

"Your left break light's out. Where are you coming from?"

"Work. I teach at the university. Well, and then the liquor store. I'm in the process of packing, and I thought some provisions were in order for the help."

"Your eyes look a little red. Have you been drinking?"

"No. Crying. I cried a lot this afternoon. I'm not a good crier. It takes a while for my face to go back to normal."

Mentioning crying to a man you don't know—cop or not— is like saying you have cramps. And in a situation like this, where you're in the subordinate position, it can be a perfect way to tone down a power play. Kate was no fool. He got just close enough to smell her breath, and then sent her off with a warning and advised her to get the light fixed within forty-eight hours.

She walked into a partially empty apartment, and poured

herself a glass of wine before putting away the liquor. She saw the kitchen table and chairs had been packed up. She ate a little supper at her counter, cleaned up, and went into her bedroom to call Sean. The phone was on the floor surrounded by dust bunnies. When Pearl said they would pack things up as Kate tagged them, she meant it. Kate swept the floor before dialing Sean's number.

"Where are you? It sounds like a tunnel."

"I'm in an empty bedroom. These movers of Anya's are dynamos. I have to put sticky tags on things tonight for their next round. They'll be stopping by every day until the place is empty."

"Any word on your moving date?"

"I'll be in Brooklyn a week from Saturday. Maybe Sunday. I'm not sure if I'll drive straight through or not, but either way, I'll be on the road that Saturday morning. The university has granted me a sabbatical through the end of the year. I haven't told them that I'm not coming back, but for some reason I think they know."

"That's great news, Kate. Do you want to tell Mom yourself or should I?"

"You can tell her, Sean. I've got a lot to do here until I leave. But I'll be in touch. Kiss Molly on the nose for me."

"Will do. Bye."

She went into her office and saw stacks of different colored dots sitting on her desk along with a note telling her to stick them on things that could be packed together. Seemed like a good system. Kate decided to tackle the books. With no classes left to teach, that task seemed pretty easy. All she needed to do was make sure not to put a dot on anything she might need to finish her new book. All the American authors got blue dots, the Irish got green, and on it went. It was working fine until the third glass of wine, when Kate realized she had placed a blue dot on Joyce's *Ulysses* and a green dot on Morrison's *Jazz*. Definitely a sign that it was time for bed. She wobbled into her bedroom, forgetting that she had to make up the sofa or else sleep on the floor.

She turned back to the living room, opened the sofa, threw some sheets on it, and passed out in her clothes.

CHAPTER 7

Kate followed a tidy routine for the rest of the week: up early, call Brooklyn to check on Molly, swim a mile, grab a coffee, tackle the book, break for lunch, let Pearl and Phil in, then go to campus and work on wrapping things up there. By the time Paul arrived Friday night, Kate had drafted two chapters and was ready for the weekend diversion. He arrived in time for dinner.

"I love what you've done with the place. How are you?," he asked kissing her on each cheek. It had become their custom after their first trip to Paris.

"I'm better for seeing your face. Come on in. You won't believe how big it all looks now that it's empty. By the way, we're on the couch. They packed up my bedroom ages ago. What do you have there?"

"Stone Crab Claws from Joe's and a bottle of cheap wine. What do you have here?"

"Goat cheese salad with pine nuts and beets and the best crusty bread I could find."

"Let's bring this feast down to the water. We can watch the sun go down. Do you have a blanket here, or did they take all of them away?"

"Blanket at the ready. Let's get out of here."

They took their loot and the blanket and headed to the beach. Kate's apartment on Collins Avenue had a lot of plusses, but proximity to the beach was her favorite by far. They were there and set up in no time at all. He asked all the right questions of concern about her family, the move, her sabbatical, and the book. As Kate was beginning to wonder if he realized this was a break-up visit, he took her hand in his and asked her what he could do to help her through things.

"I won't push it, Kate, but you might need some help getting settled in Brooklyn. My leave runs through the end of the summer, and I'll be back and forth to New York for a few talks and some research. What do you say?"

"Can I let you know once I'm there for a little while? I'll be staying at Pineapple Street until I find a place for Molly and me, and, to tell you the truth, that's all still unreal. What is real is the book. Can I talk you into reading the chapters while you're here? Better yet, can you read them when we get back to my place before I open the Jameson's?"

"Sure. Let's just wait till the sun finishes going down."

They sat together in silence, watching the sky turn reddish purple before the big ball fell beyond the horizon.

"Red sky at night, sailor's delight?"

"That's right, Kate. Let's head back." He squeezed her arm, helped her up, and off they went.

Kate got the sofa opened and made the bed up while Paul sat at the desk in her half-empty office. She grabbed a shower, and when she got out found him in the kitchen pouring a drink for each of them.

"To you, Kate. And two solid chapters."

"Really?"

"Really. You're off to a fantastic start." He handed her his marked-up copies of the chapters before picking up his drink and heading to the shower. "Let me know if my notes make sense. Back in a flash."

Kate curled up on the floor with the pages and her drink. She dug in with the same gusto she had brought to the Stone Crab claws earlier that night. When she was a graduate student, she faced marked-up pages of her writing with dread, and it was the same case with her first book. Those anonymous readers that her publisher sent the draft to were brutally honest, but she learned from that experience to take it all in. An old mentor had told her that readers wanted the manuscripts they looked over to succeed and that she should take their comments accordingly. It's possible that was one of the biggest lies ever uttered, but she approached those comments believing it was the case, and she turned in the finished manuscript in record time. The reviews were glowing, and it led to her tenure-track position. Now that she faced being on the job market again—for the first time in years—she decided to take the same positive posture.

She was lost in reading when Paul came out of the shower. God, he was gorgeous. It never ceased to amaze her just how tasty that man looked with wet hair and glasses.

"Will I ever be able to talk you out of wearing your contacts? Your face was made for glasses, you know. Very rogue intellectual."

"They're a hassle. And speaking of hassles, would you consider getting a cell phone before you head north? Refusing to own a cell phone makes you something of a dinosaur."

"Sean is after me to get one too. Don't worry, I'm going shopping for one after you leave. Unless, of course, you might want to come with me?"

"Kate, we have less than two days together. I don't intend to spend an hour of it watching you struggle with your phone issues. Besides, I hate tech stores of any kind. You know that."

"Now who's the dinosaur?"

"I'll show you dinosaur. Let's test-drive this old couch of yours."

He took the glass of scotch and the papers from her hands, and laid them both down on the floor. For the rest of the night, Paul proved once-and-for-all that the reports were right: forty was definitely the new thirty.

✦ ✦ ✦

Sunday morning came too quickly for both of them. Kate offered to take Paul to the airport and return his rental car, but he passed. On his way out the door of Kate's apartment, he reminded her to call him as soon as she got her new phone.

"I want to hear all about the drive. And call me when you get to Pineapple Street. Don't worry if it's late."

"I will. Promise. Get going or you'll miss your flight."

They shared a lingering hug.

"I love you, you know."

"I know. Me too. Get going."

Brian popped out of his apartment while Kate was still in the hallway watching the elevator doors close behind Paul.

"I don't think I'll ever see him again."

"Cut it out, Kate. You're too old to play the ingénue. You'll see him if you want to, and you know it."

"Want to come shopping with me to get a cell phone?"

"Not even a little. Just go get a smartphone. Repeat after me, smartphone."

"Smartphone. Do they come without internet access?"

Brian rolled his eyes and stepped back inside his apartment. She was on her own.

Showered, dressed, and out the door, Kate climbed into her car. She caught the reflection of her sad eyes in the mirror, and thought of Eileen. Then she thought of Molly, which brought something close to a smile to her face. She took a picture of the two of them out of her tote and tucked it into the back of the driver-side visor. Flipping the visor back up, she decided this would bring good luck as she drove to the superstore that had recently opened near the mall. She was going into what she viewed as enemy territory and wanted all the good karma she could gather.

She loved her laptop and other toys, but cell phones made her crazy. She had purchased and been given half a dozen over the years: one sat at the bottom of the River Liffey in Dublin (where she had drunkenly tossed it on her way to the airport when she was moving back to the States); another, a sturdy old number programmed only for use when traveling abroad, sat in her desk at home with her passport; the third was in a domestic violence shelter in Miami, donated when she had enough of receiving wrong-number texts; and the rest were gathering dust in her kitchen junk drawer. The main reason she was happier without a cell phone was that she liked being alone, but never felt she was with that thing ringing and vibrating at her. The propensity for people neither leaving messages nor listening to the ones she left annoyed her too. When exactly that lack of civility became acceptable she couldn't say.

The parking lot was full, and Kate had to park in the street. The doors to the big snow glove of a store were opened by a smiling millennial wearing a headset and monitoring her little phone.

"Hi. My name is Alyssa, how can I help you?" Alyssa was entirely too perky for Kate, but she looked around and saw all the staff in their blue polo shirts milling about were cut from the same cloth, so she stuck with Alyssa.

"I need to buy a new phone."

"Great! Which model do you have now? We have some trade-in opportunities!"

"Well, I don't have a phone to trade in actually!" To her horror, Kate realized Alyssa's exclamation points were contagious. She regrouped. "Do you have one that doesn't have internet access? You know, a phone that's just a phone?"

Alyssa's smile remained in place and her eyes revealed a serious case of brain freeze, but she carried on.

"Oh, yes. All of our phones are smartphones!" Alyssa apparently assumed Kate was one of those customers who didn't know what to call things. This one was slightly youngish for that, but no matter. "Is there a particular carrier you prefer? Our phones work on all of them!"

"No. Sorry. What I mean to say is that I do not want a smartphone. I just want a phone that makes phone calls. And where I can block text messages."

"Well, no, we don't have any phones like that. Are you sure

you don't want a smartphone? Take a look at the models on display, and I'll be right over there (she pointed toward the door), if you need me to explain anything!" Alyssa scurried away.

Another blue-shirted head-set-wearing kid approached her.

"Hi, my name's Ethan. I overheard your saying you wanted a plain phone. Is that right?"

"Yes. Do you have any?"

He flipped a switch on his headset, pulled a business card from his pocket, and slipped it into Kate's hand. "I have a friend who deals in what you're looking for. You can reach him on the number on the card. He only deals in cash."

"Ethan, I'm not looking to score some surplus meds here. I just need to buy a phone that's less than smart."

"I know," he laughed. "You'd be surprised what a market there is for them, but most stores don't sell them anymore. My friend and I buy them in bulk and then sell them to folks like you. Trust me, they're not stolen or anything like that. I better go." He flipped the headset switch back on and wandered away.

Kate waved goodbye to Alyssa-the-door-watcher who flashed a beaming smile in return.

Kate stopped by Brian's and told him about her adventure. "Don't call that number, Kate. I'll do it. You're hopeless."

Pearl and Phil were in her apartment sealing packed boxes and setting up the last ones she would need to pack up her worldly goods.

"Hey, Phil. Do you know anything about black-market cell phones?"

"Sure. My friend, Ethan, is the guy for that. What do you need?"

She ran back to Brian's and retrieved the business card. "Did you call the number yet? Phil knows the kid who gave me the card. He'll take care of things."

"Too late. Ethan's coming over after work."

✦ ✦ ✦

The rest of the afternoon was productive. Kate focused on another chapter of her book, while Pearl and Phil moved her sofa and some boxes down to the pod, and set up an air mattress for Kate. All that remained would fit in her car for the drive north. Phil stuck around to meet with Ethan and sort out Kate's phone needs. She spent the late hours inputting numbers into her new phone and then called Sean.

"Hi. It's me. I have a new phone."

"It's about time. Hold on a second, I have to tell Kevin he just won $20. I was sure you wouldn't get one."

Kevin came on the line. "I knew you wouldn't let me down, Katie. Which phone did you get?"

"I got a flip phone."

"Shit. Hold on."

Sean came back on the line. "Thanks, Kate. I'm $10 ahead now. You still leaving Saturday morning?"

"Yup. Everything's almost done here. I don't know how I'll ever thank Anya. These movers have been great. Can you ask Kevin to email her address to me? I want to send flowers. How's Molly? How's Mom?"

"They're both doing fine, Kate. But they'll be even better when you get here. We all will. I can't believe you're finally coming home."

"Neither can I, brother, neither can I. I'll call you from the road. See you in a few days."

CHAPTER 8

The first time a New Yorker drives through Florida on I-95, she is charmed by the availability of fresh grapefruit and oranges at practically every exit of the highway. The second time, she is busy keeping track of all the cash given to her by smoking friends in New York who have sent her on the lookout for cheap cartons on sale at every exit's convenience store. There's barely room in the trunk once the Wish List is checked off. By the third trip, she is cringing at all the cheap and readily available fireworks. From the fourth trip on, she packs her car the night before with everything except a toothbrush, goes to bed early, and gets up at dawn so the trip can start as early as possible to get out of the state as quickly as possible. The plan? Don't stop until you see signs for the Georgia state line.

Saturday started a little different though. Kate padded around her apartment in bare feet, looking in the empty cabinets, checking out the boxes, and thinking that her time here had been pretty good. The parties, quiet Sundays, movie nights with Brian, fry-ups after a day's fishing: not a bad list of memories. She slipped on her shoes, and picked up a jacket, her favorite flyrod and her tote. The flyrod, a 9-weight Sage Method, was her pride and joy.

She won it on a bet with Paul. They had been seeing each other a few weeks when she decided to call bullshit on his flyfishing snobbery. "It's not harder or more skillful than spin, Paul. It's just different. I've been fishing my entire life. I've never thrown a flyrod, but I bet I can land one of your precious bonefish on Day 1." And so one muggy August weekend, they drove down to Key West, and Kate caught and released her first bonefish—a 10-pound stunner—on a flat off the Marquesas. At dusk. On the Saturday. On her third cast. The fancy rod and reel, wrapped in a shiny red bow, were waiting at her front door within a week.

Leaving the key on the kitchen counter, she headed out of her Miami door for the last time. Brian was waiting for her in the hallway with flowers and a large, steaming-hot Starbucks. "Half-caf, no-fat latte for you, my friend."

"You're a doll. Promise you'll call me? I have this cell phone now, so I want to hear it ring, okay?"

"Promise. Yell if you need anything. I'll keep an eye out for any mail, and I'll forward it to your mom's. I'll miss you."

"I'll miss you too. But not for too long. Promise you'll visit in the summer?"

"Promise. Get going."

As Kate walked to her car, she inhaled the salty air and admired the starry sky beginning to turn orange. Nothing like the period before the sun rises, she thought. No traffic to speak of at this hour on a Saturday, except for a few pick-ups trailering skiffs south toward the Keys. Shame that flyrod would be in the trunk instead of being put to use. She loaded up the car and took a glance into the backseat. It was holding a sort of treasure chest: a little cabinet that contained all the toys Molly played with during her Florida visits. Kate tucked an old blanket around its edges.

Kate took a picture of herself with Molly, Eric, and Eileen out of her tote and stuck it to the visor alongside the one of just Kate and Molly. She wanted to see them all together and happy for the ride north. She started the engine, took one last look back, and pulled out of the parking lot toward I-95.

Driving on a highway through mainland Florida was among the most boring things a person could do. No funky swamps or mangroves, just a mind-numbing procession of exit signs and strip malls. All that kept Kate alert was adjusting the radio to keep up with the changing NPR signals. But she pressed on and made it to Jacksonville by ten. One Starbucks fix, a little gas, and she was off again. Before she knew it, the magic *Welcome to Georgia* sign was in her rearview mirror. Georgia. Georgia and peaches. There were billboards advertising all things peach: peach salsa, peach bread, peach tea, peach pie, peach smoothies, and, finally something Kate could reasonably get on board with: peach cobbler. But she didn't stop.

She made it as far as South Carolina before pulling off the highway for a proper meal. When she tried getting out of the car, she was reminded that driving ten hours was not good for the legs or the neck. She stretched and walked around the parking lot before heading inside. It was one of those Americana-themed restaurants that required a journey through a gift shop to get seated. But it was worth the kitsch. She was digging into a gravy-laden meatloaf and side of mash when she noticed her tote was vibrating. The phone. She'd already forgotten about it.

"Hello?"

"How's the drive going? Where are you?"

"Hi Mom. I'm having lunch in South Carolina. Not sure what town it is, but I've started seeing signs for *South of the Border*, so North Carolina isn't far off. How's everything there?"

"The boys have your room all ready for you, and Molly keeps asking when you'll get here. We can't wait to see you, honey, but I hope you're not still planning to drive straight through. I just never think that's a good idea. Why don't you plan on getting a room someplace?"

"I was thinking about a hotel. I've been on the road since dawn, and I'm starting to get wired. Can I say hi to Molly?"

"She's at the Aquarium with Kevin. He's been volunteering there since Hurricane Sandy. They took a hit."

"I heard. Good for him. How's Molly doing?"

"She's quiet. Quieter anyway. I bet she'll be happy to hear you're almost here. I'll tell her as soon as they walk through the door. Finish your lunch. And call me when you stop for the night. I love you."

"Love you too. See you soon."

Kate finished her lunch, paid the check and grabbed two bags of lemon drops from the gift shop before heading back out to her car. Another top-up for the gas tank, and her car was once more pointing north. Her tote danced again, and she grabbed the phone.

"Kate, it's Sean. Mom said you're someplace near *South of the Border*. Do me a favor, and stop soon."

"Yeah, I will. I just want to get into North Carolina first. These Pedro signs are killing me."

"Just pull over and get some rest."

"I will, I will. I didn't get the phone so you could nag me more, Sean. I'm hanging up now. I'll call you when I check in someplace."

She hung up, and made it just over the North Carolina border when she pulled into the first hotel that didn't look like it had hourly rates. She checked in and headed for the gym, which, thankfully, had a little heated pool that was just long enough to do a proper lap. As ever, a swim set her right. But it was a short one. She went back to her room, called Pineapple Street, grabbed a shower and curled up beneath the covers with the remote. She had gotten rid of her television around the same time she ditched her third cell phone, and she never missed it—until she got to a hotel. Then she couldn't turn it off. She passed out watching some train wreck about Americans who get arrested on overseas vacations.

Kate was up and out the door early, arriving in Virginia by lunchtime. The homestretch, she thought. The voices on the radio started sounding familiar, and she was finally realizing that this was all really happening. DC rushed by in a blur, and Maryland crab cakes were hot and ready when she stopped for an early supper at Box Hill, home of the best crab cakes on the planet. Speeding through South Jersey, she wondered—with a smile—if Pearl had made it to her ex-husband's place yet.

As she turned onto the Garden State Parkway, Kate's heart skipped a beat. Zipping through the tollbooths with the handy EZ Pass velcroed to the windshield, no traffic in sight, every mile brought her that much closer to Brooklyn. Starting over never felt so good. She drove through Staten Island, over the bridge, and was up in front of 22 Pineapple Street before midnight. Sean was sitting out on the stoop staring off into the cold winter night. Kate whistled to him through the open window.

"Lost in thoughts there, big guy?"

"Just waiting on a lady. Go on in. I'll unpack the car and get it parked. There's a few folks inside waiting to see you, and one of them is up way past her bed time."

Kate got out of the car, hugged her brother, and handed him the keys. She took the brownstone steps two at a time toward the familiar door.

PART TWO: HOME

CHAPTER 9

Stark grey skies looked down on the ferry as it pulled into the dock at Inis Mor. The bearded captain had a cigarette hanging out of the corner of his mouth. He tossed the line to his boy on shore and they navigated the ferry together, chatting away: a father and son at peace with their work. Kate grabbed her backpack and laptop, waved off the taxi and admired the monument to lost fishermen. She headed toward the guesthouse that would be her sanctuary for the week's work ahead: an overdue journal article on Leopold Bloom's confrontation with the anti-semite in James Joyce's *Ulysses*. Was there really something new to say about this episode of that celebrated novel? Kate thought so, and it involved Chekhov. Passing the cemetery on her right and a pub to the left, the driveway to the guesthouse was in her sights when...Kate felt a weight on her chest and a wet kiss on her nose.

"Bloom jew."

"Whah?"

"Blue juice."

"Sleep."

"Cuddles?"

And so the day began. Dreams of writing in Ireland would wait. Kate rolled slowly on to her side, taking Molly with her.

The hesitancy with which Molly asked for cuddles pulled a string of Kate's heart. So did the tentativeness of her posture. Molly was avoiding eye contact. Kate placed a finger below Molly's chin, raising it while she slid down the bed, bringing them nose-to-nose. Molly was still looking down, her eyes barely open.

"Cuddles, cuddles, start my day. Breakfast, dress, and then to play. Cuddles, cuddles, morning smile. When I'm big, I'll run a mile."

Molly looked up at her aunt and patted her lovingly on the cheek.

"I remember some of Mama's songs, Molly. Will I always sing them to you?"

Molly nodded and clung to Kate, her head nestling into the crook of Kate's neck.

Molly was not old enough to have accumulated a vast supply of memories. But she was holding tightly to those she possessed: especially her Mama songs. Auntie Kate didn't sing the same way as Mama, but the words were the same. Was there a word for the way a grown-up sang? Mama used to say that what Auntie Katie lacked in pitch she made up for in enthusiasm. That would make Mama laugh. Auntie Katie's singing made Mama laugh. And Auntie Kate on the phone made Mama laugh too. Mama laughed a lot. And sang. Dada laughed too. But he didn't sing. He would dance though. And swing me around in the air when he did. Then give me nose kiss and hugs. Hugs are cuddles in the daytime. They are called different words, but really they are the same thing. I like words and want to learn all of them. But my heart is too sad to do that. I love my Pineapple Street family. But if I learn words with them it means Mama and Dada are not coming back. And I want them to come back. There is room for them here on Pineapple Street.

She nudged her auntie's neck with her nose.

"Blue juice, Auntie Kate."

Kitty looked up to the kitchen ceiling, mug in hand. Eileen had made it in camp one summer. It was yellow with little playing card symbols painted here and there, more hearts than clubs, spades, or diamonds. There was one extra heart inside, and I LOVE YOU was painted sideways down the length of the many-times-glued-back-together handle. Kitty followed the sound of footsteps moving toward the bathroom overhead. They meant she could get breakfast started. Something to do.

She put the mug down, pushed her chair away from the kitchen table, and placed her palms on the table for leverage to push herself up. That was new. She had never needed a boost before. Wanted one, sure, but not needed one. These were new days. She felt older than dirt, and she didn't like it. The doctor up in Vermont had given her a prescription to help her sleep, and she had been taking a pill every few days, when the insomnia became too much. But they made her groggy the next day, and she worried about becoming dependent. She had heard too many horror stories to risk that.

She was relieved Kate was back.

CHAPTER 10

After grape juice and oatmeal served by Kitty, the three generations sat around the kitchen table looking fairly pleased with themselves. Kate left Molly with her grammy and went off to look at apartments.

She stepped out into a crisp March morning. It was almost damp enough to smell like snow. Almost. She unlatched the old gate and recalled how she used to love when a grown-up let her sit on its wrought iron bar to swing her legs as she pushed it back and forth with just the power of her own weight. She would have to tell Molly about that. And how she taught Eileen to do it, and would teach Molly when she was just a little bigger. She noticed—they all did—that Molly was quieter in little ways.

She was a real chatterbox between Thanksgiving and New Year's and had insisted on tickles so often that she would sometimes tire Kate out. Tickle requests were less frequent now, and, like this morning, often replaced by cuddles. Cuddles had been Molly's morning routine with her parents. And the chatter, Kitty and her brothers said, had been replaced by a propensity for quiet. The therapist Kitty went to said the verbal regression would likely pass as Molly worked through her grief. Hugs were prescribed. To be accompanied by the grown-ups sharing their memories, pictures, and videos of Eric and Eileen on a regular basis.

The changes in the Heights since Brooklyn became the New Something were not quite as extreme as in the borough's other neighborhoods, like Williamsburg or Bed Stuy. Heights residents had been weary of high rises for decades, and the area defied gentrification because it embodied the concept from its original settlement in the seventeenth century. It had always been a mix of professional and working classes, artists and bankers, the weary and the well-healed. The factories might have closed, but the ancestors of the factory owners and workers remained. From Vinegar Hill and DUMBO to the Heights proper, the area was—as far as Kate was concerned—the very best of Brooklyn.

But there were some changes, and they had not gone completely unnoticed by Kate over the years. Things seem to have accelerated recently. A big grocery and chain bookstore opened within a few blocks of each other on Court Street, and an independent bookshop was back on Montague Street for the first time in a long while. The indy caught her eye for its charming name, *The Page Turner*.

She crossed the street and peered in the window. It looked wonderful, and she made a mental note to check it out. The new park by the pier was magnificent, but its welcome green space was offset by a new condominium going up on Furman Street. It was so close that it cast a shadow over a long stretch of the park's jogging path. It looked ever so slightly like a prison.

She was relieved that most of her old haunts were still in business. In some cases, taken over by the children of the owners she had known growing up. These were the places she had always returned to when back visiting Pineapple Street: something she had done more infrequently in recent years than she cared to admit. It dawned on her as she walked to the corner to meet Anya that she seldom ventured out of a fairly tight circle when she was back: the homes of family and friends (all within six blocks of each other), the diners and shops that had been in business her entire life, the promenade, and the subway stations at Borough Hall and on Clark Street.

With a toddler in her life, she would have to widen the circle to include things she was now noticing for the first time. And as Anya was about to remind her, that new circle would have to include anticipating what came next.

"I've got six places for you to look at before lunch, and they're all perfect, and in your budget too. They're either two- or three-bedrooms, except one is a single, but the bedroom is huge, and you can divide it easily. Have you thought about a playgroup or preschool? I have a list here. Most of them are feeders for St. Joseph's, which you need to keep in mind. You do plan to send her to St. Joe's, right? I know it's all a bit much, but you have to start thinking about these things. You should look into the waiting list too; although that might not be an issue for your family, since so many Doyles are alumni."

Kate took the folder Anya had prepared for her. It was meticulously organized with color-coded sticky notes, and—as with Pearl in Miami—Kate was dazzled by Anya's precision.

They saw two walk-ups, one brownstone garden floor, a two-bedroom on Henry Street, and an enormous loft. The afternoon would include the third floor in Anya's building on Water Street in DUMBO, or Down Under the Manhattan Bridge Overpass. It is one of New York's great neighborhood acronyms, along with Tribeca, the Triangle Below Canal; NoHo, North of Houston; and Nolita, North of Little Italy. Sandwiched between Fulton Ferry and Vinegar Hill, DUMBO had changed radically. Kate was curious about how kid-friendly this little neighborhood on the Heights's edge might be.

They headed to Mary Lou's for lunch, where Kitty and Molly were already seated, coloring the menu as they waited for the apartment-hunters.

Ah, Mary Lou's. Chosen for its familiarity to Molly, who had been there on every Brooklyn visit since she was born, and its centrality to Doyle family big events, of which finding an apartment for Molly and Kate was certainly one. Mary Lou's had been a tradition since Bill and Kate moved to Pineapple

Street shortly before Sean was born. They had a brunch there after his baptism and the custom began.

Over pierogi and coffee, Kate narrowed the morning list down to three, and Anya began ticking off the necessities of toddler-proofing. Kate took notes as quickly as she could: outlet covers, no loose throw-rugs, window guards, child-proof clasps for low cabinets…Kate's brow furrowed at the mention of a toilet lock. Molly was two-and-a-half and potty-trained.

"I remember putting a gate at the top of the stairs when you were little, but the rest of this is new to me," Kitty said as she looked over the list and nibbled on her lunch. "A toilet lock? Really?"

Molly looked at the print-outs of the apartments, and started coloring them, while Anya texted away, and Kitty enjoyed her meal. In the safety of this place and this company, Kate allowed her thoughts to drift beyond her responsibility to Molly. Molly was always at the fore, but just behind her was Kate's career.

What if she couldn't get a job? What if her teaching career was over and everybody knew it but her? She was facing forty, and would be going on interviews for the first time in years. She had not worked outside of academia any more than she had been responsible for somebody other than herself. She wanted to freak out, but she had neither the time nor the privacy. The noshing, coloring, and texting began to swirl around her, until darkness seeped into her outer field of vision. She slid out of a chair for the second time in as many months, banging her face a little on the table before her backside hit the restaurant floor with a thud. But she was awake. Sprawled out on the floor, with a clear view of the goop stuck under the table they had been eating off of, she looked to her niece, "Well, this is not good."

"Not good, Auntie Katie," chimed Molly, looking down from her booster seat.

"Oh, dear. You have a little cut there," added her mother, who reached down and brushed the always unruly hair from Kate's face.

After checking that Kate was okay, Anya ran off to ask the hostess for something to clean the scrape.

The waitress pushed a few chairs aside, so Kate could stretch out on the floor. Her vision cleared after about fifteen minutes, and she climbed back into her seat next to Molly. The waitress returned with a glass of water, while Anya cleaned the cut on the bridge of Kate's nose.

"Kiss the boo-boo, Molly?" The little girl leaned over, obliged, and helped Anya apply a small round bandage that had the face a grinning kid.

"Dora!"

"Who's Dora, Molly?"

Molly gently tapped Kate's bandage with her little finger. "Dora here, Auntie Katie. Here. On boo-boo."

"It's a smart look, sweetie," Kitty offered. "Dora the Explorer. She's on television. I watched her with Molly this morning."

"I'll be sure to watch it with her this week. Do you like Dora, Molly?"

She nodded her head up and down. "Diego."

"Who's Diego?"

"Dora's cousin," Kitty quipped, with a smugness that elicited smiles from Kate and Anya.

"Okay, Kate. Do you still want to see the rest this afternoon?"

"No, I'd rather wait and go early tomorrow. The morning light will be the deciding factor on narrowing down what we saw this morning. Between those and whatever else you have up your sleeve, I think I can make a decision. Then Molly can come with me later in the day."

She turned to Molly. "Will you come with me in the stroller tomorrow to see the new apartment?"

Molly nodded, maybe not comprehending what a new apartment meant, but clearly grasping getting wheeled around by her Auntie Kate.

The check was paid, and—after saying goodbye to Anya, who promised to set things up for the morning—Molly, Kate, and Kitty headed down Montague Street to walk on the promenade. The wind was surprisingly strong and practically blew them over Pierrepont Place. They huddled closer together, Kitty and Kate swinging Molly between them, and admiring the view of Manhattan. Molly suddenly let go of their hands, turned to Kitty and pointed to the sky, "heaven?"

"Yes, sweetie," Kate could hear the catch in Kitty's words, "and that's where Mommy and Daddy are, up there in heaven, making sure we're all okay. I miss them though. Do you miss them too?" Kitty's eyes filled up as she reached down to hug her granddaughter.

Molly nodded, returned Kitty's hug and then just stayed like that for a few minutes, rocking slowly back-and-forth. Kitty picked her up and carried her to a nearby bench. Molly clung to her grammy, sobbing. Kate sat next to them and rested her head on Kitty's shoulder. The moment eventually passed, and Molly took their hands again and they continued their walk up the promenade, turning right at the park and up Pineapple Street. Kate tucked Molly in for a nap with her menagerie of stuffed animals. She was already dozing off when Kate kissed her forehead. She watched her sleep for a little while, wondering just how often Molly thought of her parents. Was it every waking moment? Was it in her dreams? Maybe both.

When she got downstairs, Kitty was sitting in her rocker with a cup of tea.

"Mom, does Molly ask about Eileen and Eric often? Has that happened before?"

"Yes. Not often, but it does catch me off-guard, which is foolish. I think about them constantly. Seems unreasonable to think Molly doesn't too."

Kate nodded. "I want to call Anya and thank her for that therapist she referred you to. You like him, right?"

"I do. And you will too. But there's no need to call Anya. She'll be upstairs for supper with Kevin. You can discuss it with her then." Kitty winked when she said "supper."

"What's with the wink, Mom? Something I don't know about?"

"Oh, nothing. Just a speck of dust in my eye."

Unlikely, Kate thought.

✦ ✦ ✦

Kate was up and out of the house by 8am, and Anya was already at Starbucks staring intently at her phone when Kate arrived. And, Kate noted, sipping coffee from a decidedly non-franchised cup.

"Are you ready to pound the pavement again?"

"Definitely. Let me just grab a coffee."

"No need. One half-caf, no-fat latte at the ready." She handed the paper cup to Kate.

"You're the best."

"I know," Anya smiled, "I had to reject every instinct to make that purchase for you. On the plus side, it allows me to tap into my alarmingly sanctimonious impulses. It really would be a shame not to exercise that reductive muscle from time to time. She slid the sturdy paper cup across the table with her well-manicured fingertip. "But you know you should support the independent coffee shops." Out the door they went.

Their first stop was the top-story walk-up in a stately four-story building on Remsen Street. It was close to St. Joe's, where Molly would eventually be going to school, and to Pineapple Street, which, no matter where Kate and Molly lived, would always be central. Walking up the few steps to the front door, Kate thought how nice it would be to have a stoop for summer nights: she remembered lovely old photographs of her maternal relatives smiling on their own stoops in years gone by. Entering the vestibule, Kate admired the gleaming wood paneling and ornate molding, but she also noticed it was dark and that the otherwise well-tended-to carpet—both here and up the first flight of stairs—was a bit thread-bare. Funny that she hadn't noticed it yesterday.

They took the stairs slowly, checking out every nook and cranny like prospectors in search of precious gold, which in a sense they were. Kate was adamant that they select a place for the long-term; somewhere that Molly could call home for several years. Somewhere, as Eileen said in her letter to Kate, where Molly could grow. It had to be in good condition, be big enough that Molly wouldn't quickly outgrow it, and, ideally, not occupied entirely by young, corporate hot-shots. They listened for the sound of children as they passed each apartment door on their way to the unit to which Anya held the key: not a peep.

Anya opened the door, and immediately reached for a light switch.

"No, Anya. Don't turn it on. If we need it at this hour, it's not the place for me or Molly."

"Sorry, reflex."

Anya remained near the doorway as Kate walked through the living room, both bedrooms, the kitchen, and bath. It was certainly in great shape, unlike the hallways; and the windows faced out to a court near the church, with a view of the church gardens. Anya joined Kate at the window.

"Lovely, isn't it? And you know that can never be built upon. It's part of the church property. The parish had been approached by so many developers over the years that they finally put it in writing that the gardens will remain as long as the church does; and it's a very healthy parish, if you know what I mean."

Kate understood perfectly. 'Healthy' was a polite term for a parish with deep reserves. The gardens would remain well after Molly left for college.

"I don't know, Anya. The view is beautiful, but the light just isn't right. This one is off the list."

"Onward and upward then!"

Anya locked the door behind them, and they ventured off to the first loft. As they turned right onto Love Lane, past Kitty's favorite grocery (a plus), Kate turned to Anya.

"When did this street get so developed? And where's the parking garage? Dad used to keep his car there."

"Oh, that went down about five years ago. In fact, it's condos now. Look," Anya pointed to a gorgeous faux carriage house, "that's where your old garage was."

"When did the Heights start having condos? I thought it was co-ops only here."

"Maniacal co-op boards are not for everybody. Potential buyers were becoming less willing to put up with Board snooping. When the market tanked, quite a few started incorporating condo options into their bylaws. Then the City revised some zoning laws, and, *voila!*, condos. We even have a few condops: that's sort of a hybrid of a condo and a co-op. But your dad's old garage," she pointed as they passed it, "was condo from the start."

"I can't believe I didn't notice it yesterday."

"You didn't miss it. We came a different way today. Our next building is an anomaly: it's the only co-op I know in the Heights that allows long-term rentals. So you're in luck. And it has a roof deck."

Turning left onto Monroe Place, they faced the building containing Option 2. The doorman greeted Anya with a hug, and chatted with her while he fished the key out of an old locked key closet on the wall behind his desk.

"And who is this, Anya?"

"My friend, Kate Doyle. She saw the place yesterday and is back for a final look. Kate, Mr. Best. He's been here for years."

"Pleased to meet you, Mr. Best."

"Pleased to meet you Miss Doyle. Are you new to the Heights?"

"No, I grew up here, but I've been away for a long time. Just moving back from Miami. I'll be living with my niece. Are there families with children in the building?"

"Oh, yes. Quite a few. Our in-house super has children too."

He chatted about the kids and the schools they attended. He was a rare bird: an unfailingly polite, uniformed doorman who clearly knew the goings on in the building, but oozed discretion. A good sign, Kate thought, until Mr. Best informed them of a call he received that morning from the owners of the loft they were to look at.

"They've decided to sell rather than continuing to rent it out. They've been in San Francisco for the past two years and have decided to stay. Do you still want to see it?"

Anya turned to Kate.

"What do you think? We hadn't talked about it, but is there a possibility that you want to buy?"

Kate's heart sank. "No. I can't make that kind of commitment without having lived in the place a while. And finances will be tight," she added at a lower register, "for another month or so...until the estate is settled. Would they consider renting with an option to buy?," she asked turning to Mr. Best.

"I'm afraid not. They were quite specific about selling as soon as possible. They've definitely decided to make California home."

Anya returned the key, and they headed out to see the final apartment on the day's list. Cutting through the park at Cadman Plaza, Kate marveled at the federal office building and the dozens of people coming and going. It had risen from nothing shortly after the hotel opened across from the courthouse. Together, these structures anchored the north-south line of the revitalization of Downtown Brooklyn. Anybody who remembered Jay Street before all this development couldn't help but be blown away—be it approvingly or with exasperation—at how upscale everything had become. This wasn't Hipster Brooklyn, this was Briefcase Brooklyn. As they walked over to Water Street, Kate noticed that her companion was unusually quiet.

"What's on your mind, Anya?"

"Your financial situation. And your maybe buying a place. I own the Water Street building outright. That includes all of the apartments. But I've been thinking of turning the place co-op. I want you to know that I'll give you first right of refusal, if and when I go that route. Okay? So keep that in the back of your mind."

"Will do. But I hope you don't do it anytime soon."

"Not a chance. I have too much on my plate to deal with

that; it's a long-term plan, like getting married and having children. Way down the road. So far down the road, I shouldn't have even mentioned it. Never mind."

Doth the lady protest too much?, Kate wondered.

As soon as they exited the elevator, which opened directly into the apartment, Kate was dazzled by sunlight.

"Wow."

"I cleaned the windows last night and swept the place up. Polishes up kind of nice, don't you think?"

"I sure do think. It's amazing. The light alone has me thinking it's perfect. Let's see if I can get Molly over here. Do you have time for a coffee while I call Mom?"

"Sure. Let me just pop down to my office first. I'll meet you at the diner. If you take it, the floors will be re-done and everything painted. And there's no need to sign a long-term lease. Let's keep it ten months, so my lawyer and insurance agent are happy, but I don't want you to feel stuck. I can have it all ready in about a week. Let yourself out," she said, handing Kate the key. "I have to admit I was hoping for this," she squeezed Kate's arm. "I'd love to have you and Molly in the building," she added, on her way out the door.

Kate called her mother, who said she'd be over with Molly right away. Then she took a stroll around the spacious apartment. The layout was perfect: three bedrooms, one of which could be her office; a kitchen that opened up into an expansive living room and, maybe best of all, tucked away in the corner of her office: a fireplace. An honest-to-God working fireplace. She saw herself and Molly quite happy here, but if the little one wasn't excited about it, she would have to press on. Fingers crossed. She imagined Anya could ask a small fortune for it out on the open market, and thanked her lucky stars for friends.

Anya was already in the diner by the time Kate got downstairs, holding court at the counter. Kitty and Molly arrived before Kate had a chance to take off her coat.

"Auntie Katie!," Molly shouted raising her arms in the air and struggling a little to escape from her stroller. "Big hug.

Kiss nose." She was her old self. Some days were like that.

Kate swept Molly up in the air and kissed her nose, as commanded. When Kate looked up, she saw the assembled group she rightly assumed were regulars positively melting at the sight of the little girl.

"And who is this?," one older woman asked. Molly got shy, but not for long. She was soon wandering around, exploring, and climbing on and off chairs.

"Well that's a good sign, if ever I saw one," Kitty said, placing her bag on a table. "I can't believe I've never been here; I love it. You take Molly up to see the apartment; I'll have a coffee."

Kate corralled Molly, bundled her up in her arms, and headed out the door.

"Now remember, Molly, the apartment is empty. We have to use our imaginations. And you can pick your room; would you like that?" Molly nodded.

The old elevator transfixed the little girl. Wide-eyed, she looked up to its ceiling. Shaking a little with excitement, she grabbed Kate's hand as the relic began its ascent.

"It's a cage," Kate said, showing Molly how the buttons and accordion handle worked. When it opened directly into the apartment, Molly was even more delighted. She walked around the apartment, looking out the living room window— "bridge!"—and exploring the closets.

She wandered into each bedroom, with Kate following closely behind, delighting in her niece's enthusiasm. After checking out each bedroom a few times and then returning to the living room, she reached up for Kate's hand.

"Come, Auntie Katie." Every time she felt that hand in hers, Kate fell in love with her niece all over again.

Molly guided them to the biggest bedroom (not that there was much difference from one to the other), stopped in the middle and pronounced: "your room."

Kate looked down at Molly, "Why, thank you. Yes, I like this room very much."

She then went into the room next door, "my room."

Kate nodded, "yes, your room. It's perfect."

Entering the last bedroom, Molly looked up at Kate again, "my room."

Kate laughed. "Can we share this one?"

After a round of tickles—their first since Kate arrived from Miami—Molly agreed that they could share it.

They collected Kitty downstairs and headed back to Pineapple Street. Kitty retired to her sanctuary downstairs, and Molly was left, very happily, with her Uncle Kevin. He was finally done with the long days he pulled for a week straight. He completed a lobby renovation early so that he could take a full day off to spend with Molly. It would be a special day with his goddaughter: no phone, no email, no work. Just the two of them at the aquarium and a stroll on the boardwalk at Coney Island. And that day was tomorrow, so they took the afternoon to look at pictures of fish. Kevin was a planner, no two ways about it.

Kate welcomed a few hours on her own. She drove over to the new apartment to drop off the boxes and toy chest she had driven up herself. Returning the car to Pineapple Street, she saw her flyrod on the floor of the back seat. She grabbed the tube, locked up the car, and headed back to Water Street. The walk would do her good.

She'd been on the verge of tears since breakfast. At least the heavy fog that sat in her lungs and on her heart wasn't with her twenty-four hours a day anymore. In true Doyle fashion, she had kept the tears at bay until she had some privacy. Losing it in public was not her thing.

She was halfway down Columbia Heights, barely at Dog Park, when tears began to slide down her face. They fell up Middagh Street and down the tail end of Hicks, across Old Fulton and over Dock. No street was able to damn the fear that overwhelmed her, nor capable of providing comfort. They only slowed down some when she turned onto Water Street. The irony did not escape her. As she fidgeted with her front door key, her phone rang. It was Gillian.

"Speak at your own risk. I'm the proverbial hot mess, and I

have boxes to unpack."

"I can help you unpack boxes. I am a woman of many talents. I'm also about twenty feet behind you, and I have booze and a care package from Katz's. And a pack of cigarettes, one of which I'm smoking."

Kate wiped her eyes and turned around.

"How did you know where I was?"

Gillian tossed the cigarette, "Kevin told me."

She set her two shopping bags on the sidewalk, and wrapped her mittened hands around Kate's face.

"You weren't kidding. You are a mess."

Kate shook her head. "I am. And your grungy mittens aren't helping. Can I wipe my nose on them?"

"You wouldn't be the first." She palmed up to Kate's nose. "That is one snotty shnoz. Now blow."

Kate blew.

They examined the content of the mitten together.

"Not bad," they said in unison, laughing.

Each grabbed a bag, and headed inside.

CHAPTER 11

Kate got up early and left Pineapple Street while everybody was still asleep. Sitting at Starbucks with the morning paper, she reached into her tote and grabbed the new apartment keys. The week spent refinishing the wood floors had flown by. Kate also noticed, when she stopped in yesterday to check on the progress, that the bathroom fixtures had all been updated and the tub and floor re-tiled. Nice touches for which she was gratefully surprised. She finished her coffee and strolled over to Water Street to check out what mornings were like on her new block. She firmly believed that morning was the measure of just about any place or anyone. As she approached the building, she saw Anya at her desk and tapped on the glass of the big picture window. Anya smiled and waved Kate into her office.

"The flowers are absolutely gorgeous, Kate. I know I should say 'you shouldn't have,' but I'm going to ignore that nicety." She kissed Kate on the cheek, "you should have! And I'm glad you did. Have you heard from Pearl?"

"No, but I expect to at any minute. She should be here this morning with the pod. Where will they park that thing?"

"Don't worry. One of the great perks that came with this building is curb rights. Didn't you notice the street signs in front?" She pointed to the pole directly outside. Sure enough, a sign said *Parking by Permit Only*.

"They're pretty much obsolete now, but it was part of the deal when I agreed to fully renovate the building. I have a permit sticker here for Pearl's truck and the pod. But she said she'd have it all unpacked within twenty-four hours. Do you have time for a coffee next door?"

"I'll pass on the coffee. I stopped for one on the way over."

"What will it take for me to get you away from the corporate coffee bean?"

"You'll be wasting your time, Anya. I'm hooked. But I promise to support the diner too."

"Okay. I forgive you. Go upstairs and look around. The painters finished yesterday, so it's all in tip-top shape. See you later."

As Kate waited for the elevator, she looked around the lobby and admired what Anya had done with the place. She had started her real estate firm over ten years ago in what was then a ramshackle warren of artist space occupied by painters who had been priced out of Soho, Chelsea, and the East Village. They were soon priced out of DUMBO too and moved further along to Red Hook, Williamsburg, Bushwick, you name it. Painters, textile designers, writers…the crafts were many, and constant mobility is more likely to impede than inspire. Contrary to romantic notions and screwy biodramas, a little security goes a long way in the arts.

Anya understood this, and she worried that the clock was ticking faster every day on just when the rents in those Brooklyn neighborhoods would also prove too steep for the community. She dreaded the idea of rents resigning even one artist to taking out a loan to cover tuition for a coding class: walking away from the artistic impulse in favor of the security of a 'real' job. Anya watched that clock with disdain and guilt. She had seen friends and neighbors move away and mom-and-pop stores close as a result of escalating prices, and felt no connection to the hedge-funders, trust-fund kids, and designer boutiques that took their places. The guilt was because she profited handsomely from the hedge fund, trust fund, and hipster invasion of Brooklyn. She had entered the real estate business just as the boom was about to start.

By the age of thirty-two, she was a millionaire twice over and left the firm she started with to open her own place. Along the way, she bought this six-story building nestled between the Brooklyn and Manhattan bridges that Kate was about to call home.

Anya renovated each floor as tenants of the previous owner moved out, taking the top for her own home, and the ground floor for her business. She shared the street front with the family-owned coffee shop that had been in the building since the 1950s. She gave The Bridge Diner a 25-year lease at a steep discount in part to assuage her guilt, but also to guarantee that its coffee and babka would always be nearby. They thanked her on a regular basis, catering fundraisers for local schools and charities with the profits they now enjoyed thanks to all those hipsters, who shared counter and table space with the DUMBO long-timers.

But her little oasis sat amidst evidence of the property boom. Surrounded by *Roast This!*, a coffee-granola-kale co-op, and *Safety First*, which sold everything from condoms to bicycle helmets—and with curb-side parking neither those shop owners nor their customers could use—she maintained a charm offensive to help temper their entitlement-tinged hostility.

If those building owners ever took the trouble to find out that she had paid a full 60% less per square foot than they had, all attempts at civility would certainly have been futile. Whenever a business owner on the block did become hostile toward her, she presumed (usually correctly) that they'd looked up the tax records. Anya didn't let it get under her skin though. She was not going to apologize for having the guts to bet on this neighborhood.

Anya had come to real estate following a brief career on Madison Avenue, where she learned that it's a business less about selling products and more about a constant jockeying of people desperate to be relevant. She only looked back on those years when she bumped into a former colleague. The leaving was a messy affair that dragged on for several months.

She had told her boss that she decided to move on to other things, but he talked her out of it. Who else would he manipulate into covering up the fact that his expense account cash for "tips" went to gratuities of another kind? He talked her out of resigning by offering her a paid month off. She took it happily. The sun and rest definitely recharged her batteries, but they also confirmed that she wanted out of advertising.

She ran toward a career where she would never again have to be surrounded by people who were fixated on yesterday. She always loved architecture and buildings and took a real estate course just to test the waters. She passed her exams and never looked back. Kate admired Anya for her refusal to dwell on the past and what was a genuine Auntie Mame approach to life. The woman *lived*.

Entering her new apartment, Kate was dazzled by all the work that had been done in just one week. Kate had rented her share over the years and was always at the mercy of landlord's tastes, but Anya was clearly a unique breed of landlord. The hardwood floors were in pristine condition—the new matte finish glowing warmly in the morning light—and every wall in every room was another shade of magic.

She saved looking into Molly's room for last, and it didn't disappoint. The walls were periwinkle, the door green, and the windowsill pink. Little stars were affixed to the ceiling, and a lace curtain hung on the window. Kate saw a note pinned to the curtain, and she bent down to read it:

Dear Molly, welcome to your new room. I hope you like it. But be sure to let me know if you want new colors...or more stars! Love, your Auntie Anya.

Kate took a framed picture of Molly, Eric, and Eileen out of her tote, kissed it, and placed it on the window sill. The ringing phone helped her shake away the teary fog threatening to move in. The caller ID made her smile.

"Pearl! Where are you?"

"I'm stuck in traffic on the Outerbridge Crossing. Is Phil with you?"

"No."

"He called me a few minutes ago from a diner on your block. Bridge Diner maybe? Something like that."

"That's right downstairs. I'll go meet him and make sure the cones are out so you can park right in front."

"Anya's already taking care of the parking. Go get a coffee with Phil. I'll call you back when I'm nearby. If this traffic ever improves. It's worse than the Palmetto during rush hour. Oh, it's starting to move. Hanging up!"

Kate skipped the elevator and ran down the three flights of stairs, stopping at every landing to check the view from the wonderful little rose windows that graced each one. Anya had explained that these windows had a direct link to the Cathedral of Saint John the Divine, but it was a strictly secular connection.

The west rose window of that landmark Cathedral, uptown in Morningside Heights, is a colorful, intricately constructed marvel that sits above the main entrance, welcoming visitors in from Amsterdam Avenue. It was installed in 1932, and, like the opening of the Brooklyn Bridge some four decades earlier, drew the appreciation of throngs of New Yorkers. James McCann, then the owner of Anya's building, was one such admirer. He went back every few days, from Thanksgiving to Christmas, and stared at that window. He saw it in the daylight, at dusk, and in the dark of night; in the rain and in bright winter sunshine.

McCann ran a speakeasy behind the space that was now Anya's office, and a lucrative wholesale market where the diner now stood. Between these two enterprises, he was rolling in money during the last few years of Prohibition.

He was also a romantic who loved the sea and all things nautical. These interests collided one night in December of 1932, when he decided that miniature versions of the Divine rose would be perfect on Water Street. He paid the local glass and iron works to create a design he drew on an old bar rag. When his new windows were ready, he recruited a group of carpenters and painters to lay them in on the wall facing the harbor. Holes were knocked out on each floor, the west-facing wall as luck would have it. With their metal casings and thin iron lines, they resembled the portals of a ship.

Kate looked forward to showing them to Molly. Below each one was a sign that Anya—ever the kitsch fan—had affixed. At the third floor, now home to Kate and Molly, there was vintage Macy's: *Santa Has Gone to Feed the Reindeer*. At the next floor, an old subway sign announced the N and Q trains to Coney Island; and the final floor reminded people to *Keep Calm and Carry On*. She went to open the lobby door, but it wouldn't budge. Was I supposed to get a key to this?, she wondered. When she pushed it again with all her weight, it swung freely—and quickly. She staggered into the chest of a dark-haired man cradling his cell phone between his shoulder and left ear, and holding two bags of groceries. He had greyish blue eyes that made Kate catch her breath. She knew instinctively that her reaction had not gone unnoticed. And she blushed.

"Whoa! Sorry. You okay?"

"Yes, I'm fine. Sorry too. You okay?"

"I'm grand." He put the bags down and said "call you back" into the phone. "Finn. Howiya?"

Yikes. There were Dublin accents and then there were Dublin accents.

"Kate. I'm good, how are you? I'll be your neighbor on three, have to go meet the movers."

"Welcome. I'm just up on five."

He made no attempt to hide the full appraisal he was giving her, and it made Kate cringe. But just a little. More out of habit really. He tilted his head a little and squinted, looking at her face and forehead intently. "What's with the…," he tapped the bridge of his nose.

The little scrape had healed, but Molly insisted on applying a little sticker after Kate took her shower. She had quite a collection. Today's featured a cat.

"Oh, that's nothing. Nice to meet you, Finn. Gotta' go. Sorry about the crash there."

She walked quickly through the lobby and out the front door, without looking back—ripping off the sticker on her way and shoving it in the front pocket of her jeans.

Anya was on the street putting out the cones. She smiled as Kate skipped toward her.

"Where you off to in such a hurry?"

"Next door. Just got off the phone with Pearl. Her son flew up ahead of her. He's here already, and she'll be by with the pod soon. She called from the Outerbridge."

"I know, I know…yell if you need anything."

Kate stopped. "I will. And thanks so much for Molly's room; she's going to love it." She kissed Anya on the cheek. "Later, gator. Oh, and remind me to ask you about the Irish guy on the fifth floor."

"He's single!"

Phil was sitting at a table with his laptop open and an old duffle bag at his feet. She took the seat across from him.

"Hi, Phil. Your mom's on her way."

Phil stood up beaming. "I know. I just got off the phone with her." He shook her hand then sat back down. Kate absolutely loved his manners.

"What's put that big smile on your face?"

"I was checking my email. Look," he said, spinning his laptop around so Kate could see the screen. "Look at this. I have a job! A real one. I've been subbing at my old high school for a lady on maternity leave. She came back last week, but it looks like she's decided not to stay. They're offering me her job. I can't believe it."

"I'm so happy for you, Phil. When do you start?"

"Monday. I start Monday. I'll get three full months before summer break. Wait till I tell Mom. She'll go nuts."

"Go ahead and call her. I'll grab a coffee."

"No, no. I want to see her face when I tell her. I'll wait until she gets here. Excuse me for a minute."

He ran outside, jumped up and down in the middle of the sidewalk and then rocked what was apparently his happy dance. Folks at the counter watched this over their papers, forks, and mugs; smiled, and then turned in unison toward Kate, with brows raised.

"He just found out he got a job he's been wanting for years. Give him a break, okay?"

When he came back inside, everybody at the counter applauded, and one old man got up to shake his hand.

"What's the big job?"

"I'm going to teach English at my old high school. I can't believe it."

Phil took a seat and started telling him about the school, and how long he'd been substituting there. He forgot all about Kate, who took the opportunity to check her email on Phil's laptop. She hadn't realized there was free wifi in the diner. That would come in handy until she got around to getting her cable set up, which, in New York, could be a waiting game of epic proportions. But living in a city where early morning diners rated enthusiastic sidewalk dancers was more than worth the hassle. She felt like a million bucks, and opened an email from Paul:

How's the move? Call me when you can. P.

If she had five minutes to think about it, she might have missed him too. He was due in New York tomorrow for a seminar at NYU, so she would see him soon enough. An email from the publisher of her first book caught her eye:

Dear Kate, I ran into Paul at the airport last week, and he said your new book is taking shape. We'd love to have a first look. If you have an outline and a few chapters, please send them along. We lost a title from our next fall schedule and have an opening. If the timing is good for you and the material is good for us, it could be a win-win. Give me a shout a soon as possible. Best, Jennifer.

This surprise was the first professional optimism she'd felt in months. With her sabbatical in place, her tenure review had to be pushed back—it was now two years away—and Miami didn't know that she had no intention of returning. She was playing this very close to the vest. The Doyles, as was the family practice, didn't ask. They figured she would tell them the status of her job when she was good and ready. Not a word to Brian or anybody else either. No, this one she had to work through on her own. She was for all intents and purposes about to voluntarily become one of thousands of under- or unemployed PhDs. Finishing the book, it suddenly dawned on her, would allow her to see what working as a full-time researcher/writer would be like. Could she do that? Pearl's voice snapped her out of What If land.

"I need coffee, Phil. Phil? What are you doing?"

Kate turned around just in time to see what she would have thought an impossible feat. Phil had his mother in a bear hug and the slight young man was lifting his 6' tall mother—easily 200 pounds—clear off the ground.

"Put me down."

The counter regulars started cheering and began, all at once, to tell her about Phil's job, creating a cacophony of good cheer. Kate said a quick hello, grabbed a key from Pearl, and headed out to see the cube, leaving the diner buzzing and giving Phil a chance to fill his mother in on the good news.

It was parked directly in front of her building, and she opened it to peek inside. Everything appeared in good shape, as far as she could tell. She had just sat on the curb to wait for Pearl and Phil when her brothers appeared from around the corner.

"Give me the combination. The men have arrived," Sean winked as he reached out to give Kate a hand up. "You've packed on a few, Kate."

"Oh, leave me alone, and get to work. How did you know

my stuff was here?"

"Pearl called Anya, and Anya called Kevin. We're waiting on a delivery to finish a job, so we thought we'd help out. And the truck from Vermont will be here by lunch. We want to take care of Molly's bedroom furniture and toys ourselves. Step aside."

The boys removed a dolly from the pod and loaded it with boxes. Kate was about to roll it inside to the elevator when Pearl and Phil joined them at the curb.

"What are you doing? Phil will take care of that. Hey, handsome," she said addressing Sean, "grab your friend there and help me get the sofa off-loaded."

She turned to Kate, "are these the brothers?"

"They are. And brothers," Kate turned to a bemused Sean and Kevin, "this is Pearl."

Leaving Pearl clearly in charge, Kate took the dolly into the elevator. Phil joined her with an armful of area rugs and a lamp. It was a tight fit, but they managed to get everything up to the third floor with no trouble. When the elevator opened directly into her apartment, Phil was impressed. He had never seen such a set-up.

"This is cool, Kate. But how do you get in—or out—if the elevator's not working?"

"There's a stairwell over there," she said, pointing toward the far living room wall. "That door opens right into it. You should check it out, there's these little windows on each landing, and they all face out to the Brooklyn Bridge."

Phil bolted to the stairwell, while Kate laid the area rugs in the bedrooms and stacked boxes in her new office/guest room/playroom. A three-bedroom apartment with windows in every room, including the kitchen, was all new to her. She was bragging about the space and the luxury of it all to her mother last night, when Kitty warned her to enjoy it while it lasted. "If Molly's at all like Eileen was at that age, you won't have a spare inch."

The morning flew by, with the pod unloaded by the time the Vermont truck made an earlier-than-expected appearance.

The living room and Kate's bedroom furniture were in order and the most important contents of the Vermont truck—Molly's bedroom—nearly done by the time they stopped for lunch at the diner. Everything else went to storage for when Molly was older, except a few pieces that Kevin, ever the sentimentalist, insisted on keeping close to him at Pineapple Street. Kate was touched by the care the boys gave to setting up their niece's room. They assembled the bed, unpacked the boxes and filled her toy chest, hung some clothes in the closet and folded others into her dresser. Kate caught Kevin removing a small stuffed penguin from his jacket pocket.

"What's that?"

"Molly and I went to the aquarium last week. Remember? She liked the penguins, so I picked this up for her new room. The tag says his name is Pete."

He placed Penguin Pete on Molly's pillow and reached back into his pocket. He retrieved a photo of him and his goddaughter, placed it next to the penguin, and then put his hand on Kate's shoulder to steer her out of the room: a sweet ending to a good morning's work.

Anya joined them all for lunch, with Pearl entertaining the rowdy group with stories about her ex-husband, Walter. Phil blushed through most of them, occasionally interjecting a "he's not that bad," but mostly enjoying the tales as much as everybody else. Halfway through Pearl's telling them all about Walter getting their skiff stuck on a sandbar in Biscayne Bay, Sean turned and whispered to Kate: "Anya's hand is on Kevin's knee."

Kate dropped her napkin to get a better look while picking it up from the floor. Yup, definitely touching there. She caught Anya looking at her, a little flustered, when she sat back up.

"Oh, this is good," Kate whispered to Sean. Mom doesn't miss a trick, she thought to herself.

They were interrupted by Pearl. "I'm done. Let's get back to work."

"The queen has spoken," Sean said smiling. "To the queen!" he added, raising his water glass. "To the queen!"

everybody laughed.

Pearl took it with good nature, but she also sat up a little straighter and, if the diner lighting hadn't been working in her favor, the rest of the group would have seen a prideful blush.

Anya went back to her office and the crew returned to work. In three hours the apartment was filled with boxes and ready for its new occupants. Kate surveyed the place; it looked great…mostly. Her dining room table and its four chairs, while fine in Florida, looked like dollhouse furniture against the scale of this space. Besides, they would never accommodate what she hoped would be regular visits from her family and extended family here in Brooklyn. She made a note to start looking for more chairs and a table that would fit ten. Too tired to do more unpacking, she decided to stay with Molly at Pineapple Street one last night, before officially making this Home Sweet Home.

CHAPTER 12

For the first time since arriving in Brooklyn, Kate was up
before Molly. She took care not to wake her little roommate,
and went to the kitchen to put on a pot of coffee. But Kitty
had beaten her to it. She was seated at the kitchen table with
her laptop, in a chair draped with her treasured Reese jersey.
Pee Wee Reese, Boy of Summer, and team captain. Kitty was
busy replying to queries on the Brooklyn Dodgers fansite.

"Morning, Mom," she mumbled before kissing Kitty's
cheek.

"Morning, Kate," she replied without looking away from
her work. "Pour yourself a cup. I'm replying to a man in
Munich who's writing a book about New York baseball...in
German. Isn't that wonderful? Turns out he came to America
for graduate school and fell in love with baseball when he lived
here. Now German readers can learn all about Pee Wee and
Jackie."

Kate sat down with her coffee. She was relieved to see her
mother reconnecting with the world. Her vail of grief was
lifting, if only a little.

"Mom, I was thinking about having a housewarming dinner
tonight. You know, for good luck. There's a lot of boxes
around, but the dining room and living room furniture are all

set up. And I'll have the kitchen unpacked this morning. What do you think?"

"I think it's a great idea. Give us all something to celebrate together." She patted Kate's hand. "Who do you want to invite? I can get the word out for you, while you're over there unpacking." She handed a notepad and pen to her daughter.

Kate wrote down the names, while she said them aloud: "You and Molly, Sean and Margot, Kevin and Anya." She looked up at Kitty. "What's going on with those two, do you think?"

"Oh, they've been together since the summer. They'll be married by the end of the year. I think that losing Eileen and Eric moved things along for them."

"What?! When did they tell you that?"

"They haven't. I don't think they know it yet. But they'll figure it out soon enough. Let's not talk about it though. It might jinx things. I could use a family wedding." She logged out of her blog. "Can I have the crossword puzzle?"

Kate tore the puzzle page from the paper and slid it over to her mother, who never ceased to amaze. Kate turned her attention back to the guest list.

"Gillian's in town. So, call her too. That's thirteen, including Glen and the kids."

"Unlucky number for a housewarming. Are Pearl and Phil still here?"

"Yes, they're staying downtown until tomorrow. You can get their number from Anya. Mom, do you mind if I take a look at the old furniture in the basement? My dining room set is too small for the new space. I definitely need a table. And more chairs. As it is now, a few people will be sitting on the floor tonight, with dinner plates in their laps."

"That's fine. Take whatever you can use. Just don't take things with a letter K stuck to them. They've been claimed by your sentimental brother."

Kate finished her coffee, and, armed with a flashlight to make up for the dull wattage in the stairway, ventured down to the basement. It was packed. Her parents had never been successful in begging Kevin, Sean, Kate, and Eileen to clear out the odds and ends they left down there. Both officially gave up when they retired to North Carolina.

Kate smiled at the memory of her father announcing one night that "it was all Sean and Kevin's problem now. Let them deal with it."

Kate found two folding chairs, an old metal-backed number that she recognized as the desk chair of her teenage bedroom, four sturdy oak chairs that would work fine with what she already had, and a small wicker one that she could put in Molly's room.

As she was about to go up the stairs, she noticed something in the corner, covered with an old sheet. It was small, maybe three feet high and only about two feet wide. Lifting the sheet, she pointed the flashlight on a little table with two drawers, each with a carved *claddagh*, the traditional Irish symbol of loyalty, around a recessed handle. Looking closer, she saw little harps carved in the legs, along with letters. She could make out D, L, and O. But the fourth one was too hard to see. And there was something she couldn't quite identify in the center of the table top.

"Mom! Can you hear me?," she shouted up the stairs. She put her hand on the tabletop, and the whole thing wobbled, but just a little. One leg was a touch shorter than the others, and it looked just slightly lighter in color. She ran her hand over it searching for a carving. Sure enough, another harp, and she could feel two letters: MM.

"Yes, I can hear you. What is it?"

"Come down. There's something here I want to ask you about."

Kitty came to the top of the basement stairs.

"I don't like going down there. Can you bring it up?"

Kate slipped the flashlight under her arm and lifted the little table. It was heavier than she expected, but she still had no trouble getting it up the stairs and into the kitchen.

"Mom, what is this?"

"It belonged to your Grandma Edna. Do you remember

her?"

"Of course. She took me to my first Broadway show. How old was I when she died?"

"You were around ten or eleven, I think. She told your dad that this table was to go to you when you were older. I forgot all about it. Isn't it lovely?"

"It is. Do you know what this symbol is, here on the top?" She traced it with her finger.

"That's St. Brigid's Cross. St. Brigid was—maybe still is—a patron saint of Ireland. If memory serves, her feast day is the 1st of February," she said, staring at the table, continuing to slowly trace the Cross's edges. She looked up at Kate.

"People used to hang the Cross over their front door or by windows—any opening to the home they would have had—to keep the evil spirits away. It was meant to keep the family safe when they were inside. I always thought it was an odd thing to have on a piece of furniture. Your father said that Edna was very fond of this. It went back a few generations on her side to the family that emigrated here in the 1800s. Your grandmother always kept it by the front door. If you open the drawer, you'll find a note in there."

Kate's excitement was tempered by the Feast Day. February 1st was also the date of Eileen and Eric's car accident. She was sure that wasn't lost on Kitty. She pulled on the top handle, but it was stuck.

"Leave that. It's not a drawer. It's called a secretary—a little extension of the tabletop for when you need more room to lean on. Let me try." She jiggled it, with no luck.

"There's too many years of grime on that. You'll have to clean this up to get it open. The second handle down is the drawer. That's probably okay"—she pulled at it—"because it would have been used more often, I expect." It got stuck at the halfway point. Kitty slid a few fingers inside and retrieved an old, yellowed envelope with *For Liam* scrawled across the front. She handed it to Kate and smiled. "She always called your father by his Irish name. Read it to me."

"*My dear Liam, This is your family history, treat it with care. Your loving mother.* That's it?," Kate flipped the paper over.

"Your grandmother wasn't one for a lot of words. Your father got that from her."

"It's just what I need next to the elevator. And I'd love to take the chairs too. Okay?"

"Sure," Kitty said inspecting the table, "this needs a serious cleaning though. The chairs too. I'll get some mineral spirits and clean rags for you to take. Be careful with the top. That's bog wood inlaid on the leaves and cross. Edna was serious about it needing to be treated carefully."

Kate brought the chairs upstairs while Kitty went to gather the cleaning supplies. Her mother was right, the chairs were pretty grimy. She heard footsteps overhead, but didn't want to disturb Sean, Margot, and Kevin when they were heading out soon to work. She called Sean's phone instead, and got his voicemail.

"Hey Sean. I'm taking some furniture from Pineapple Street. I need you and Kevin to take it over to my place in your truck after work. Or before work. I'll take whatever you can do. And I hope you and Margot don't have plans for dinner. I want to christen the new apartment. Mom will give you the time when you stop by for the furniture. Bye."

Molly tiptoed into the kitchen. "Gammy? Auntie Kate?"

"In here, sweetie," Kitty answered from the hall closet. "Come give your grammy a hug."

"And don't forget about me, Molly," Kate said.

Molly dispensed the hugs, and climbed onto a chair.

"Blue juice?"

Kate poured the grape juice and got the oatmeal started on the stove. As the three of them sat down to breakfast, Kevin and Sean came through the front door.

"We're in the kitchen," Kitty called out in their direction. "Come have some oatmeal, there's plenty."

The five of them had breakfast interrupted by Molly taking turns sitting on everybody's lap.

Sean turned to Kate, "So, today is the official moving-in day?"

"It is. I just left you a message. Any chance you can take a few things from the basement over this morning?"

"Not a problem."

"Good. I need a bigger dining room table than the one I brought with me from Miami. I'll go over to Macy's this morning and find something. Can you meet me there with the van in an hour or so?"

"Will do. Call us from the store."

Kitty took Molly upstairs to get dressed for the day, while the boys said their goodbyes to Kitty. Kate headed to downtown Brooklyn in search of a table. She saw a furniture store on the opposite side of Henry Street, and it had a great big, beautiful farmhouse-style table in the window. It was perfect. The shop wasn't open yet, but she saw somebody inside and tapped on the glass to get his attention. He let her in, and she made a beeline to the table. It had a clearance tag— nice—but she didn't see any obvious reason for the mark-down.

"There's two scratches," the salesman said, watching her.

"Where?"

"Near where the leaves meet. It was dropped when we moved it. It's a bargain at that price."

Bargain or not, it was more than she planned to spend. But she liked it, and she hated to shop for anything other than shoes and books.

"I'll take it." She gave him her credit card.

"Do you want it delivered?," the salesman asked as he waited for her card to be approved. "I can have it out in two days."

"I actually need it today. But not delivered. My brothers will come to get it."

She called Sean again.

"Change of plans. I'm in that furniture store near the Clark Street subway, and I bought a table. Can you stop here on the way?" She looked at her watch. "Why aren't you at work?"

"Because it's Saturday, Kate. You need to get back to work. Have a schedule. You're worse than Mom. We'll be there in ten minutes."

"Hold on a second." Kate looked at the salesman, "can you get this outside in ten minutes?"

He didn't miss a beat. This might be the fastest and easiest sale at this price point that he would make all week. "Done."

"I'll meet you in front, Sean." She hung up, signed the credit card slip and waited while two guys from the backroom came out to move her beautiful new Table for Ten. It would fit the Doyles easily, with room for more if everybody squeezed together. She was thrilled, but Sean was right. Not having a work schedule was giving her pudding brain.

✦ ✦ ✦

With the new furniture in place, and the boys on their way to Good Will with her old table, Kate looked around the apartment. A lot of work still lay ahead, but there would be plenty of room for people to sit tonight, with two at the counter and a body or two on the couch. She looked at the boxes stacked up against the living room wall and sighed. Then she looked at her watch: 11am. She grabbed the boxes labeled *Kitchen* and two marked *Miscellaneous Crap* and got to work.

Two hours later, the boxes were unpacked and everything she needed for the night was run through the dishwasher. She had just started on the bathroom boxes when there was a knock on the stairwell door. She slid over the deadbolt.

"Who is it?"

"Finn. Your neighbor from upstairs. Anya said you were moving in today, so I brought a little house-warming. Wanted to make up for yesterday's crash."

Kate didn't hesitate to open the door. There in the stairwell was the dishy, gray-eyed man from the lobby. He was holding a bouquet of bodega flowers. And he had a happy face sticker on the bridge of his nose. Kate laughed.

"What's with the...?," Kate asked, tapping herself between the eyes, before reaching out for the flowers. "These are gorgeous, thank you."

"You're very welcome. Can I come in?," he asked, removing his sticker and looking around. "This place looks a lot better than when I came around in the fall. What a difference."

"Of course, come in. I don't even have a cup of coffee or tea to offer you though. I need to get to the grocery store right after lunch. There's absolutely nothing here."

"Can I look around while you get the flowers sorted?"

"Sure, I'll just be a minute."

Kate rummaged through the kitchen cabinets—where had she put that vase?—and kept half an eye on her new neighbor as he roamed about the living room.

"Look at this," he whistled, checking out the little table by the elevator and recognizing the cross on top. "It'll keep any bad luck away. Where did you get it?"

"It was in my mother's basement. My grandmother left it for my dad, and then he left it for me."

"It could use a scrub. I helped my uncle in his furniture store back in Dublin in the summers. Second-hand furniture mostly. And he restored for the real antique shops too. I love this old stuff."

She handed him the mineral spirits and rags, "have at it. But, before you get started…what can you tell me about St. Brigid? All I know is she's supposed to keep a home safe."

"There's that. And her Feast Day marks the start of Celtic Spring. In Irish mythology, she was a fire goddess, that's a powerful woman. She's the patron saint of all sorts of powerful figures: midwives, sailors and mariners, poets…babies too. She keeps an eye on the little ones when there's not an adult caring for them. And there's the St. Brigid's ribbon. My gran was a believer in it. She'd hang a ribbon out the window on St. Brigid's Eve, and then keep it for curing headaches. She'd lay it across the forehead. Swore by it."

He started on the table while Kate unpacked the bathroom boxes. She was hanging the shower curtain, when Finn called out, "Kate, come here. There's a paper stuck beneath the top. Wait, there's more stuck above the drawer. Letters maybe?"

She went out to find the tabletop a full shade lighter than it had been less than an hour earlier, and Finn sitting on the floor with papers in his outstretched hand.

"Careful, they're delicate."

Kate took the papers from Finn and walked over to the dining room, unfolded them carefully, and laid them out on the table.

"They're definitely letters, and here's one envelope. It looks like they're in Irish. Mine is rusty. How's yours?"

"Sketchy at best, it's twenty years since I sat the Leaving Cert. What do you mean it's a little rusty? What do you know *as Gaeilge*?"

"I went to graduate school at Trinity. I was never fluent, but I learned some Irish when I lived in Dublin. Now it's pretty much gone though."

His head tilted in amused curiosity.

"Graduate school? You'd be interested to know then that Brigid is also the patron saint of scholars. Let's have a look."

Finn skimmed the letters, some of which had words or parts of words that had faded or been torn away. But he was able to make out some sections fairly easily.

"It's addressed to somebody named Seamus."

"It could be any number of relatives. Seamus is James, right?"

Finn nodded.

"There are Seamuses and Jameses all over, on both sides actually. What else can you make out?"

"Kate, the letter's in a mix of English and Irish. Something about a boat, that's in English, and Átha Cliath—that's Dublin—and Brooklyn. It looks like the sender was letting this James know that he or she was on the way to Brooklyn. And it says thanks for letting us know that the Delany brothers arrived in Brooklyn 'agus na cosa ina bpócaí.' With legs in their pockets? That's a new one. They must have been legless from the boat. Drunk or seasick, I don't know. I'll ask my sister about that. She's kept up with her Irish. Great expression, either way. It's dated January 1880. I can't tell you the sender though, the name is torn off. Where's the envelope?"

She handed it to him. It contained the fragments of a foreign stamp and a Dublin return address.

"It was sent from somebody at Siúlán Bhaitsiléir—that's Bachelor's Walk—in Dublin. You know that part of the Quays maybe from when you were at Trinity?"

Kate nodded, she knew that stretch better than a little. She lived just up the river from it for three years, passing it every day she went to campus.

"It's to James Somebody on Gold Street here in Brooklyn. That's not far down from our building: Vinegar Hill, just on the edge of the Navy Yard. Did you know the Vinegar Hill neighborhood got its name from the Irish Rebellion of 1798? Battle of Vinegar Hill against the British. Lost that one, of course. I can't make out the last name here. Wait a second. The letter says 'a dhearthair,' so James is a brother." He set it aside and reached for another letter. There were three altogether. "I don't think this envelope goes with that letter. Look, the handwriting is different."

"You're right," Kate agreed. "This handwriting matches that first envelope though."

Finn was busy reading the second letter when his phone rang. Just a second later, so did Kate's. Finn took his out in the stairwell, and Kate went into the kitchen.

"Hi, Mom. You'll never believe what we found stuck inside that little table. It looks like letters from whichever one of Dad's ancestors came to America. It's amazing. What do you know about the ones who came here from Ireland?"

"Not a lot. Only that they were Stanleys, and they came over in the mid- or late-1800s. You can look things up easily enough. Irish records are everywhere online. It's funny, I always spent my research on my side of the family. Your dad was never interested in that sort of thing. Actually, I don't remember your grandmother Edna ever talking about it either. She was born here, so was her mother. Her mom was an Edna too. Edna O'More. Can we talk about all this at dinner? I've got Molly all packed, and she's getting antsy to go to Dog Park and then over to see her new room. And I promised we would stop at the diner for a treat."

"Of course…and her room is amazing. You won't believe the colors. Anya did the whole thing." Kate looked at her watch. "I've still got to go grocery shopping. Is everyone a 'yes' for tonight?"

"Every single one. You're going to have a full house, my dear, wait, did you say *we* found? Who's *we*?"

"My upstairs neighbor. He stopped by with flowers to welcome me to the building."

"Name? What does he do?"

"His name is Finn, and I have no idea what he does. But he started cleaning St. Brigid for me. He used to do this sort of work for his uncle back in Dublin."

"Dublin? Invite him to dinner, Kate. You've got to."

"I don't know. He's on the phone, maybe he has plans."

"Well you won't know until you ask him. Do that. And get to the store. You've barely got time to shower and cook. Molly and I will come early to help. See you at six."

Kitty hung up, and Kate looked around for Finn. He was still out in the stairwell chatting away on his phone. She gathered the letters, placed them inside the drawer, and slid it shut. This mystery—as much as she wanted to know more— would have to wait.

"Kate, I have to go. That was the boss. I wasn't supposed to go to her place until tonight, but she's moved up the reading. Some dinner plans came up."

"Reading? What do you do?"

He tilted his head and looked at her, not for the first time, with some degree of bemusement.

"Are you putting me on?"

"No. Why?"

"Nothing. Never mind. I just haven't been asked that in a while." Was he blushing? "Can we pick this up tomorrow?"

"The cable guy's supposed to show up, and my niece will be here. I don't think it'll work. Rain check?"

"Rain check. Take care."

He left before Kate realized she hadn't invited him to dinner. And she still didn't know what he did for a living. She stacked the dishes on the counter and ran out for provisions.

CHAPTER 13

Kate made it home with food for an army by five o'clock. Three pounds of spaghetti, sausage, meatball mix, a hunk of fresh parmesan, two loaves of seeded bread (still warm), olive oil, stewed tomatoes, the works. And a parsley plant. Kate had a fondness for fresh parsley. She thought it tasted like oxygen, so she put it put it on everything from pasta to scrambled eggs. Her preoccupation with this handy herb made growing her own a practical hobby. She had not shown any evidence of inheriting Kitty's green thumb, but she had proven herself capable over the years of keeping parsley alive on a number of window sills. It was Brooklyn's turn. She removed it from its plastic bag and placed it on the counter, turning it around to find the most promising bits to clip, chop, and add to the sauce. She only had one bottle of wine, but the liquor store would deliver in an hour: all systems were go.

She had the groceries unpacked, sausage browned and soaking in a pot of sauce, and meatballs made and wrapped in wax paper with enough time to spare for a very quick shower. She was getting dressed when the buzzer rang.

"Is that you, Mom?"

"Yes, it's me and Molly. Let us in, it's cold out here!"

She buzzed them up and unlocked the elevator.

"Look at the two of you, all bundled up," she said, taking Kitty's coat and hat and hanging them on a hook by the elevator. She reached down and felt Molly's nose. "Very cold, bug."

Molly nodded her head in agreement. Kate unhooked the stroller's little seatbelt, and Molly climbed out. She slipped off her coat and mittens. Kate showed her that one hook was just her height, and a pleased Molly hung her own coat up all by herself. Just like in Vermont. Kate stuffed Molly's mittens and hat in the hood of her coat. The basket on the back of Molly's stroller was crammed full with shopping bags.

Her mother gave her a hug, while Molly made a dash for her room.

"Be sure to unpack your old winter things, Kate. It smells like snow out there. Oh," she said, looking around, "I just love it. Here," she handed over one shopping bag filled with her biggest pot and two boxes of spaghetti, "I thought these might come in handy. And this," she handed over another, "has a few of Molly's things. But I kept plenty for Pineapple Street sleepovers."

Kate was calculating pasta per person when Molly re-appeared.

"Gammy! Gammy!" She made no sense beyond her gammy's name. She was shaking a little from excitement, and her eyes were so shiny that they appeared on the brink of spilling over. She couldn't process her emotions, but she grabbed Kitty's hand and dragged her to see the ceiling that glowed in the dark.

Kate followed them into Molly's room, and unpacked the tiny, little-girl clothes. The tops and bottoms were mix-and-match in every color of the rainbow. She was distracted though by the tomato-y smell from the kitchen. She left Molly flipping the light switch up and down enthusiastically for Kitty, to show the stars appear and disappear.

She poured a small glass of wine and set about tackling the meatballs. Her one big skillet had seen better days, but it was the only pan big enough to cook them. She wiped it down with a tea towel, poured in a few tablespoons of olive oil, and turned on the heat. One by one, she unwrapped a meatball from the waxed paper and set it into the warm oil. She transferred her sausage and sauce to the big stock pot that Kitty brought and added in the meatballs as they finished cooking.

When she went to put a favored old tablecloth on the Table for Ten, she discovered she had more table than cloth. The buzzer sounded while she dug through the *Kitchen Stuff I Will Probably Throw Away* in search of a second table cloth to combine with the first. She ran to the buzzer, mumbling "let the games begin," good-naturedly under her breath.

"Who is it?"

"It's Margot and Sean," Margot shouted. "Let us in, it's freezing out here."

Molly heard the intercom and trotted out of her room. Kate met Margot and Sean at the elevator, and was surprised to see Margot holding a box of booze, and Sean lugging an old, pink rocking chair. Molly reached her arms up toward her uncle, "Big hug. Kiss nose!"

"This is great!," Margot said, opening the gate into the living room while she juggled the heavy box. "There's an old elevator like this at City Hall, but I've never seen one in an apartment before." She kissed Kate and handed over the box. "We arrived as your delivery pulled up. And, here's a little extra," she said, retrieving a bottle of red from one coat pocket, and a bottle of white from the other.

Sean swooped Molly up, and placed her on his shoulders. "Now, show me this room of yours, Goose. I heard there's stars in there. I brought a chair for you to sit in and watch them twinkle." They went off to join Kitty, who welcomed a little break in the old chair Sean had dragged over from Pineapple Street. Kate opened the wine, and poured a glass for Margot and one for herself.

"Want the nickel tour?"

"You bet I do. And did I hear there's an actual working fireplace?"

"There sure is. It's in my office. But don't call it that, Molly says it's her room, but that I can share it." The tour was interrupted by the intercom.

"I'll get it," Kitty yelled out. "In fact," she said, sticking her head in the office, "I'll take door duty for a while. You girls sit for a bit."

It was a shivering Pearl and Phil, with traces of snow on their shoulders and bare heads.

"I checked the weather before leaving Florida, and I promise you there was no mention of things being this cold...let alone any word of snow," Pearl said, running her hands through her long gray hair. "Where's the bathroom? I need to clean up," she handed her soggy Miami Dolphins jacket to her son. Kitty pointed the way, and Pearl was off, leaving Phil with Kitty.

"I guess you're not used to this kind of weather, are you, Phil? Give me your mom's jacket. And take off that sweatshirt. I'll find you something warm to put on. How about a cup of tea?" Without waiting for an answer, she hung up the wet clothes, grabbed an old flannel shirt from Kate's closet for Phil, and got him settled in the kitchen before putting the kettle on the stove and stirring the sauce. "Now, tell me about this new job of yours."

The intercom buzzed as Pearl emerged from the bathroom with her hair fixed and a big smile on her face.

"I'll get it. I'm together now." Pearl's 'together' took the form of a boxy white shirt with a tuna fin emerging from the bottom hem. Just above the fin, it said NETS in big letters, with a red circle and a line through it. Pearl apparently had strong feelings about commercial tuna netting.

She buzzed up Kevin and Anya, who were barely in the apartment when Gillian phoned Kate's cell.

"We're here! I hope you're ready for us. Glen's just parking the car with the kids and one of my actors. Kate, do you mind if we bring him? He lives in your building. We gave him a ride home, and he's on his own tonight. He says you've met. Finn."

Kate turned just a little pink.

"Yes, we have. One of your actors? He's working for you?"

"Well, *with me* is more accurate. We wrapped a film together in December, and he's part of the new show at the Vanguard. Can he join us?"

"Sure. The more the merrier. Should I know who he is?"

"Only if you live in the world and are remotely aware of Hollywood. Really, Kate, you do live in a particularly selective bubble. Finn Murphy. He inherited the Irish Bad Boy label in the press when Colin Farrell outgrew it. But those days are well over for him too, and he's actually a great guy. And a fantastic actor. We'll be up in a bit."

"All rightee then."

She ended the call and understood why Finn said he felt foolish this afternoon, now it was her turn. She thought back to the look on his face and realized he had probably wondered if she was being coy. Two seconds later, her phone rang again. It was Paul. She was about to let it go to voicemail, but she thought better of it.

"Hi there. Where are you?"

"At my hotel. Free for dinner tonight?"

"Actually, I've got dinner on the stove. I wanted Molly to have family around for her first night here, so I'm cooking for the lot of them." The dinner party dangled across the phone line for a minute, while Kate wondered what to do. Invite him? Not invite him? Paul saved her.

"That's a good idea, Kate. Get back to the kitchen, and call me tomorrow if you have time for a visit. I'm in town for two more days."

Kate bit her lip and asked, "Why don't you come by for lunch tomorrow?"

"I'd love to, but it has to be more like a late breakfast. I'm giving a talk downtown at one o'clock."

"That's even better. I'll get bagels." She gave him the address and directions and headed back to the kitchen, fully aware that she was, with relatively little regret, more engaged with the prospect of tonight's company than she was with seeing Paul.

✦ ✦ ✦

It was an absolutely perfect evening. Phil and Pearl were stunned to find themselves having dinner with two *bona fide* celebrities, and both Gillian and Finn sat still for selfies with mother and son squeezed between them. Before long, everybody got in the act and dozens of pictures were taken. Phil even went around with his phone collecting quips for a video of the night. Sean and Kevin disappeared to the local bodega after dinner to get some ice cream, with Gillian and Glen's two sons along in an advisory capacity. They returned with ten cartons of assorted flavors and enough starter logs to break in the restored fireplace. It took a while, but, with Anya's help, the boys eventually managed to get a blaze going and everybody squeezed into Kate's office. They sat on the floor passing around the ice cream, staring into the flames, and chatting away the hours.

Molly had taken her co-hosting duties very seriously and helped with everything that was within her reach. When the dessert was done, she and Gillian's kids disappeared beneath the bedroom stars and made noise until it was time for them to head home and for Molly to turn in for her first night on Water Street. Kitty got her ready for bed, with the help of Gillian's daughters, while the rest of the party cleaned up.

Kitty joined them in the kitchen, "That little one's going to nod off without a bedtime story, if you don't get in there soon," she said to Kate. "And it's time the rest of us got going. Are we going to walk off the dinner, Sean?"

He finished drying the last of the pots and turned to his mother, "The roads aren't that bad, and the truck can make it through anything anyway. I'll bring it around and meet you downstairs. And Pearl, I'll drop you and Phil at the hotel. Great time," he said to Kate, giving her a hug.

"Kevin, you coming with us?"

"No, I'll help Kate tuck Molly in. Meet you back at Pineapple Street."

"Okidokee," Kitty said, with an arched eyebrow in Anya's

direction. "See you later." In fact, they all looked toward Anya, who held her breath then slowly exhaled, delivering a "jig is up" look recognized the world over. Kate had to give credit where it was due. Anya regrouped in a flash, kissed Sean smack on the lips, said her good nights and excused herself to head upstairs to her place. It was a nice exit.

Glen and Gillian managed to corral their brood, and adhere scarves, hats and mittens to the appropriate child.

"Love you, pal," Gillian waved from the packed elevator.

"Love you, Kate!," her kids added.

"Me too," Glen said, waving as the old cage began its descent.

Kate and Kevin went in to read Molly her bedtime story, but she was sound asleep, curled up around her new pal, Penguin Pete, and a favorite book.

"She is the cutest kid in the world," Kevin said, pulling her blanket up closer to her chin and giving her a kiss.

"I know," Kate agreed. "Can we do this, godfather-of-the-cutest-kid-in-the-world?"

"Of course we can. We promised Eileen, and she thought we could. I just never imagined we'd actually have to deliver on the promise," Kevin said, turning off the light. "And I hope that she never really imagined that either. Come on, let's help Finn. I think he got left on kitchen duty."

They went into the kitchen to find the cleaning up done and Finn sitting at the counter drinking a whiskey.

"Am I a cliché or what?"

"Well, then I am too, and so is my sister."

Kate joined Finn at the counter, while Kevin grabbed two glasses and placed an ice cube in each one. He poured two fingers of whiskey over each cube and passed a glass to Kate.

"To the new digs," he raised his glass.

"The new digs," Kate and Finn echoed. Kevin finished his in two gulps and then said his goodnights. Finn walked him to the door, while Kate checked on Molly.

"Well, that just leaves me," Finn said from the living room. Kate returned to find him putting on his jacket. "Thank you for letting me crash. I can't remember a better night since I moved to New York."

"You're more than welcome, Finn. And I'm glad you joined us. I expect Molly will insist on your coming to the next party too. You have a real fan there."

"It's a mutual admiration society then."

They stood there, inching a little closer, sizing each other up and wearing the slightest of grins. Kate took a step back, tilted her head, closed the gap between them and brushed back the hair that had been mopped across his forehead for the better part of the evening. She realized, in this gesture, that Finn wasn't much taller than her. She lifted her heels, leaned in, and brushed her lips against his. But she reserved the kiss for his ear.

"I hear you have a bit of a sordid past. Any truth in that?"

He nuzzled her neck and slid her sweater aside far enough to leave a trail of little kisses to the tip of her shoulder.

"Some truth, and some a bit of make-believe." He traced the length of her arm and wrapped his fingers in hers. "Will you hold it against me? I've sometimes thought a woman like you might."

"A woman like me?" She was amused. "I never really thought of myself as a type."

"You know yourself. You're accomplished, educated...and, I hate to speak ill of the women I tend to meet, but you're entirely level-headed and that's pretty fucking rare."

"Don't mock the sisterhood, Finn."

"I wouldn't dare. I'm every inch a feminist. It's the work I do and the constant travel. Relationships are a bit fast and furious. I don't get the chance to see day-to-day normalcy, I know that. But I'm also pretty good at seeing when someone— women mostly, but men too on occasion—are drawn to me to be seen with me. And I don't call that a sign of level-headedness."

"Fair enough."

Kate raised their joined hands and kissed the back of his.

"And who's this now?" Finn whispered over her shoulder.

116

Kate turned around, and there was Molly with Penguin Pete.

"Hey there, Goose."

Molly lifted her arms, and Kate scooped her up. "Want to sleep with me tonight?"

Molly nodded against Kate's neck.

Finn rubbed Molly's head, "Good night Molly." He looked to Kate, "and goodnight to you. Let's pick this up soon, okay?"

"Deal."

Finn saw himself out.

CHAPTER 14

Kate was awakened by a wiggling lump of a Molly.

"Are you looking for cuddles?"

"Cuddles."

Kate snuggled Molly close, both of them facing away from the morning light creeping around the blinds. It was crazy bright from the snow.

"Cuddles, cuddles, jammies, juice. This morning's already on the loose. We will learn, and play, and sing. We'll climb in snow and everything."

Molly giggled.

"Ready for some breakfast?"

Molly nodded and climbed down from the bed.

The morning's unpacking did not take long. Kate put away the last of the Miami car load, and flattened the empty boxes. Then she tackled the remaining kitchen boxes, poured a cup of hot tea, and joined Molly watching the snow fall through one of the big living room windows. The bright and cheery view was appreciated, but it also reminded Kate that she had to go shopping for curtains. Nothing from Miami would fit these; they had to be five feet tall at least. A closer look outside revealed that the snow had really piled up; it must have been falling all night.

"Want to go out in the snow? My Florida friend, Paul, is visiting, and I have to get bagels."

Molly bounced up and down. Kate wasn't sure which the little girl loved more: snow, bagels, or company. Likely, it was a perfect trifecta. Molly played in her room, while Kate cleaned out the fireplace and got showered and dressed. Once they were all bundled up, they rode the elevator down to the lobby and went looking for the trash room to deposit the remnants of last night's dinner and fire. As they were about to open the door—labeled, in Anya style, with an old sign bearing the logo of the New York Department of Sanitation—Kate heard a familiar Dublin accent from inside.

"I know...no, I don't want to wait...yes, I understand. But offer the asking price anyway. Thanks, Sam."

Kate and Molly opened the door on Finn sorting his recycling, with his phone cradled between his shoulder and ear. He was ending his call as they entered the musty room, and looked up, smiling at Kate and Molly. Kate returned his head-to-toe appraisal and smirked. She and Finn shared in the humor of two very adult adults knowing they'd get their hands on each other eventually. And somehow understanding it would be worth the wait.

"Well, if it isn't last night's charming hostess," he said, tickling Molly's chin. "Are you off to play in the snow?"

Molly nodded.

"We'll only play a little for now. I have a friend in town, and he's coming by for bagels. And I need to stop by the hardware store. It's a busy day."

"So it is. I had a great time last night, thanks again for including me. Is your friend here for a while? Our play opens this weekend, and I can leave you tickets."

As Kate was wondering if he was fishing for information about her friend, Molly forced the issue.

"Boyfriend."

"What's that?," Finn asked, bending down to get a better listen.

"Florida. Boyfriend. Bagels."

Kate looked at her niece. "Who said Paul was my boyfriend?"

"Mama said."

Kate was flustered. Was this a cue to talk about Eileen and Eric? The therapist had advised the family to take leads from Molly. "Did she, now?"

Molly nodded. "Bagel?" And with that, the moment passed.

"Yes, sweetie, let's put the trash out, and we'll go to the store."

Kate turned her attention back to Finn. "No, he's not staying for the weekend. But I'd love a ticket for myself."

"We open Friday, but that night will be mad. And if you'll really be on your own, why don't we make it Saturday? We can grab a drink after. Maybe finish that chat we started last night?"

"Love to." They exchanged details, and after Finn tickled Molly's nose, he kissed Kate on the cheek and squeezed her arm.

"I'm not bothered by a little competition, Kate. Just so you know." And he was off.

The sidewalks were clear enough to get to the hardware store and bagel shop easily, but stops to jump in the big piles of snow slowed travel considerably. By the time they returned to Water Street, Paul was waiting outside, and Molly still wanted to explore this winter wonderland. She was in her element.

"I was just about to phone you," he said, kissing Kate on the cheek. "You look great. And," he said, reaching down toward Molly, "you must be Molly."

Molly shook her head up and down and held tightly to Kate's arm. Anya popped out of her office to say hello, as the trio was about to head inside. Molly reached up for a hug.

"Good morning, bug! How are you today?"

"Play?"

Anya smiled at Paul, "Hi stranger. Not exactly Keys

weather, is it?"

"Far from it. I'm freezing. But," he looked to Molly, "I think somebody wants to stay outside and play in the snow." Molly was inspecting the gray edges of the snow pile.

"It's good to see you, Anya. How long has it been? Two years?"

"Just about. It was Kate's 38th, and we crashed your birthday plans for her. Kevin's idea, by the way, not mine. And you were a great sport. Quite a weekend, wasn't it?"

"Memorable for the food, sunburns, and hangovers— pretty much in that order," Kate replied. "God, I love Islamorada."

"Me too. Hey, all of my showings were called off today, and I've run out of emails to delete. Kate, can I steal Molly for a little while? I think it's a perfect morning to make snow angels in the park." She stole a glance to Molly, who agreed enthusiastically.

"Dog Park?"

"No snow angels at Dog Park." Anya pulled a face, "poo there."

Molly giggled.

"But we can make angels at Bridge Park. We'll go to both!" Anya looked at Kate with the best doe eyes she could muster, "Two hours or so? Please? Pleeeaase Auntie Kate?"

Molly smiled at Anya's antics.

With a promise to have Molly home in time for a late lunch, Anya set off with the bubbliest toddler in DUMBO.

"This place is amazing," Paul said, admiring the lobby as he and Kate walked toward the elevator. "It's *The Iceman Cometh* meets Edith Wharton."

"I know. Anya said the building had barely been touched in decades. She preserved all the crown moldings that were still intact and restored whatever had broken off. She used old photographs from the Historical Society for the renovations. And they aren't done yet, by the way. She's renovating every floor; there's still two to go. My brothers are starting on the floor above mine next week. Anya's determined to work with what's here as much as possible. And, wherever the previous owners or tenants stripped out original details, she's trying to restore what she calls the building's 'integrity'."

Paul was listening thoughtfully, but stopped nodding approval long enough to ask, "her integrity ends at electrics and plumbing, I hope?"

"It does, don't worry. The City required her to upgrade both as a requirement of the purchase. Along the way, she installed solar panels, insulated window shades, and planted those trees outside. Her next big project is the roof. She wants the building as green as possible. She said that's one reason she restored the fireplaces. I can't believe I have a fireplace."

Kate continued chatting about the building during their ride up the elevator, acutely aware that the old flutter was absent. She wasn't unhappy to see him, but he looked out-of-place somehow. Catching their joint reflection in the little mirror as they entered her apartment, she saw that it framed dual expressions of uncertainty. Kate left Paul to explore the apartment, while she unpacked the curtains, rods, and bagels, and put on the coffee. She kicked completely into busy mode, and even went searching through her boxes for a hammer and screwdriver.

"Want help with those curtain rods?" he asked, joining her in the kitchen. "We can eat while we work." He was all about avoidance too.

The windows, each measuring 7' by 5', absorbed every bit of the white sheers that Kate had picked up at the hardware store. Kate was delighted by the bright sunlight—accentuated by the newly fallen snow—that still managed to filter through. The sheers reached to the floor, pooling ever so slightly on the hardwood. It was a dramatic effect that gave the room the look of a feminine vacation lodge: perfect for an academic angler and a little girl from Vermont.

"Those windows are crying out for your desk, I think."

"You're right. It would be a perfect place to write, but my office has to be contained. We've lived here less than a day, and Molly's things are already creeping out of her room."

"Speaking of your office. When will you go back to the book?"

"Next week, if I can get the unpacking done. Jennifer emailed me again. I promised to send the outline and two chapters by tonight. The chapters are drafts, technically speaking, but they're definitely clean enough for readers to look them over. Thanks for sending her my way. It's got me re-focused. Mom's agreed to keep Molly at Pineapple Street for a few hours each day, so I'll have time to work. She can't wait, and I need the structure. I've given myself through July to get it totally done. Then I'll have to start thinking about finding a real job. If I can focus on just one big thing at a time, I might be able to keep my wits about me while Molly and I find our way around this new world of ours."

They kept the conversation in the safe zone of work and gossip and enjoyed the bagels and coffee. It felt good. They were interrupted by a knock on the door. It was Finn.

"Sorry to interrupt, but my rehearsal was canceled for today—the weather has people thrown off—and I thought I'd work more on St. Brigid." He reached a hand out to Paul, "Finn Murphy, furniture restoration. Good to meet you."

"You look an awful lot like an actor of the same name," he said, smiling and shaking Finn's hand. "My mistake?"

"No, you're right about that. Acting's the day job."

The two men took the measure of each other, trying to gauge the other's relationship to Kate. Finn turned down Kate's offer of coffee, picked up the table and disappeared back through the hallway door.

Paul turned to Kate.

"Let's hear it."

Kate was filling Paul in on her neighbor, Gillian's connection to him, and the mysterious letters when there was a fresh knock on the hallway door.

"It's us!," Anya shouted through the door. "Cold and wet. Let us in!"

"Let us in!," Molly echoed. She was becoming a world-class mimic.

Both of them were pink-faced, soggy, and hungry.

"Is there any firewood left from last night?," Anya asked. "If not, I'll go get some from my place. We need to warm up."

"Yup, still a few logs here. I'll get it started. You get the coats and boots off."

"And I have to get going, or I'll be late for my talk. Anya, great to see you again. Molly, it was very nice to meet you." He looked at Kate, while slowly buttoning his coat.

"Let me walk you down. The fire can wait a few minutes."

They took the stairs. One flight down, he stopped and turned to her: "NYU has offered me a year's Visiting Professorship. What do you think about my taking it to see how things might work out if we lived in the same city for a change?"

"That's a lot to say on your way out a door."

"I know. I know it is. But what do you think?"

As Kate gathered her thoughts, Paul watched her expression. Then he took her face in his hands and kissed her. "Kate, you would be the world's absolute worst poker player," he said sadly, but grinning. "I'll find my way out."

Kate watched his back as he walked away from her, this time, no doubt, for good. She followed him down the rest of the stairs.

"I'll think about all this later," she uttered to the front door as it closed behind him. He turned back and raised a hand to her. She stepped forward and raised her hand back, then placed it on the cold glass door. Bye, she mouthed. He nodded, and took off toward the subway.

She returned to her apartment to begin the cable company waiting game, and maybe indulge in some hot chocolate with Molly and Anya. Whipped cream and marshmallows seemed like a good idea. But first, there was a fire to start.

CHAPTER 15

Kate woke up with a stiff neck, a book on her head, and the remnants of a whipped cream mustache. Her teeth were wearing socks. She cursed the sofa and listened for Molly. Too quiet. It turned out to be entirely innocent quiet though. Molly was curled up with her stuffed animals on a blanket that was spread out on her bedroom floor. It was set up for what looked like one fabulous tea party. There was a note attached to Penguin Pete's beak with a paper clip.

> Hi Kate. You passed out on the couch first, but Molly wasn't far behind. She has been fed and watered. Finn left St. Brigid and a note for you in the kitchen. Said to tell you he found another letter, and he's got his sister translating it. Hugs, Anya. PS I'm writing this at 6pm. Cable guy was a no-show. Good luck with that.

On her way to the kitchen, her phone rang. It was Gillian.

"We had a blast last night. Great house-warming! A good sign of things to come, I'd say."

"I agree; perfect party all around. Can you guess who stopped by this morning?"

"Male or female?"

"Male."

"Irish accent?"

"No. But I've seen him too. He invited me to your play this weekend."

"Opening night?"

"No. Saturday. And a drink after."

"Perfect. I want all the details Sunday. Don't forget to call me…but not too early. Glen's taking the kids to the Museum of Natural History, so I can sleep in. Can Molly go too?"

"Definitely. She'd love it. But come on, guess the visitor."

"Did he stay long?"

"No. Just for brunch. And he helped me hang curtains."

"Profession?"

"Academic. But that gives it away."

"Paul is in town? I figured that was over when you left Miami."

"It is. He's up from Atlanta for a talk at NYU. This was an official good-bye, I'm sure of it. But it was good to see him."

"Well, I'm glad you two ended things like grown-ups. I hate de-coupling with unnecessary drama. I have to run, but thanks again for dinner. Find me after the show Saturday. Even if it's only for a quick hello. I want to know what you think about it. And, Kate, Finn's a good guy. Don't take any gossip you hear to heart. Have some fun. You might even be good for each other."

"I know you're right. A diversion would do me good. Break legs, Gillian."

"Cheers."

Kate eyed the French press on the counter. It was a little late in the day for a caffeine jolt, but she couldn't resist. She slid across the floor as fast as her bare feet allowed. Cold bare feet at that. She prepared the press, put on the kettle, and returned to her room for a pair of socks.

Her room. She sat on the edge of her queen-sized bed to pull on her socks and looked around. It had rounded edges and fresher paint than her old place, but the size and furnishings were exactly the same. The white, three-drawer dresser could generously be called shabby chic. She'd found it in the back room of a used furniture store on South Street in Philly. She got it for a song. Sand paper, a few coats of paint, and a set of glass drawer pulls had managed to give it an air of gentility. A tall chest, nightstand, and reading chair filled things out. Nothing matchy-matchy here.

She filled the press with hot water, and took it, a favorite mug, and the envelope left by Finn into her office. He had gone ahead and had the January 1880 letter fully translated. His note thanked her for a reason to call his sister and uncle after too long a time:

> Somewhere along the way, I fell into a bad habit of only touching base with family when I'm on my way there or they're on their way here. My sister is glad to put her Irish to use. And it was great talking to Ciaran. He said to keep with the mineral spirits and be sure to rub it, not scrape it. I told him it's oak and that your mom thinks the inlays are bog wood. He said that would locate it in the midlands or maybe Kerry. Probably early or mid 19th century. He asked if your ancestors might have been military. Or maybe made furniture for the military? The design is off, but the materials and shape of things remind him of what they used to call campaign furniture. Officers took it from one posting to another: easy to reassemble apparently. See you after the show, Finn. PS You have an amazing face.

She smiled—he had a pretty amazing face himself—and placed the first letter on her desk and turned on the lamp.

Somehow, the letter looked even older—a little shy even—with the light washing directly over it. But there it was. A direct link to her family's past, not quite as sturdy as the table, but just as tangible and so much more personal. It opened with thanks for sending a dollar and with relief that James had arrived safely in Brooklyn back in September. And now it was early January, according to the date on the top. For three months, the Dublin family had not known how their son and brother was getting on. Or even if he had arrived safely. Kate thought how worried she would be under those circumstances.

She considered the father's eyes being in bad shape. Had he been ill? And then there was the part that Finn had laughed about when they first read the letter together: "Tá mé sásta gur tháinig muintir Dhúshláine slán. Agus cosa ina bpócaí acu! Maolaíonn an cluiche seo an cumha…" According to the translation, "the Delany brothers arrived safely—and with legs in their pockets! This game tempers the sorrow." Finn had thought the Delanys were probably wrecked from the long crossing, but Kate didn't remember him saying anything about "this game," so maybe there was more to it. And what was "the sorrow" that the sibling referred to? Family sorrows maybe? No short supply of those then. Or now. It took the wind out of her sails. She put the letter down, turned off the light, and went to check on her niece.

Still sleeping on her picnic blanket. Kate picked her up, and tucked her into bed. It was close enough to her real bed time that she would probably sleep through the night, and she would get a kick out of waking up in her play clothes. She filled a sippy cut and left it on Molly's nightstand. Kate went back to her office, to the coffee, and to the letter.

She turned on her laptop, hoping for some juice from the diner's wifi. It didn't show up, but Anya's office did; apparently she kept a public line for clients. It was slow, but still…lucky Kate. She googled *legs in pockets*. All the search turned up was advice on reducing fat pockets from one's thighs.

Then she searched for games—Irish or otherwise—that involved legs. Nothing useful there. She had better luck searching for games with pockets, but still nothing that she could reasonably connect to a nineteenth-century transatlantic journey. So she turned her attention to the geography questions raised by Finn's uncle Ciaran.

Doyle was a County Carlow name, as far as she knew. But

the Stanleys, her ancestors that owned St. Brigid, were from County Westmeath, which was well in the Midlands. In fact the county was practically smack in the middle of the island. Her father once told her that there had been two Stanley brothers, and they had a falling out. One stayed in Westmeath—he was dad's ancestor on the maternal side—and the other went off to Belfast. The Westmeath brother, the one who went to the States, had lost his wife when she was fairly young, and he raised his son and daughter alone. One of the few family stories passed down was about that marriage: a legendary love match. The husband never re-married; he couldn't bring himself to. The James/Seamus of these letters could well be their son, and the father with failing eyesight that heartbroken widower.

She popped back online and sifted through the National Library of Ireland and a few other genealogy zones, writing down the names of ships that sailed to New York from late June through August 1879, the best guess Kate could make as to when James would have left for America. The names that appeared as she scrolled down were fantastic: the *City of Chester*...the *Bothnia*...funny...that seemed to be the extent of ships sailing that last summer of the 70s.

She tried a few more websites, but they only had the two ships also. The same ones. She shook her head. It was impossible that only two ships sailed to New York during the summer of 1879. Well, improbable at the very least. Granted, the Great Famine was over in the 1850s, but Irish immigrants kept coming.

She scanned a few more websites and learned that there was to be one more major blight after the Great Famine. And it occurred in 1879. Its physical impact was less severe than the events of some twenty years earlier, but the psychological impact was great. Memories of the 1850s were fresh in the minds of those who survived, and stayed behind on Irish soil. Fear of what could be led to another emigration run. Kate thought perhaps her ancestors came that year to flee this mini famine, known as *an Gorta Beag*. She was still struggling to find ships for the period when her eyes fell on *Perseverance*. Great name for a ship of emigrants to sail upon. She hoped that her ancestors came over on a vessel with such a gritty name. She turned her attention back to the letter, and its fear, joy, and heartache contained in the small details of tedium.

She found that the trauma of emigration could not be truly studied, no matter how well-intentioned the scholar. The experience had to be witnessed. This letter's closing lines were proof to Kate. Time had faded the ink and dulled the weight of the pen's impression, but a sadness, apprehension, and wonder remained. It seemed to Kate that the sender planned to join the Brooklyn brother at some point in the future, and he or she—probably a sister, Kate judged by the handwriting and the language—was wondering what awaited. Kate was struck by the sibling not asking about what was *there*, but rather about what remained from what was *here*: "An airíonn tú uait an teanga? An mbíonn tú ag brionglóideach i nGaeilge?" She checked the translation, "Do you miss the language?," the brother was asked. "Do you dream in Irish?"

The letter was written in a mix of Irish and English, but the family was from the English-speaking midlands, not the west of Ireland where Irish would have been more commonly spoken. This made her curious about where the siblings learned Irish. Might some older relative or a neighbor have been an Irish speaker? She looked at her watch and saw it was well past ten o'clock. Too late to call Kitty, so she sent an email:

> Mom, you said grandma used to call Dad by his Irish name. Was she an Irish speaker? Or was it just the name? G'night, Kate.

She reviewed the pages in her spiral notebook, and was about to turn off her laptop, when a reply from Kitty appeared.

> You're still up too? Kevin's upstairs cursing at the Knicks, and Margot and Sean are at some City Hall

thing. I guess it's a late night all around. I'm glad you
emailed. That table of yours got me thinking, and I
grabbed an old file of your father's. Call me if you're
staying up for a while. Just give me a few minutes,
I'm putting on some tea. Love, Mom. PS No, your
grandmother wasn't fluent in Irish. But she could
swear in it. She was a character.

Kate scanned all the originals on her copier, and placed the
originals in a folder for safe-keeping. She took the carafe and
mug to the kitchen sink, then changed into sweats and a t-shirt.
She curled up on the couch and called Kitty, who picked up on
the second ring.

"You've opened a Pandora's box, Katie, but one where
good things pop out. I haven't looked through this stuff since
Sean was in high school, when he had to write a paper on his
paternal family tree. I remember he was thrilled to find an
ancestor with the same first name as his. Of course, his
homework assignment was way before the internet, so you can
find a lot more now. But I'll put this aside for you to take
tomorrow when you drop off Molly. There's a family tree in
here that's more detailed than the one in your Dad's old Bible.
It shows Sean and Marcella Stanley were married in 1857 in
Westmeath. They had two children: a daughter born in 1860,
that's all it says, daughter, no name; and a son born in 1859.
His name is here: James Thomas, with Thomas spelled the
Irish way, you know T-o-m-a-s. And there's an accent mark
over the 'a'. What is that called again?"

Kate scribbled *Sean and Marcella Stanley, Westmeath m. 1857:
check parish records for marriage certificate* into her notebook.

"That's a fada, Mom. It's weird though that one of his
names would be in English and the other in Irish, and the letter
is posted to Seamus rather than to James. The letters from St.
Brigid are a mix of both languages too. But I'm pretty sure
Westmeath was not a Gaeltacht region—that's an Irish-
speaking district—even back then. And now one child's name
is half in Irish. It's peculiar. Not impossible, I guess, but

definitely a little off. I wonder if one of them—Sean or Marcella—was an Irish speaker and the other wasn't."

"Well, the father's name is Irish here, but I guess it can be read either way. I doubt there was any other spelling of Sean back then. You'll have to ask your brother about all this. There are some copies of things here, and he may also have a file someplace. You know he never throws anything away. And I'll give you your father's family Bible."

"Thanks, Mom. I'll check in with both of you tomorrow."

They said their good nights, Kate looked in on Molly again, and then threw herself on the bed in her own room. On top of the covers. Without brushing her teeth.

CHAPTER 16

Kate woke up to Penguin Pete's beak tapping her on the nose, courtesy of Molly.

"Time to get up," Molly whispered, tickling Kate's ear. "Time to get up," she started laughing. "Pete says, 'get up,' Auntie Kate...up, up, up."

It was nothing short of glorious to hear Molly being chatty again. Kate gave her a big hug.

"Blue juice for you, oh child of the increasing vocabulary?"

"Oats?"

"You got it. Let's get you in the tub first though. You're long overdue, stinkbug."

One thing that hadn't changed from before their worlds did: Molly loved the tub. Kate got her settled with toys and bubbles, and caught a glimpse of herself in the mirror. She washed her face, brushed her teeth, and piled her hair in a messy bun before heading to the kitchen.

With coffee in-hand and oatmeal on the stove, she started breaking down the few remaining moving boxes, when she heard "It's Finn...hello?" through the door.

"One minute." Kate threw on some clothes, and let him in. "Let me guess: you smelled the coffee in the stairwell?"

"I did not. And this, I regret to say, is not a social call." He rubbed the small of her back. The gesture was as natural and relaxed as if they'd known each other for years. Neither hesitancy in its delivery nor surprise in its receipt. "Wish it was though."

He stepped back and, with mock seriousness, announced, "No, I'm here this morning in my antiquities capacity. Ciaran says he's sure it's a relic, but he can't get his head around the piece. He's dying to see it in person. Threatening to visit even: and that would be a first. Definitely working-class, he said. But the carvings are first-rate. Whoever made it, knew what he was doing. Maybe worked in a shop, but made this for himself. He recommends Harrison's down in Chelsea, says they have a good reputation for Irish antiques in New York. They can probably identify the wood for you. The big news for right now is that I actually found two letters last night, not one like I told Anya. But I couldn't get the second translated fast enough. It was too late to call on you, once I had it sorted with my sister. Here's the email she sent, and this baggie," he pulled it out of his pocket, "has bits I peeled off the secretary and from behind the drawer. I've got to get to rehearsal. We're still on for Saturday?"

"You bet. But I think the drinks have to be on me to pay you for all your work."

"Not a chance." He brushed the side of her cheek before turning toward the door. "See you Saturday," he called over his shoulder. She followed, and watched him hop down the stairs, taking them two at a time. Then he turned around and came back up two at a time. "Kiss me, Kate."

She laughed. "You know *The Taming of the Shrew* is not exactly the Shakespeare play feminists most adore."

"Well, this feminist sees the heart that's in it."

"And the mess that is Petruchio?"

It was Finn's turn to laugh. "Yes, that too. Poor man."

"Kiss me, Finn."

"At your service, Kate…coffee…nice."

"Minty…nicer…get to work."

He bowed, turned, and hopped back down the stairs.

The man had a lot of pep for 8am. She closed the door, and threw the dead bolt. When she turned around, a naked, sudsy Molly was daring Kate to catch her. She took the oats off the stove, covered the pot with a tea towel, and roared toward the screaming kid. Breakfast would wait.

Kate had Molly washed, fed, dressed, and to Pineapple Street in plenty of time for lunch. Then she practically ran to the subway, thrilled at the prospect of devoting a full day to getting a handle on St. Brigid's mysterious letters, and relieved to have her mother's NYPL card at her disposal. Exiting at Times Square, she found there was no snow to speak of left on the midtown sidewalks. She walked east, took a left onto Fifth Avenue, and there they were: Patience and Fortitude, guarding the main branch of the New York Public Library, and welcoming Kate back. As had been her tradition since her school days, she stopped to tap each on the right paw before making her way inside.

The security check was a disappointment. The days when she could glide across the shiny marble floor and only face a bag inspection on the way out were apparently over. Now, in addition to the security check, there was a rope line, a little café, and tourists. The lobby was packed with people admiring its beauty and causing minor traffic jams while stopping for the obligatory selfie.

She found a chair on the back wall in her favorite reading room on the third floor, and took her spiral notebook, laptop, all four letters, and the translations out of her tote. She set her phone to vibrate, and fished around for a pen while her laptop powered on. A lemon drop surfaced with the pen. Good sign. Then she realized that she had forgotten the bag of fragments Finn gave her this morning. Bad sign. She swore under her breath, but didn't let it deter her.

The earliest letters were dated January 1880. The first, as Finn translated the day he began cleaning it, was from

Bachelor's Walk in Dublin to a James—probably Stanley, she thought—at 125 Gold Street in Brooklyn. She did what she always did, she made a list:

1. Who was the Bachelor's Walk sender?
2. Confirm James's last name
3. Find ships from Dublin or Queenstown/Cork
4. Legs in their pockets???

The second January letter, from Brooklyn to Dublin, was addressed "A dheirfiúr, a chroí"...dear sister...so the Bachelor's Walk sender was solved. It was the daughter Stanley from Sean's family tree, which meant the Gold Street brother had to be James T. Like the first one, this letter was written in a combination of Irish and English. Trying to avoid being distracted by the language fluctuations, Kate read on, and Finn's sister's translation confirmed that there was again mention of a "game":

> Dear sister,
> The Lawless brothers arrived yesterday, and with
> them the sum of a...Donald was sick from the travel
> but proud to deliver his portion. The game of this
> makes the worry of friend's crossings a little more
> tolerable. There is much excitement...news of a
> bridge to connect Brooklyn with Manhattan.
> Hundreds of men are needed...the work, and I will
> go with the Delany brothers tomorrow to see if we
> can sign on. With the dollars enclosed I trust you can
> now book passage in the spring. I am sorry to hear
> that father's eyes are not improving. I hope we can
> get help for him when you both arrive here in
> Brooklyn.
> > Yes, dreaming in Irish,
> > Your loving brother, Seamus T

The Lawless brothers brought "the sum" of something.

Money? For James? That was odd, since James was clearly sending money to Dublin to help his sister and father with the boat passage. And what "game" was he talking about?

The Lawless brothers arrived yesterday. Donald was sick, but "bróduíl as a sciar a thabhairt leis": proud to deliver his portion. His portion of what? "Baineann an cluiche seo cuid den imní nuair a bhíonn cairde ag trasnú," the letter continued: this game makes the worry of friends crossing a little more tolerable. She googled *games played on immigrant ships to America from Ireland*, with mixed results. There were articles devoted to passengers spending their time writing letters home, singing, and gossiping. But all mention of games was limited to stating that the playing of games was a common pastime: no specifics.

At the time James made the crossing in the summer of 1879, steamers were increasingly replacing sailing vessels and had reduced the length of the voyage by more than half. Only one decade before he left Ireland, sailing to New York took more than a month. That was over thirty days to miss home, and hear rumors of what was to come in New York. Over thirty days to question the wisdom of your decision, be seasick, and watch fellow passengers—like Donald Lawless—fall ill or maybe die. It all reminded her of an old essay by Thoreau that she tried reading ages ago about the wreck of the *St. John*, a famine ship from Galway that wrecked off Cape Cod in 1849. It arrived in early October, at the same time as a terrible storm. Over 145 people died, many of them children.

James's bridge job paid well: "Tá an obair ar an droichead marfach tuirsiúil...ach taitníonn sé liom, agus fostaíonn siad an-chuid leaids ón mbaile." It's exhausting, but he loves it, and he thinks he can get the Lawless brothers a job there, because "they hire lots of men from home."

Bridge job? The Brooklyn Bridge maybe? It had to be. Kate checked the dates online. No other bridges were being built in New York, let alone Brooklyn, in 1879. The Manhattan Bridge was newer than the Brooklyn Bridge, and construction on that link to Canal Street had not begun until 1901. The Williamsburg Bridge maybe? No, also newer than the Brooklyn

Bridge. She checked the library catalogue to see if there was a copy of *The Great Bridge* by David McCullough. Of course they had it. She filled in a reader's ticket, and was rewarded with a "love McCullough" when she handed it to the clerk.

"Me too," she said. "Have you read this one?"

A nod. "It's a classic. Give us twenty minutes. When you see the last four digits of your library card number on the screen, the book is ready for you to collect."

"I'm going to grab a coffee first. Can I leave a few things to hold my seat?"

"Sure. But take your wallet and phone."

Kate ran off to the lobby café for a little pick-me-up.

The prized McCullough was ready when she returned. It confirmed that construction, which had begun in 1869, was still underway a full decade later. Immigrants, particularly the Irish, were among the majority of the bridge workers, all of whom were paid better than most laborers in the city. The Bridge Company's hiring of Irish workers might not have been the case if John Roebling, the celebrated engineer whose design linked Manhattan and Brooklyn, had not died in the early days of the project.

One of Roebling's last big commissions before what was originally called the East River Bridge (it wouldn't be known as the Brooklyn Bridge until well after it opened) was for a bridge in Cincinnati. In 1857, Irish workers went on strike in protest of the poor pay. Roebling replaced them all with German immigrants like himself. He swore the Irish were disloyal and vowed not to hire any of them ever again. Whether he meant just on that job or well into the future was unclear to Kate. But plenty of Irish showed loyalty to Roebling's son—the decorated Civil War veteran Colonel Washington Roebling—who took over from his father and, with his wife, Emily, saw the project through to completion.

The Irish workers were mostly from the tenements on the

south side of the Brooklyn Navy Yard, an area known as "the flats," in the small neighborhood of Vinegar Hill. An online map of the area showed that James's address at 125 Gold Street was indeed south of the Yards. Finn had told her that Gold Street was not far from where they lived in DUMBO, so she made a note to walk over there and see what, if anything, remained.

James was earning money, and he included a dollar with the letter, but there was "still not enough saved for a ticket" to get the rest of his family to Brooklyn. He wants her to put the money toward that, but not if their father needs a doctor. If James maintained a pace of sending one dollar every three to four months, it would be a good two years before the family would be together again. Kate also wondered what was causing the father's eye problems. Something about his work, but what did he do for a living?

Before signing off, James wrote, "bím ag brionglóideach i nGaeilge." He was dreaming in Irish. If not literally, then perhaps figuratively, reassuring his sister that Ireland was still with him, here in this new place.

Finn had suggested that "agus cosa ina bpócaí acu" (legs in their pocket) was a joke of some sort about being legless, and the "What fun!" that followed indicated that he might be right. But it wasn't an expression she had ever heard before. She would need Finn to ask his sister about that.

The next letter, the shortest of the lot so far, brought an abrupt change of tone:

17 February 1880
De.....
I write with sad news. The ship carrying Brid and
Edward O'More could not make it past
Newfoundland. Worse still, Brid has fallen ill.
Edward is keen to bring her to Brooklyn, but she is
not well enough to travel. Keep them in your prayers.
Dollar enclosed. Best to father, Seamus

Her tote vibrated with a text from Sean asking if Molly could spend the night at Pineapple Street. Kate hadn't realized the hour, and she still wanted to check out the Roebling house and Gold Street. She scrawled *Dreaming in Irish* across the cover of her trusty notebook, stowed everything back in her tote, put on her coat, returned the McCullough, and made her way toward Fifth Avenue.

She headed toward Bryant Park. Once a no-go zone, with dealers surrounding the place, it was thriving since being adopted by the fashion industry. There was a visitor's booth, food stands, even a sit-down restaurant. And the manicured gardens, pristine paths, and elegant benches were spectacular. She paid the ridiculous price of $4 for a bottle of water and sat on a cold bench to call Sean.

"Of course she can sleep over. Get her in bed by seven o'clock though. Deal?"

"Deal. I'll call you in the morning."

As she hung up, Kate decided to snoop around the Heights and DUMBO for remnants of the Bridge's history. She wanted to see the houses where people connected to its construction actually slept at night. She would start with 110 Columbia Heights, home of Washington and Emily Roebling. It had to be close to Pineapple Street, but she would resist the urge to check in on Molly.

Water consumed, bottle recycled, MetroCard located, she headed toward the subway steps closest to her, but then stopped abruptly, turned around, and went back toward 42rd Street. That entrance would put her in the James Joyce tunnel, so named for the tile mosaic celebrating *Finnegans Wake* that adorned its walls. She had not seen it in years and was feeling nostalgic.

✦ ✦ ✦

Her first stop was a failure. The old Roebling address on Columbia Heights, a tree-lined street that ran parallel to the promenade, no longer existed. All traces of what she imagined had been a stately brownstone were gone. The house from which Washington, too ill to visit the site himself, watched the Bridge's progress through a window; in which husband and wife discussed how to handle the latest crisis; and where they received President Chester Arthur on the day of the Bridge's opening celebration had been replaced by a lump of brick. It was a lump with which Kate was already familiar. But she hadn't known that the ugly building down the street from where she grew up had replaced what should have been protected as a historic landmark. The cornerstone said 1949. Somebody should have known better.

Kate walked the length of Columbia Heights toward Dog Park, and then down the hill to the old Ferry slip, stopping to admire its tribute to Walt Whitman. One stanza of "Crossing Brooklyn Ferry" was punched out of a metal panel that ran the length of the pier. The panel was surrounded by faux steel cables that mirrored those supporting the actual Brooklyn Bridge, which was way up in the air only a few hundred yards to the right. She blew it a kiss and sauntered toward Gold Street, taking the block behind Old Fulton Street past St. Ann's Warehouse, Jane's Carousel, and her own apartment building. Through the big plate glass windows facing Water Street, she could see Anya powering down, and the manager of the diner running the day's receipts through the register. Closing time. She cut across the culvert under the Manhattan Bridge anchorage, loving its eerie dampness and shadows.

Gold Street was a disappointment on par with Columbia Heights. The entire block that Kate estimated had once contained the house where James Tomás Stanley rented a room was now a construction site. A high rise with adjacent parking garage was under construction, and, from the look of things, nearly finished. A billboard advertised Luxury Studios starting at $4,000/month. More than James would have made in—what?—ten years? Kate was too amused to actually do the math. She wandered the block, trying to recall what Vinegar Hill was like when she was growing up. She mostly recalled derelict factories and weedy lots. And the projects, which she saw were still there, as were coffee shops and a deli. The area seemed to be thriving. Sean called to remind Kate that Molly was going to the museum tomorrow and sleeping over with Glen and Gillian's brood.

"Sure you can spare her for two whole days?"

Kate hesitated, but only briefly. It would do Molly good to be around kids more. She had been almost exclusively in the company of adults since February.

"Of course. Have fun. And give her lots of kisses from me."

"Will do."

Kate took a picture of the building and headed home. As with all efforts so far to get through the mystery of St. Brigid, the lady would have to wait. Kate had a busy day tomorrow.

CHAPTER 17

Kate had given herself a good look in the mirror before turning in last night and realized more than a little maintenance was in order. Anya—who knew absolutely everybody and could do positively anything—came to her rescue with a last-minute appointment at a Montague Street salon for the works: haircut, facial, brows, leg wax, nails, and a massage. It would take most of the day, but she hadn't been on a first date in ages, and she wanted to polish up. After a few hours of pampering, she stopped at a little boutique and treated herself to a red cashmere V-neck before heading home to a quiet apartment.

Rounding the corner onto her block, Kate noticed a man and a woman standing on the sidewalk across the street from her building. They were giving it a serious once-over. The tall and bespectacled man appeared to be counting the floors. His companion was grinning at him and shaking her head. Then she took his hand in hers, seemed to correct his counting, and they laughed together. He reached across her shoulder with his free hand, and rescued the long pink scarf that was sliding down her arm. He tied it expertly around her neck and kissed her cheek. Elegant, Kate thought to herself. They crossed the street, passing within a few feet of Kate, and delivered nodding smiles in her direction before strolling, hand-in-hand, toward St. Ann's Warehouse. Kate grinned. Maybe, like her, they were looking forward to a night at the theater and a romantic drink. She breathed in the clear winter air: it was perfect weather for an evening of stagecraft and shenanigans.

Kate headed to the elevator, checking the mailbox along the way. Empty still. She rode upstairs, tossed her coat on the sofa, and laid the new sweater on her bed. It was flawless. Not a pull in sight. She turned it over. More perfection. She snipped off the tags.

Kate removed the hairpins and shook her hair out of its messy bun. Then she peeled off the sneakers, t-shirt, and yoga pants that served as her spa uniform, and tossed it all in the hamper on her way to the shower. She let the water run hotter than hot before stepping in. She closed her eyes, touched her lips and thought of Finn, Finn's lips, Finn's mouth, and Finn's hands. And then, for just a second, it was Paul's lips, Paul's mouth, and Paul's hands in there with her. Whoa…steady girl. She finished the task at hand and toweled off. One handful of curl reviver-frizz control mousse later, she fluffed her hair out and stood in front of her closet.

Grey-wool trousers—cuffed, very Hepburnesque—were hanging over the closet door, with a pair of chunky, black patent leather brogues on the floor nearby. What seemed like a good idea this morning now looked like work clothes. She pursed her lips and said to Penguin Pete, who was observing from the nightstand, "I think not." Pete was noncommittal.

She reached into her closet for a pair of black jeans, pulled them on, and surveyed the view—front and back—in the mirror. Better. She reached in again. This was a night for what Eileen had dubbed her Bad Ass boots. They were an impulse buy in Paris that cost her what was then two month's salary. But they were a splurge she never once regretted. Her toes wiggled of their own volition at the very nearness of them. Her body always remembered luxury, and these were the epitome of it: perfectly arched but so wearable that she could keep them on all day; suede-soft leather with hand stitching at the zipper; and a magical interior lining that protected her feet from ever once making a bad first impression. Perfect footwear. She pulled them on first, then slipped on the new top. It felt good to feel good. She sipped a small glass of merlot and listened to *Stevie's Underground Garage* while applying what constituted make-up for her: moisturizer, a touch of concealer here-and-there, mascara, and rose-tinted lipstick. Then she piled her hair on top of her head, spritzed on her favorite grapefruit perfume, and headed to the subway with time to spare in making the 8pm curtain.

She got off the train at West Fourth Street and wandered over to Washington Square Park. Apart from a renovation that involved the enormous fountain in the middle of the Park having been given a facelift, it was much the same as it ever was. The birdman was still giving pigeons a perch, chess hustlers worked the southwest corner, and aging folkies with songs and pamphlets held court by the Arch. In short, still pretty much whatever you wanted, even on a crisp night. More trees than she recalled though. A nice improvement. Her only disappointment was that the temperature was keeping visitors to a minimum. But the hush of it all was magical, and she thought of a song about somebody seeing Bo Diddley strolling through the park. Willie Nile, maybe? She hummed it quietly to herself and bounced happily toward Gillian's little theatrical paradise on Sullivan Street.

She collected her ticket from Will Call, and squeezed through the crowd to her seat in the packed theater. Before folding her coat in half and placing it on her lap, Kate checked below her seat. She doubted most of the occupants noticed the small brass luggage tags affixed to the left hinges. Each contained the name of somebody or something that Gillian wanted to honor. An entity to whom she felt gratitude for exposing her to New York theater. Kate was delighted that her tag said The Drama Book Shop. She and Gillian spent the better part of their high school Sunday afternoons there, browsing the shelves and hoping for a find on the discount table. She didn't have to flip the tag over to know who sponsored it, but she did anyway. Gillian's mom and dad. Long gone, but still much loved. Kate herself had sponsored the Shakespeare in the Park tag, which, if memory served, was just a few rows behind the house seat she occupied.

Only ten years ago, this was a derelict space in such bad shape that when it came on the market even NYU didn't want it. And they gobbled up buildings in this neighborhood like pigs after truffles. Anya negotiated a deal for Gillian and Glen, who then spent two years and most of their savings stripping it down and building it up. The result of their efforts—and a fair amount of fundraising and volunteer labor from their wide circle of family and friends—was a modern, but intimate theater that had a three-show season, a summer school for teens, and an engaged board of directors that helped keep the coffers flush and the subscription base growing. Vanguard Arts was the envy of more than a few small independent arts organizations.

Having Gillian and Finn's names above the title had generated plenty of advance buzz for the play, but the glowing opening night reviews pushed sales through the roof. There was a smiling face in every possible nook and cranny; even the standing room tickets were going fast. College kids—definitely there for a Finn sighting—and seasoned subscribers mixed in anticipation. It was a two-act play, with a cast of four; Gillian and Finn; Pauline Allison, whose star was very much on the rise; and the journeyman character actor Craig Stadler.

The premise as far as Kate could figure out from the little *Playbill*, was of a Manhattan matron calling her three adult children together to collect old belongings from the Upper West Side apartment in which they'd grown up because the mother decided to downsize. Hardly compelling on paper, but Vanguard always delivered good theater. So Kate made no presumptions about the plot.

A slip of paper fell to the floor as she closed her *Playbill*. It was an announcement of the next season's schedule, and it included Chekhov's *The Cherry Orchard*. That play's Ranevskaya appeared on Gillian and Kate's list of *Great North-of-40 Parts*, a list that was ever-growing as they themselves aged and looked more closely at how older women were portrayed in theater and film. It was topped by Winnie in *Happy Days*, Gertrude in *Hamlet*, and Bernarda Alba in the García Lorca play. Gillian intended to play them all before too much time passed, and she was diligently ticking them off one by one. She played a Winnie two years earlier that Beckett fans were still gushing over.

The lights dimmed, everybody settled down, and the curtain went up on Gillian, barely recognizable in costume as the 70-something society matron, seated in the center of a long sofa, sipping from a martini glass. A doorbell got things moving. When Finn entered the stage, Kate was stunned. He absolutely filled the space. The other actors held their own, but there was no denying the magnetic presence of Finn. Playing the older son (and family black sheep), he cajoled, flirted and charmed his way through 90-minutes of internal family bickering that ended with old wounds being laid to rest. It was a witty crowd pleaser, and the audience erupted in cheers at the end, as the old woman danced with her children and the curtain fell on them in a unified heap on the sofa.

One standing ovation and several curtain calls later, Kate made her way backstage. There was Gillian, still in hair and make-up, answering a reporter's questions. Kate stayed back, not wanting to interrupt, gave her old friend a wave and blew her a kiss. As she turned to head down the hallway, Kate saw Finn, already in street clothes, with his coat draped over his shoulders. It wasn't an easy look to pull off, and she admired his gumption. He put a finger to his lips, "shh, let's slip out before that reporter sees me. Gillian won't mind if I wait until tomorrow to do press. Come on."

He took her arm and led her to the backstage exit, where a crowd of theater kids—not bothering at all to contain their enthusiasm—were in search of autographs.

"I have a car waiting," he said, pointing toward a black town car at the curb, "give me a few minutes, and I'll meet you there. Go ahead. It's cold."

He nudged her toward the car, slipped on his coat, and turned his attention toward the young crowd. Kate got in the car and watched as he took the time for pictures and signed every *Playbill* thrust his way. It was almost an hour later when he joined her in the backseat after first introducing himself to the driver and, if Kate's eyes were right, slipping the uniformed gentleman some cash in apology for the delay. Kate approved.

"I'm sorry. That took a little longer than I thought it would. Hungry?"

"Not really."

"Thirsty?"

"Parched," she said, leaning in to kiss him.

"Shameless," he whispered, returning her kiss.

They drove through a bustling Manhattan Saturday night, heading uptown and over the 59th Street Bridge in the direction of Queens. The car pulled up in front of a nondescript bar.

"Welcome to Woodside, Kate," Finn said, before jumping out to open the car door for her.

They entered the bustling bar, and Finn waved to the bartender, who waved back and nodded toward a flight of stairs.

"That's Gerry. Great guy, but strange taste in music. Only plays Cole Porter and the Clash."

Finn guided Kate up the steps to a small room, with a table set for two and a bottle of Jameson sitting in the middle. A waitress appeared, set two candles, a plate of fruit and cheese, a bowl of ice, a bottle of water, and two glasses on the table. She dimmed the lights, and slipped away.

"I'm a cliché again, Kate, but this is the best pub in the city. Besides, it reminds me of home."

With music from the jukebox drifting up the stairs, they sipped their drinks, nibbled on the food, and honored the ritual of all first dates: questions and answers about the past. What Gillian had not already told Finn about the deaths of

Eileen and Eric and about Kate's career had largely been filled in the night of the housewarming dinner, but he still had questions, and he was a great listener. They realized that their paths might well have crossed when Kate was living in Dublin, if she had spent less time in the library and more time at the pubs.

"Woodside actually reminds me of Ringsend a little. That's where I grew up. Very working-class then. Do you know it?"

"Not at all. I probably got there a time or two on my walks down the Liffey, but I have no memories of it."

"Well, it's gas. Changed some over the years, of course. Lots of industry now on the Docklands: recording studio, tech firms, like that. Some very pricey flats too." And when Finn filled Kate in on how he came to acting and how embarrassed he was now about his wild days, Kate admitted that she had looked him up online him over the morning's coffee.

"How much of it is actually true?"

"More than I care to admit, I'm afraid. And then some," he added sheepishly. "Water under the bridge though. I'm pretty much done with rehabilitating my reputation. I'm lucky that most of my crazy days happened before everybody walked around with smartphones. I'd be finished if that were the case. Or at least mortally embarrassed. It's taken years to turn things around; back to stage work and taking smaller character parts. It's paying off though. My next film—that'll be with Gillian again—would never have been open to me otherwise." He told her about the movie, and said he and Gillian would be shooting in California and Canada for all of June. Before that, he planned a trip to Dublin as soon as the play closed, to see his family and attend an old friend's wedding: "best man, that's me. Nick and I have been friends forever. He's my Gillian. I just have to make a quick stop in London on the way to take care of some business."

That gave them just a few weeks to get to know each other and then he wouldn't be back to New York until July.

"So, how much time will you have to put up with me before I take off?," he asked cautiously. "And what's with your man who came to visit? Is he still here?"

"No. And we've said our goodbyes. Great guy, but we were best long distance: me in Miami, him in Atlanta. To tell you the truth, I've only been in long-distance relationships for most of my life. Except very briefly when I lived in Dublin. But he turned out to be a drunk with a writing problem: talk about clichés. I stole that line from somewhere, but it really fits, and I got over that so fast I don't even remember his last name. I've always preferred keeping my personal life at arm's length. Fewer complications."

"I'm a little out of practice myself, contrary to the gossip blogs. If you don't mind my asking: how's living with Molly and so close to your family working out with the arm's-length business?"

"Completely destroyed. I'll play psychiatrist and say that it's probably why I keep banging my head. It seems whenever I'm faced with my nice little worlds colliding, I hit the ground. You'll notice, though, that I'm without a scratch now."

"I had noticed," he said, taking her hand while Tony Bennett began to sing *Just One of Those Things*. "Dance with me." It wasn't a request.

They rocked slowly in each other's arms.

"So, tell me, Finn, how out of practice are you exactly?" She liked whispering into his ear and claimed the left one for this very purpose. She noticed the remnants of an old piercing and stroked it. Pushing his hair back, about to take a little neck nibble, she saw the raised skin of a scar. "And what happened back here? It looks like it might come with a story."

"It's from the first play I was in." He laughed.

"What's so funny?"

"I was dancing—badly—and tripped over my own feet. Went down like a ton of bricks and landed against a prop."

Kate looked at his face. The memory of that first show was clearly a fond one. She liked that he laughed as easily as he did. Bennett gave way to Ella Fitzgerald's rendition of *Don't Fence Me In*, and he twirled Kate out to a gentle snap before pulling her close again.

It was Finn's turn to explore Kate's ear, and he opted for her right. "Ah, no earring. Good. I hate an obstacle course. Did it fall off or did you come prepared for me? Let's see the other side…mmm, no obstacle there either. Nicely done."

Kate was finding it hard to focus. His mouth and hands were as warm as the whiskey. They had nixed the ice on the last pour.

He reached to the table and plucked a strawberry from the bowl. "Matches your cheeks."

She opened her mouth. He fed her half and took the rest for himself. "More?" Kate nodded slowly.

"My turn though."

She dipped her fingers in the bowl and retrieved a grape.

"Peel me a grape…," she sang to him.

"And the professor sings…sort of. You are a find." He paused, "and not an altogether bad dancer. But your grape song isn't by Cole Porter."

Sinatra's version of *You Do Something to Me* flowed through the air and the lights flickered.

"Barman's warning. I'm afraid this is almost our last dance." He slipped his hands into her back pockets, and she reached behind him, returning his move in kind.

"We should leave while we can still stand, luv. But I do think a proper kiss is in order first."

But there was nothing particularly proper or orderly about it. They were up against the wall, obliterating any sense of cool. Kate's jeans were halfway to her knees and Finn's down around his ankles. She braced herself against an old *Guinness is Good for You!* sign, making the Bad Ass boots she was now teetering in worthy of their nickname. Finn was biting her shoulder, and he had Kate rocking to the strains of *Police on My Back* until she shook to wake the dead. They beat the Clash to the punchline—what have I done?—just in time. The lights came up on the two of them panting like teenagers after a first feel. Once they caught their breath, they laughed so hard they could barely get their pants up.

"Your hair's a sight, Kate," Finn sputtered, brushing it out of her eyes before tucking in his shirt.

"General messy or I just had a quickie in a bar messy?" She reached up to get a sense of things there.

"The latter. Definitely the latter. Would you get to the ladies and fix yourself up? I'll be in the gents."

He steered her toward the bathroom door.

Kate peed and, when she left the stall and caught a glimpse of herself in the mirror, she started laughing all over again. She blotted her face with a tissue, and tried to fix her hair. She found two hair pins stuck in her fancy new sweater, but there was no sign of the rest, so she just tied it all up in a knot and put the errant pins in her pocket.

Finn was waiting for her right outside the door.

"You clean up okay for a lady in a rush. Come on," he took her hand. He grabbed their coats, left cash on the table, and they headed downstairs. Slightly drunk, still tingling, thoroughly amused, and a little sleepy. Nothing quite like a middle-age walk of shame.

They dozed on and off in each other's arms on the drive back to Brooklyn, and a silent Water Street greeted their arrival home. Kate reached the elevator before realizing that Finn had stopped by the stairwell door. She turned and looked back at him.

"Will you take the walk with me?"

It dawned on her then that he always knocked on her door rather than taking the elevator. She assumed it was because he was just one flight up, but now she saw his discomfort.

"Are you, by any chance, claustrophobic?"

"I am," he said, looking down at his feet and then back up at her. "Do you find that a bit sad?"

"Not sad. A bit sweet actually."

She took his hand, and they wandered upstairs side by side, taking the steps slowly. He knew Molly was at Pineapple Street, but he made no move to come in when they got to her floor.

"It's your call."

"I call yes. But," she shifted her feet a little, "I need to grab a shower before we crawl into bed. I think some of that sign adhered itself to my ass."

"You're a class act all the way. Let me see to that."

And he did, until eight o'clock when he went to his place in search of some pre-matinee slumber and to give Kate the luxury of sleeping in, with the entire real estate of her big bed all to herself.

CHAPTER 18

Kate woke up to a bright, crisp April morning that matched her happy mood exactly. Armed with the *Times*, bagels, and coffee, she curled up on the couch and opened the magazine to the back. The crossword puzzle had once been a Sunday ritual that posed a challenge she could usually meet over the course of a few quiet hours. But as she poured her third cup of coffee, she was less than halfway done. It was work, which had no part in her plans for this particular Sunday. It was a rare day: no planning, packing or running around to be done. Or laundry. A single person with no kids has absolutely no idea what it is to do laundry. Kate was in the basement laundry room every two or three days. It seemed never-ending. As she stretched out the aches from her 39-year old body, and contemplated the happy prospect of a quiet Sunday, the letter fragments took up residency in her brain: not so fast, they seemed to say.

Putting down the puzzle, she took the bag of fragments, scanned them, and put the originals in her folder before cutting up the copies so that each piece could be matched up against the letters.

Every bit as thankful now for the Table for Ten as she had been on the night of her house-warming party, she placed the photocopied letters side by side, then poured the fragments over them. Matching things up proved a more productive Sunday puzzle than the *Times* crossword. She had all the pieces fitted together in less than an hour. She reviewed them, taping small bits to larger ones, and her heart hurt when she saw that first letter from Dublin was signed "Your loving sister, Eileen."

The desk and its hidden treasures were pointing her back to her sister as much as they were directing her to a family history of which she was embarrassingly ignorant. Everything seemed to be swirling around family—her family. Kate was coming to believe that if she kept herself receptive to the echoes of the past then they would help her be the tour guide for Molly that she had promised Eileen she would be when she agreed to be godmother. Maybe these family heirlooms would offer some peace at losing her own Eileen.

She had a sudden urge to visit Kitty at Number 22.

Kate peeked in the lower windows. There was Kitty, busy in her post-Mass gardening routine. She was diligently tending to the enormous red geraniums on the front windowsills, which were all of a foot above street level. The potential lack of privacy didn't seem to worry Kitty any more than it had Kevin or Sean, when the garden apartment was their shared post-college crash pad. Covering the windows in old concert posters had been the only nod to modesty that they ever made, and that was strictly in response to the requests of various girlfriends. When they renovated the place for Kitty, they took the time to install window boxes on the inside sills, so Kitty could plant her way to a little discretion. They also put in some very fancy blinds that she could operate with a remote. She loved them, but only turned them down at night. Kate knocked on the window. Kitty smiled and pointed to the front door, mouthing "it's open."

Kate let herself in and hung her coat and scarf by the door before heading in to join her mother.

"What a nice surprise. You're just in time to help me with these monsters. Grab the potting soil from under the sink, will you?" She appraised her daughter's face. "Good night at the theater was it?," she asked with a raised brow.

"Is there anything that gets past you?"

"Not a lot."

"I'm happy to help you with the plants," Kate shouted back on her way to the kitchen. "But I've got a bunch of questions. I've finally gotten around to looking at all the letters in St. Brigid. I need your help figuring out who these people are." She returned with an enormous bag of dirt and a spoon.

"I'll do my best, Kate. But, you know your father was never interested in tracing his roots. I found his Doyle family Bible like I said I would. That should be useful with names and dates. Add some soil to those plants, and I'll go get it."

Kate took a close look at the geraniums, and even she could see that they needed more than a little attention. It was a running joke in the family that none of her children inherited Kitty's green thumb, so Kate took some pleasure, the second Kitty returned, in teasing her mother about the windowsill's dubious state of affairs.

"Really, Mom. It looks like wild animals have been digging in these things. I think we'll need two bags of dirt to fill these planters."

Kitty took the bait.

"Oh, stop it. It's just a normal amount of erosion. And don't think for a second that I don't know you have absolutely no idea what you're talking about. Give me the spoon and the dirt, and you take the Bible. Go make yourself useful, and put the water on. I'll join you in a few minutes." She shook her head, as she dug into the dirt.

It was not the first time in her life that Kate was sent away from plants and toward tea. She had the letters out and the Doyle Bible open just as the kettle began to whistle and Kitty popped into the kitchen.

"I think this project of yours deserves coffee cake. Agreed?"

"Agreed."

The Bible had more names and dates, but, like Sean's tree, only "daughter" for the second child of Sean and Marcella Stanley. When Kitty joined Kate at the table, Kate showed her the first letter, now with the fragments taped to it, so her mother could see who sent it. Kitty's eyes widened at the sight of the name.

"It's Eileen then. Give me a pen." She drew a thin line through the word *daughter* and wrote *Eileen* above it. She patted the Bible, then rested her hand upon it. They sipped their tea.

"I think that Eileen and James are the people in an old photo your grandmother kept in her china cabinet. I have it in with your father's papers. There's no names written on the back, just a date: December 1883. And they do sort of resemble each other. It was taken on the Brooklyn Bridge. I'll dig it out tonight. Double-check the Bible, but I think this Eileen is your great, great grandmother."

"She's the one responsible for my being born in Brooklyn?"

"Well I had a little something to do with that, but she is one of many responsible for your being on the planet. As for being in Brooklyn, your letters indicate that her brother—your great, great, great uncle James—came here first. I doubt she'd have come over on her own. Is that right? Three greats?? Oh, and look, the Bible has their father dying in Brooklyn. Maybe he came over with her. The letters suggest that was the plan too, and it must have worked out that way. See here," she said, pointing to the family tree, "Sean Stanley, born Mullingar 1825, died Brooklyn 1883. And I can assure you that none of them came through Ellis Island, so there's no point checking those records."

"How do you know that?"

"Many—maybe most—of the Irish did come through there. But a lot entered through Castle Garden, or, like my own illustrious ancestors, via slightly less official channels. But we know the Stanleys didn't come through Ellis Island because it didn't open until 1892. Our Bible here says Sean died in 1883, and I think it's a safe bet he came here with his daughter."

"If yours came through unofficial channels, how did you gather so much information about them?"

"My dad and aunties knew a lot going back two generations. Then, as the years went by, I discovered that the National Library of Ireland had a genealogy service, so I stopped by there when your father and I went to Ireland for our 25th. Remember when we did that?" Kitty reached over and patted Kate's hand. "You came home from college to stay with Eileen while we were away. And then, of course, the internet happened and those ancestry websites are a gold mine. Connecting the dots is so easy now that I've traced my father's side back eight generations, and my mom's back nine. You'll have no trouble with the Doyles. I'm sure of it."

"I don't have Dad or any chatty aunties to get me started though."

"No, you don't, but you have these letters and the Doyle Bible. Trust me, this will be painless. And fun. Give you something to do when you take breaks from that book of yours. How's that coming by the way?"

"Slowly. What I have is good, but I don't have a lot. St. Brigid keeps drawing my attention away from it."

"And you need the new book to get a new job? Do I have that right?"

"It will help."

"That's that then. You need to get Brigid out of the way. I'll help. Let me see that third letter again, the one dated February 1880. Who were the couple stuck in Newfoundland?"

"Brid and Edward O'More."

"Look at this Bible entry: Eileen Stanley married Edward O'More in Brooklyn in December 1883." Kitty, always one to whisper bad news, leaned closer: "Brid must not have made it."

Kate nodded.

"So we know Eileen Stanley arrived here from Dublin by the end of the year, which confirms that the Stanleys all arrived in America before Ellis Island opened. The Bible also says they had four kids, including your great grandmother Edna. She's the first of the Ednas, your grandmother is the last I suspect.

It's just not a name you hear much anymore, is it?" Kate had to agree that it was uncommon.

"Pass the coffee cake. You know, your father and I seriously considered naming you after her, but the name just didn't suit you." Not wanting to insult the memory of her late grandmother aloud, Kate silently thanked her lucky stars. Kitty continued: "Marcella Stanley—that's Sean's wife—died in Ireland. Find out the name of the parish where they married: it's more than likely where she's buried. Parish records there might give you some information to look back even further. What do you make of the letters being in both Irish and English? I hope you're still curious about that, because I sure am...I'm correct to say Irish, right? Not Gaelic?"

"You're right, Mom. It's Irish. Gaelic is the full family of languages, including Irish, Scottish, Welsh, a few others. You know, it's the strangest thing. I'm used to hearing people switch languages when they speak, but I've never come across it in writing before. It's disorienting. I feel as though I'm in the room with these people. I'm not sure about some of the phrases though." She sipped her tea, "do you know anything about the O'More family?"

"They were active at St. Charles over on Jay Street. But, you know, all their kids and grandkids—the grandkids would be your dad's cousins—moved away. Ours was the only family to stay in Brooklyn. And, of course, your father was an only child. It's unfortunate. It would have been nice to have a bunch of cousins and in-laws around." Kitty slid the Bible over to Kate: "this has Edward buried at St. Charles in 1937, and his wife is there too. Check the parish records. You can do it tomorrow, after you drop Molly off here. Speaking of which...did you hear the front door?"

"I sure did. They must be back from the Museum. I take it Kevin went with them?"

"Of course—you can't keep him away from that place. Having Molly here has turned him back to being a kid. And," she added, raising an eyebrow, "Anya went too. Married by Christmas those two. Wager?"

"How much?"

"Five dollars?"

"Okay, moneybags. You're on."

"Let's go upstairs and beg some lunch off them. You just know they came back with goodies."

"Go ahead. I'm going to take advantage of your wifi and check my email. I'll join you in a few minutes."

Kate heard footsteps running across the floorboards above as the kids welcomed Kitty. She logged in to her university email and was equal parts relieved and alarmed that there was so little sitting in her Inbox. Happy that it would only take a few minutes to reply; distressed to think that in only two months she was already falling off the professional radar. She dug her cell phone out of her tote and called Brian.

She had been avoiding him out of guilt. He was a good friend to her, and she didn't like withholding her certainty that the sabbatical was permanent. But she had to keep that to herself for as long as possible.

Brian was a notorious gossip. Golden otherwise, but he was just insecure enough to believe that telling you another person's secrets could potentially curry your favor. He crossed a line in telling her about a colleague who destroyed her credit score after a dozen sperm bank purchases, and Kate had actually screamed at him at the top of her lungs to put an end to the gossip. It was, to this day, their only falling out. He'd had the decency to be embarrassed, and he kept right on gossiping, but he limited it to less private content, at least with Kate.

Maintaining a university affiliation was essential in academia. Things were changing fast, but, for now, 'independent scholar' remained something of a scarlet letter. This was a shame because some cutting edge work was being done by people who earned their living outside of universities. The idea of doing that herself—opting out of what she knew first-hand to be a deeply flawed and sometimes vicious system—was intriguing.

"Well, hello, stranger! How's everything going?"

"Great. We're settled into the apartment, and I'm starting back on the book this week...all systems are definitely 'go'. You?"

"All good here too. But I miss you. The woman who moved into your old apartment is a nightmare. A bunch of us are trying to figure out whether she's truly disturbed and needs help, is a few points shy of average intelligence, or mean. She blasts music every night—and every night the guy below her asks her to turn it down. Every single night, Kate. Wouldn't you—if you had the music on, I don't know, say volume 7— and neighbors said it was too loud, wouldn't you at least start keeping it at 6?"

Kate laughed in spite of her best efforts not to. "I know it's not funny to all of you, Brian, but you're approaching this like she actually cares about the people who live around her. It's quite possible she's all of what you say—in need of medication, not too bright, and mean—but from the cheap seats here, I think you've just got an asshole on your hands. Tell the guy downstairs to move. Or to get earplugs until she moves."

Now it was Brian's turn to laugh in spite of himself. "God, I miss you. Is your offer for me to visit over the summer still good?"

"Definitely! There's plenty of room, and Molly loves company. When are you thinking of coming up?"

"Late July, early August. I'll email you dates once I figure things out. Now, gossip. Me first...," and Brian filled Kate in on department activities and intrigues, none of which she regretted missing. He quickly cured her of the mini-blues caused by her paltry Inbox. "Your turn."

"Guess who I had drinks with last night?" She was about to feed his gossip appetite for a week, and she knew it.

"Not a clue."

"He's an actor I think you've heard of. Irish. Fortyish. Co-starring with Gillian in a play at the Vanguard...can't you Google as fast as I can speak?"

"Hold on, my browser's slow as shit...Finn Murphy?!"

"Yup. He's nice, Brian. You'd like him. Although he thinks

jogging is bizarre and Florida completely…I think the word he used was 'daft.'"

"Well, he's right on both counts. Will I meet him when I come up?"

"I hope so, but it depends on when you visit. He's shooting a movie with Gillian that's supposed to finish in June, but she told me once that these schedules are always flexible to allow for weather and things like that. We'll have to see how things go. It may be purely platonic by then, but he lives upstairs, so it's likely you'll at least run into him. However this goes, I have a feeling he and I will be friends."

"You and your friends with benefits," he said under his breath. She could hear him typing away. "According to IHaveTooMuchTimeOnMyHands dot com, he partied it up with his—and I'm quoting here—'gorgeous, young co-star Pauline Allison' last night in some club in Williamsburg."

"Really?"

"Seriously. I'll send you the link."

Kate smiled. "No need. Listen, I have to head upstairs for some free lunch. I'm so glad you're coming up soon. Big hug, my friend."

"Back at you, Kate. Be good."

Content that she was still connected to the land of the living—even if not via the voluminous emails she had regrettably grown accustomed to—Kate headed upstairs to join what was beginning to sound like an honest-to-goodness party.

✦ ✦ ✦

Getting Molly back to Water Street was no easy task. As Kitty suspected, the group returned with treats, and a pizza party was in full swing when Kate joined them. Gillian's family, Kevin and Anya, Sean and Margot, Kitty, Kate, and Molly added up to one very full house, and Molly was in no hurry to leave. But it was Sunday night, and home is where you went on a Brooklyn Sunday night.

The two of them set off to Water Street. The temperature

had made a steep climb during the day and very little snow was left. The warmer air brought with it rivulets of water in the gutters and drains as well as a thick fog. Molly squealed with delight as they headed down the hill by Dog Park, Kate pushing the stroller as fast as she could. They were unable to see the Manhattan skyline that usually dazzled. The magical sight delayed walkers probably more than car traffic on the BQE down below. It was impossible to say whether the suddenly warm temperatures after a big snow storm or the fog still rolling in off the water brought the neighborhood out in droves, but the sidewalks were packed. Kate didn't have the heart to say no when Molly asked if they could turn back to the park and play on the swings. It was dark when they finally opened the door at Water Street, and a little past her bedtime when Molly nodded off to sleep.

CHAPTER 19

Standing in her sunny kitchen in stocking feet, Kate stared at the kettle, willing it to boil. She was hoping for just a little alone time before Molly woke up. Kitty had registered for Grandparents Week at the parish, and that week was to begin this bright Monday. While the older kids prepared for Communion classes, the younger ones—including Molly—would have play-and-story time under the supervision of their Grannies and Grampies. Kate wandered over to the kitchen window and drew a happy face in the morning condensation. Smiling to herself, she wondered who would have more fun: Molly, who would have a chance to start meeting some neighborhood kids, or Kitty, who would be able to show off her beloved granddaughter.

Molly had been baptized, but Eileen and Eric agreed to let her choose her religion for herself when she got older. Their will's mention of a religious upbringing was limited to "we trust her godparents will make the best decisions regarding spiritual and religious guidance." Kevin and Kate had sat down one afternoon to map things out, expecting it to be the first of several lengthy discussions. They talked about their own Catholic upbringings and discovered that although they had to one degree or another fallen into that dubious category of semi-Catholic, they remained grateful for having the church as a touchstone in their lives. And Kevin considered the new Pope a good sign of things to come. He was getting up early on Sundays for the first time in years. Kate had to admit that since returning to Brooklyn she was drawn back to the church herself, but stopping in to light candles for Eileen and Eric was as close as she had gotten to attending mass.

They agreed that Molly could—and likely would—still make her own decisions when she got older, but they saw only positives to her having a Catholic foundation, especially since Eileen and Eric had opened that door with her baptism. When Kate and Kevin shared their decision with the family over supper that night, everybody nodded approval, even Margot: Pineapple Street's favorite atheist.

"I know you all probably thought I would be the dissenter here, but"—Margot had looked toward the godparents—"I really do think it's a good move." She then put her palms together in a mock prayer, bowed and smiled. "You have my blessing."

Kitty reached over and put her hand over Kevin's. She had said nothing, but was clearly pleased.

The kettle finally cooperated, and Kate poured the water into the French press just as Molly's feet could be heard padding across the living room floor. Kate turned around to see her little niece rubbing the sleep from her eyes.

"Kisses, Molly?"

"Kisses, Katie," she said, reaching up for a morning cuddle.

Kate sat Molly up on the high barstool the little girl loved to call her own, filled her Molly mug with some tap water, and watched her slowly wake up to the new day.

"Will you make the coffee for me, sweetie?"

Molly nodded. It was one of her favorite chores. She would ever-so-slowly depress the plunger, watching the steamy sides of the press get erased by the filter as she gently sank it lower. A bit of magic for Molly, leading the way to Kate's first cup of the day. It was a win-win for them both.

Fed, washed up, and dressed, Molly helped Kate make the

beds, packed up her little knapsack and announced she was ready to go Grammie's house.

"Well, she's not expecting you for another hour. What will we do until then?"

"Swings?"

✦ ✦ ✦

They waved to Anya through her office window and to the seniors sitting at the window counter in the Diner, as they made their way up Bridge Street. Molly loved people watching from her stroller. The park was already filling up. Little kids too young for school were running around under the watchful eyes of moms, dads, and nannies all holding tightly to insulated travel mugs. Kate joined two dads on a bench, while Molly shyly ventured over to join two little girls—twins for sure—in the sandbox. The three of them set about brushing away what little snow was left, before peeling off their mittens to make castles in the sandbox.

"Look at those little fuss budgets making everything neat and tidy," said one father to the other, who nodded without looking up from his phone. "They take after you."

"Never get between a broker and his gadget," the first father said to Kate. Reaching out his hand. "Those are our girls—wave hello, Emma and Adelaide!—there with your little one. I'm Joe, and this is Robert. You are?"

"Kate. Nice to meet you. That's my niece, Molly." She leaned over and conspiratorially whispered, "I call them gadgets too."

"I heard that," Robert said, looking up to shake Kate's hand. "But I'll be nice to you anyway. Robert. Pleasure to meet you."

As Kate and Joe began exchanging their reasons for disdaining portable technology, Kate's phone rang. Joe rolled his eyes.

"Go ahead, take your call. Traitor."

He winked at her, smiled, and went over to join the girls in the sandbox.

The Caller ID showed it was Finn.

"Good morning," Kate answered. "How are you on this beautiful day?"

"Better for hearing the sound of your voice. What's got you so cheerful?"

"The sun is shining. I'm at the park with Molly, and we're making new friends. It's all good."

"Well, I'm stuck inside reading a script and fielding emails from my sister. She's trying to get my bid through on a house in Greystones in Wicklow. I've had my eye on it for years, and it finally came on the market. Wish me luck."

"Luck. When do you leave for Dublin?"

"Week after next, just after the play ends. Give some thought to what you want me to bring back?"

"Chocolate. Bring me back a box from Butler's, and I'll be forever in your debt."

"Consider it on the list. And I left a little something outside your door."

"Oh?"

"In honor of Saturday night. I'll let you get back to your new friends."

Kate ended the call, looked at Molly playing with Joe and his girls and thought the world was looking brighter than it had in a while. And Finn was a part of that. Gillian was right: they just might be good for each other. He seemed to need the distraction as much as she did. She was well past the age of pondering where Saturday night would lead. But his mentioning it did curl her toes a little. Maybe long-term, maybe not. Either way, any man willing to promise her a box of Butler's was okay in her book. Then she looked at her watch and realized her world was dangerously close to running behind schedule.

"Come on, Molly. It's time to go to Grammy's."

She exchanged numbers with Robert and agreed to a future play date, before gathering Molly for the short walk to Pineapple Street.

One quick cup of coffee with Kitty later, Kate was heading

to *The Page Turner* on Montague Street. She passed by it constantly, but had yet to make it through the big doors, with their quill pen door handles and the *Warning: Bookworms Inside* sign stenciled across the middle. It might well be a perfect bookstore, and Kate had been wanting to get inside since noticing it her first week back.

It had only been in business for a year or so, but it had the look of a well-visited establishment. Her curiosity had been piqued by looking through the large picture window as she zipped past the shop on almost daily dashes up one side of the Heights main shopping drag and down the other.

From the sidewalk, she had appreciated over-stuffed chairs, a community bulletin board encased near the front door, floor-to-ceiling bookcases, and four-sided shelved cubes for used books throughout the shop. She had been ogling its insides from the outside for too long. It looked like her Holy Grail. Enticingly close, but just out of reach because of its peculiar hours: no pages were to be turned there after 7pm. Kate seldom got Molly to bed much before then, and collapsed into bed herself by eight. As for the mornings, the constant picking up and laundry meant they inevitably got away from her.

Today's mission: her own copy of McCullough's *The Great Bridge*; a new, preferably annotated, copy of Hart Crane's *The Bridge*; Betty Smith's *A Tree Grows in Brooklyn*, which, when it came up at the pizza party last night, she realized that she had never actually read; and anything the shopkeepers recommended to help her get reacquainted with her home turf.

Her own book needed to get done, but her family history was begging for attention; and she couldn't shake the feeling that the little table held secrets she wanted to know. Kitty had a point about solving the mystery first, but Kate intended to try juggling both. She decided to split her afternoon between the two projects, with the family history coming first.

She pulled on the door handle, but it wouldn't move. She squinted through the glass door and saw two men—one middle aged and the other in his late twenties—walking so purposefully in her direction that she checked her posture. The younger man stood aside while the other one unlocked the door.

"I'm so sorry—we're a few minutes late—a delivery came in this morning, and we got stuck in the back checking things in. Make yourself at home, and yell if you need any help."

"Will do. My list should keep me busy for a while though." And she took that list out of her pocket and went hunting upstairs.

The non-fiction section was divided into People, Places, and Things. After years of being programmed into the nichiest of niches by enormous chain bookstores, Kate was taken aback. She would have to do a little thinking in *The Page Turner*. Nice. She meandered over to Things, and sure enough, to the right of *Bees of North America* by Amanda McCullough and the left of his own *The Path Between the Seas: The Creation of the Panama Canal, 1870-1914*, sat David McCullough's *The Great Bridge*, which she happily tucked under her arm. The journey to poetry took her past Children's Books, so she grabbed a new *Curious George* for Molly. She found an annotated Crane that looked perfect, and she added that to her loot. Fiction took up the entire main floor, so back down she went.

Kate was surprised to discover the entire Fiction section was just that: fiction. In alphabetical order by author. No more little categories here than had been upstairs. She found the letter 'S' and a dozen shelves of Smiths, including an entire row dedicated to Alexander McCall Smith, whose London and Edinburgh series she adored. Kate grabbed the most recent of each, before browsing her way to Betty's *A Tree Grows in Brooklyn* and then the check-out.

Both gentlemen were bent over their desks, and the set-up was priceless. They faced each other from across a pathway of about seven feet, and each desk was orderly but well-used. There were catalogs, trade magazines and an assortment of bookstore-type tchotchkes that Kate suspected would never find their way into this meticulous shop: they were likely sent to entice *The Page Turner* into joining the industry move toward minimizing shelf space of actual books. No, Kate didn't see this place going that route any time soon: she was thrilled to see that this bookshop sold only books. There was not one game, tote bag, reading light, puzzle, plush toy, or magazine (except *The Paris Review*, which was on sale near the desks) in sight. The desks of these bibliophiles were equipped with a touchscreen check-out and a laptop. A comfy leather chair was beside each desk should anybody wish to have a rest or a chat.

The shop's one concession to marketing—a bookmark bearing the shop's logo—was slipped into each purchase. And if you asked for a bag, you received one with the shop name printed on the side. The civility of it all made Kate's knees buckle. She found herself checking her hair as she approached the older man's desk, and wishing she had popped a mint after drinking that coffee earlier. Both men seemed lovely, but they were so well turned-out that she felt a little frumpish.

It was noon by the time she got to her place, where, on the floor outside her door, she found a copy of *Sandinista!* She cracked up, and flipped the CD case over. Sure enough, *Police on My Back* was one of the tracks. She popped it into her old boom box and got to work.

While she was now armed with a source that would answer her bridge questions, and two others that would put her in a Brooklyn frame of mind if and when she ever went back to her pre-Molly luxury of reading before sleeping, she needed to devote the next four hours to her professional life. She found the *This is Your Book on Drugs* box and carried it into her office.

What was so familiar to her in Miami now seemed completely foreign. She would have to get reacquainted with the material all over again. Was it worth the time? She emailed Jennifer, the publisher who seemed interested, to see if anybody had the chance to read the outline and two chapters yet. The email was purely professional in tone and subject. Just as she was about to hit *send*, Kate decided to tack on the sort of personal note that academics shy away from ever writing, particularly when a new book contract is on the line:

I recently became guardian to my young niece and

moved back to Brooklyn. I'm finding 24-hour days much too short. And an eighth day in a week would not go unappreciated. There's just no time for me these days to have a 'maybe' book contract. And, let's face it, my work is too solid and your press too good (and really the only one I want to work with right now) for either of us to linger simply for the sake of lingering. Let's not dance the academic contract tango on this one. Can we agree on a decision date? I propose 5pm one week from Friday. What do you say? Best, Kate.

She hit *send*, knowing it probable that a reply would come her way filled with phrases like "editorial schedules being what they are," "if it were only up to me," and "best of luck to you in the future." But she felt good about it. It wasn't only her new-found financial security that let her be herself, she was certain being back in Brooklyn had something to do with it. She felt comfortable in her skin for the first time in years. Really comfortable. Being on no treadmill at all—not the student track, the tenure track, nothing—for the first time in twenty years actually afforded Kate time to think. Just think, not plot the next move. The starting over that she spent most of a lifetime getting charged up by, she now felt was a game. So this is what financial security meant: the luxury to think and to choose. No wonder the wealth industry lobbied so aggressively to limit admittance into its club. It was the surest way to curtail free expression and, dare she say it, revolution.

She unpacked the box and made a special place on the bookshelf just for this project. She would know next week if she had a contract. If she did, great. With family and friends pitching in with Molly, she could reasonably have the book done by Christmas. If she didn't, that would be just fine too. It would mean she could finish it at a leisurely pace, and send it out next summer. She backed things up on a little flash drive, labeled it, and stowed it on the shelf with the three files of material she had accumulated to date.

And then she noticed an email from Jennifer, whose reply reinforced every ounce of faith that Kate had in human nature:

> I say, *yes*. And until we get an eighth day in the week, know that I have your back. I will be in touch by the appointed day and hour. No academic tango today, and good for you. Best, Jennifer.

CHAPTER 20

"Men who keep their highlights up more than I do should never be trusted. And that guy," Margot pointed to a former co-worker sitting at the end of the counter, "always kept his up. And I'll bet you he definitely had them done within the past week."

She dunked a donut into her coffee, glared across the table, and then turned back to Kate, daring her to so much as hint at challenging this Margotism. Kate agreed enthusiastically, grateful for the mouthful of bagel that prevented her from actually uttering a word. When Margot was on a roll, it was best to let her keep rolling. When she appeared to have exhausted her disdain for highlighted men generally and that highlighted man in particular, Kate waded into the waters.

"I'm glad I ran into you this morning. We haven't had time alone together since I got here. Everything's good?"

"Right as rain. I don't agree with a lot of this administration's policies, but it's been an exciting time and I'll say this for him, he's not afraid of long hours or hard work. No chance of getting re-elected though. The silly season already started, as you know. But I'm gearing up now for the final stretch and hoping to be able to say Madam Mayor on the first of January."

"You think she has a real chance of winning?"

"Absolutely, and it's about time we had a woman mayor too. The boy's network in this city is completely freaking out—which I find fun, don't get me wrong—but the truth of the matter is she's the best candidate for the job. She'll do great things for the city. Did you register to vote yet? The deadline isn't until September, but you don't want to put it off or you'll risk forgetting until it's too late."

"It's on this week's To Do list, along with some other housekeeping things. Then I have to get back to work on my book. Today though is about St. Brigid and her letters. You've heard about them?"

"Of course. And I eavesdropped on you and Sean looking over that old school project of his too. I was hoping you'd ask me to tag along to St. Charles. I went to school there from first through twelfth. I left the church the second I graduated, but I'll take you over there, if you want. The nuns were actually a very nice bunch."

"I'd love the company. Sure you have time?"

"No time to stay, but I'll show you into the parish office, and I'd actually like to see the place again. I wonder if it will be smaller than I remember. You know, like schools always are."

Margot and Kate paid the check and wandered over to Jay Street. They fell into spontaneous laughter when they turned the corner and ran smack into three girls in uniforms sharing a cigarette behind the school.

"Some things never change," Kate said to Margot.

"I know, I know. I was one of them. You?"

"Of course. You really had to ask?"

"Ever think about being one of *them*?," Margot asked, pointing to the nuns entering the school.

"No. Definitely not. You?"

"Of course I did. Only somebody who was totally immersed in the church could have run away from it as fast and furiously as I did. I was sure I would become a nun, and that conviction lasted a while."

"Well, you still have the zeal of a convert...only now it's

pointed toward politics."

"Your brother would agree with you. Come on, there it is."

They walked toward an old wooden door with smoked glass in the middle and gold stencilled lettering announcing it as the Parish Office.

"Exactly the same. I like that," Margot smiled. The door swung open from the inside just as Margot was placing her hand on the doorknob. Standing in the doorway was the oldest, toughest-looking nun Kate had ever seen.

"Sister Gemma? Is that you?"

"It is," the old nun replied, looking at Margot sideways, her features softening. "I know that face, help me with the name though."

"Margot…" was all the reply Margot managed before both women said "Smith!" in unison. They each covered their mouths in shock before reaching out for a hug. For somebody who ran away from the church, Margot had clearly not let it taint any fond memories. And from the look of things, the fondness was mutual.

"Kate, this is my absolute favorite teacher ever, Sister Gemma. She's also the reason I left the Church. I could never have measured up."

"Oh, stop it, Margot. Pleased to meet you, Kate," she said with a warm smile and shaking Kate's hand. "What brings you here today?"

"Family history. I came across some old letters and they mention an O'More family. Then my family Bible," she took it out of her tote and handed it to the nun, "has a tree that says they were communicants here and buried here too. See that page with the sticky note? You'll find it there. I'm just looking to get a picture of who these people were, and I'd appreciate copies of any documents you might have."

"Well, you won't leave disappointed. There's plenty on them here. Come with me. You too Margot, you'll recognize this room, I think."

She led them down the hall and toward double doors that were just as old and etched-glassed as the other had been.

They could see from the hallway that the room was dark inside. "It doesn't officially open until two o'clock, but it's never locked during the day," she said, reaching inside for the light switch. "See," she said, as the lights slowly came up, "the sign over the Check-Out desk?"

"The O'More Library?" Kate turned to Margot, "did you know about this?"

"Of course I knew. I spent half of my life for twelve years in this room, and I know every nook and cranny. Although I can see it's had some upgrades," she said, admiring the work stations. "No computers in my day. Have fun ladies, I've got to get to work. And Sister Gemma, I'll be in touch."

They exchanged numbers, hugged good-bye, and Our Lady of Ancestor Searches was out the door and heading to City Hall.

Gemma grabbed a big binder from behind the Check-Out desk and directed Kate to take a seat. Sitting in a chair next to her, Gemma opened the book and laid it all out for Kate.

"Eileen and Edward O'More joined the parish when they got engaged, and they're buried down the block in the old Parish Cemetery. I can get you copies of every single record we have here about them before you leave. This though," she said, pointing to the first two pages in the binder, "gives you a little background. Their daughter, Edna O'More Egan, put it together when she and her husband, Dennis, raised the money to open this library. They're the ones who named it after the O'More family. They even left a little annuity so that it could keep going after they died. And, as you can see," she said, waving her arm, "it's still puttering along. Keeping kids like Margot out of trouble." She grinned.

"Eileen and Edward married here in December 1883. He was a widower, and she was a spinster—that's the term they used then for a single lady. They had seven kids, all were baptized here, but you can see one died after just a few weeks. I doubt that was uncommon. But six lived, including our Edna. Edward passed in 1937 and Eileen, oh. She actually predeceased him. I forgot that. Look, it was by a full decade.

She died in 1923. This page," she said flipping to the next one, "has their obituaries from the *Brooklyn Eagle* and the one from the Church Bulletin. Their daughter must have put those in. Oh, there's an obituary in here for a James Tomás Stanley too. It says 'Uncle James, brother of Eileen Stanley O'More,' in pen across the top." Gemma let Kate read them to herself, while she stepped down the hall to order copies of the O'More and Egan parish records from the office.

Kate read that her great-great granduncle James T. had worked for the Brooklyn Bridge Company through May 1883, when construction on the Bridge was completed, and then for the City building subway tunnels. He retired from there in 1920 and died five years later. A short retirement after all those years of physical work, Kate thought, shaking her head. What a life. It said he was survived by five children and twenty grandchildren. All the names were listed, which Kate copied into her notebook to look into once she sorted out her direct line to his sister and parents.

Eileen's obituary, from 1923, had her being survived by six children (and as many grandchildren). Kate read the survivor names again in both Eileen's and her husband Edward's obituaries, and discovered that a son named Francis was missing in Eileen's list. The grandchildren weren't named, so she made a note to try to figure that mystery out later.

The next page had a neatly typed summary by Edna Egan Doyle about her parents and her great grandfather, Sean Stanley. Sean, the document confirmed, had indeed emigrated from Ireland to America, specifically Dublin to Brooklyn, with his daughter Eileen. They arrived in November 1882, and he died on May 25, 1883, with "his eternal soul at rest in Co. Westmeath Ireland beside his loving wife Marcella."

She writes that a Father Michael Dempsey was traveling back to Ireland shortly after Sean passed and, at the request of Sean's children—Eileen and James of Brooklyn, who were also communicants of St. Charles—accompanied the body back to Ireland for burial. It had been his dying wish to be buried alongside his late wife. Sister Gemma returned as Kate was digesting this.

"It's too sad, Sister. Sean spent years trying to get to America, he had bad eyes that made working to feed his kids hard, his son in Brooklyn had to send money for the fare and his daughter worked at God-knows-what in Dublin for at least two years to help raise the rest. He finally gets here—when he's what, 57? 58?—and less than a year later he's taken back to Ireland in a box."

"Well, that's one way to look at it. Another way is that maybe he never wanted to leave at all, but his coming to America was the only way his daughter would leave Ireland, so he did. You have a lot of reading to do. You'll find there's pictures in here too. Take the whole thing. Copy what you want, but bring it back. We like having it here. Before you go, you should know that I knew Edna O'More Egan, Sean's granddaughter and, I presume, your great grandmother. I was training to be a nurse at Brooklyn Hospital—this is before I took orders—and we used to make home visits. I went to a call at her house with my supervisor, and we wound up going back a few times. She got well, but we stayed in touch. She had a gaggle of kids, grandkids, neighbors and friends, but she liked meeting new people, and before I knew it, we were old pals. She was the first one I told—after my parents of course—that I was going to the convent. She tried to talk me out of it!"

"Seriously?"

"Yes, yes. Anyway, her husband, Dennis—lovely man by all reports—had only recently passed when we met, and she talked about him a lot. I can tell you that he went to City College at nights and became a pharmacist. He apparently worked at the hospital for years, but then opened his own pharmacy over on Flatbush in the 1920s. Edna loved telling stories about the bootleggers trying to cut deals with him during Prohibition. Apparently those two professions did a fair amount of business together back in the day."

"My apartment building was supposedly a busy place during that period too."

"Oh this whole neighborhood was. That's a fact. There's

plenty about the pharmacy—and its clever ways of staying on the good side of the bootleggers—in the binder here, but not a lot about Edna. She was more interested in talking about everybody else. But I want you to know that she changed my life. If it wasn't for her, I think it's likely the world would have had one miserable nurse instead of a reasonably content nun. She was always dishing out advice, and she told me that if I found work I loved then the coins in my pocket would always make music for me to dance to. Isn't that lovely? She herself regretted never having a paying job she loved. She was in her twenties when she got married, so she'd done some work, of course, but nothing she was passionate about. Nothing that made her want to dance. That got me thinking. I was only studying nursing for the work, not because I was called to it in any way. I wanted to be of service, but in many ways, not just in one way. Not just tending to the sick. That could be part of things, but I didn't want it to be the only thing. Well, you can see where I landed. I don't think she ever thought I'd stick to it, but here I am almost sixty years later. Never any coins in my pockets, but there's been a lot of dancing these years. I promise you that."

The old nun got up to go. "I'm so glad you came to see us. You use that for as long as you need," she said patting the binder. "Come back with any questions. Or give me a call. Maybe we can meet for a coffee?"

"I'd love that. And you can meet my niece, Molly. She'd be your Edna's great-great-granddaughter."

"I'd like nothing more." She shook Kate's hand, held it for a minute, and left her in the library to finish her reading.

Kate flipped through pages and pages of newspaper clippings, pictures from parish parties and, way in the back, a picture of Edna and Dennis with all six of their children in front of the Egan Pharmacy on Flatbush Avenue. There was an address on the window that she couldn't quite read, but she made a note to bring the photo to the Historical Society over on Pierrepont Street, to see if they could help her figure it out. As she was closing up the binder, a young woman from the

Parish Office came in with a manila envelope filled with copies of every form of parish certificate imaginable, including the big five: baptismal, first communion, confirmation, wedding, and death. It had the weight of generations.

She took a detour on her way home. Needing to stretch her legs and get some air—it was as mild as last night, maybe even a little warmer—she decided to "do a full lap." That was Kevin and Sean code for walking across the Brooklyn Bridge and back as quickly as possible: a game they'd played as kids. She cut up Tillary Street, turned right onto the bridge and didn't stop until she touched the traffic island on the Manhattan side. Turning to head back, a sign caught her eye. She had passed it hundreds of times in her life, but hadn't actually read the thing in decades.

It was the Bridge Memorial marker, dedicated to Emily Warren Roebling, wife and daughter-in-law to Colonel Washington Roebling and John Roebling respectively: the engineers responsible for the bridge's design and construction. Kate dug her notebook and a pencil out of her tote to trace the marker. It took three pages to capture every detail, and she made sure not to cut off the ending lines:

> Back of every great work we can find
> The self-sacrificing devotion of a woman
> This Tablet Erected 1951 By
> The Brooklyn Engineers Club
> With Funds Raised by Popular Subscription

Kate made a mental note to learn more about Emily Roebling and the Bridge. She needed to properly lean in to that newly purchased copy of McCullough, and she would get on that first thing in the morning.

A stone marking the grand opening of the Bridge on May 24, 1883 was just a little further along. The date rang a bell. She stopped long enough to fish out her notebook. There it was: Sean died on May 25, 1883, the day after the Brooklyn Bridge opened. She put away her notebook, looked out across the water and started her walk back to the borough that was such an integral part of her family's history.

CHAPTER 21

Anya, appearing slightly more caffeinated than usual, popped out of her office as Kate walked by on her way to the diner for a cup of tea.

"Kate, will you be working at home today?"

"I just delivered Molly to Pineapple Street, and now it's all me all the time. Until two o'clock anyway. I'm going to stop by the Historical Society on my way to collect Molly. Why? What's up?"

"I have workers coming over this morning to clear out the fourth floor. It will be the first day's racket in a week's worth, I'm afraid. But they'll never start before 9am. I laid down the law on that. Including with your brothers, who take things over tomorrow. I bet they'll be in full uncle mode. You might find them knocking on your door, sniffing around for a free cup of coffee."

"I wouldn't be surprised. And Molly would love seeing their morning faces over breakfast. Don't worry about noise today, or tomorrow for that matter. Molly will be at Grandparent's Week with Kitty, and I can work at the library. New tenant I take it?"

"Two of them actually," she nodded. "Mr. Best—do you remember him from the Monroe Place building you looked at?—he sent over a couple who had an offer on their apartment there and want to rent for a while until they figure out their next step. I showed them my place and Finn's: they loved them both and are willing to take the fourth floor even though it is a work-in-progress. They're both just recently retired from the New York Philharmonic: cello and violin."

"Which played which?"

"I didn't think to ask. But you can. They'll be stopping by today for some sort of ceremony. They want to put a little spell on the place before their piano is brought in: and that's happening this afternoon. I wonder if they're Buddhists...," she trailed off, distracted by the phone in her hand pinging for the fifth time in as many seconds. "I have to get back to work. Sorry again for any noise...and the piano will live in the lobby for a few weeks. Should be fun! I gave the Vogelmanns—they're the musicians—your number. In case they can't find me for some reason and have questions, or hit a snag supervising the piano. Be nice to them, Kate!"

Kate watched Anya through the plate glass window. She was actually doing three things at once. With a smile on her face. And nobody else in sight. Kate was impressed. "I will smile more even when nobody is around to see it," she said to the empty sidewalk, "and I will begin now."

She walked through the diner door wearing what looked more like a smirk, and it raised the suspicion of the old timers who sat near the front door. But they kept their thoughts to themselves. Kate grabbed a *Daily News* from the window sill on her way to the counter. What was becoming her favorite seat, the last one away from the front door, was empty and waiting for her. She ordered a coffee and retrieved the last two letters, the ones Finn found stuck behind the drawer, from her tote.

The one dated February 1880. She'd only had time to skim it in the Main Branch, but its "sad news" had made her feel a little embarrassed then, as if she were snooping through somebody's diary. Aware now that Brid O'More would soon die—and that her husband, Edward, was Kate's own great, great grandfather—added a new layer of voyeurism. Before signing off, James asked his sister to "coinnigh I do chuid paidreacha iad." Kate wondered if that request to Eileen "to keep them in your prayers" ever haunted her once Edward became her husband. On some level, it must have. After all, she had kept this letter with personal items precious enough to have been passed along the generations. There was a story to be told about them for sure.

Kate was about to fold it away, when she noticed James had enclosed another dollar. And this was just a month after the first dollar he sent home. She grabbed her McCullough to find out what she could about salaries among the men who worked on the Brooklyn Bridge. Maybe the book could tell her what kind of work James did there. Was he way up high in the air, or down in the caissons, where some, she knew, died of the bends? Whatever he was doing, it paid well enough for him to potentially have his sister and father to Brooklyn in just one year's time. She settled in.

As expected, McCullough delivered the goods. By the time James arrived in the fall of 1879, those men who worked on the caissons—Irish, German, and Italian immigrants mostly—had moved on to other bridge jobs or to safer lines of work. Kate learned that they had earned $2/day: a fortune for young men from the tenements, including the Irish living over in "the flats" on Gold Street. The men in the air, cable wrappers, made half of what the sandhogs had earned, but it was still more than they were likely to make anywhere else. Less dangerous too, but certainly not without its risks.

From what she read, it seemed most likely to Kate that James worked on the road building and the finishing work. These projects stretched out longer than was planned, due first to delays in materials coming from Pennsylvania and New Jersey, and then to some local political jockeying. She made a note to share the politics with Margot, who would no doubt comment that some things never change. The combination of these delays compromised Roebling's position as Chief Engineer. He had to fight on a regular basis for more than two years to keep his job. It made Kate wonder what James might have endured in order to keep his own. Day labor was hard work, but the competition must have been fierce. Irish immigrants were seldom at the top of a manager's hiring list.

Her phone rang, not a number she recognized, but it was local. She grabbed it, hoping to find the elusive cable man on the other end.

"Hello?"

"Hello! Is that Kate? This is Anne Vogelmann, your soon-to-be neighbor."

"Yes, this is Kate. Are you at the building?"

"I am. Here with my husband, Mike. And I understand from Anya that you might be able to help us. We can't seem to get her on the phone. The apartment is open, but we forgot our key to the building in all the commotion this morning."

"Give me two minutes. Where will I find you two?"

"On the sidewalk. We're the couple standing next to the Steinway." And with that she hung up.

Kate paid her check, gathered her things and headed outside, where, sure enough, four movers and a familiar looking couple—she with a fabulous pink scarf sliding down her arm—stood staring at a piano.

"Hello everybody, I'm Kate."

"Mike Vogelmann, cello. Have we met before? I never forget a face," he said, extending his right hand and placing his left on Kate's forearm.

A charmer. But how was it possible that Anya didn't know what instruments each one played?

"Not *met* exactly. But I think our paths crossed on Saturday night. Were you here looking at the building?"

"We were! I'm Anne, violin. How do you do? And these," she beamed at the movers, "are the crème de la crème of the Philharmonic's stage crew. Doing us a favor...don't tell the union! The piano will have to come into our apartment through a window, but Anya doesn't want us to do that until the weather's a little warmer. We couldn't agree more. For now, you and our other neighbors-to-be will, I'm afraid, have to put up with her presence in the lobby."

"And," Mike added, "we will make up for the inconvenience with evening performances as often as possible. Starting tonight at six o'clock."

"I can't wait. And my niece will absolutely love it."

"That's settled then. Now excuse us as this beautiful beast is moved inside."

Kate opened the door and invited the Vogelmanns to stop up for tea once they were done supervising the transport of their prized Steinway. Kate knew absolutely nothing about music or musical instruments, but she could see this was no run-of-the-mill piano. Even with covers—they had one for the piano as well as the bench—it took some faith to leave it unattended in the lobby until they moved in. Kate watched them get it settled near the corner, then returned to her work while they went about theirs.

She put three proper tea cups out on the counter, with a cookie in each saucer for good measure, filled the kettle, and settled in to read the translation of the fourth and final letter. Dated December 12, 1882, it was from Eileen to her father:

> I can hardly believe that I am here. I arrived yesterday and spent the whole night up on the roof talking with Seamus. We watched the sun rise! He said he stayed up all night when he got here, and so I had to. He is thriving, but I worry he works too hard. He is on the bridge—you cannot imagine this bridge—with the other men from dawn to dusk and sometimes later. He was promoted and he will have a ticket for you very soon. I hope you are well looked after … I miss you and worry about your eyes. Waiting for your legs to be set right, Your loving daughter, Eileen

She came over without her father??

The idea of James goading his younger sister into staying up all night struck a happy chord with Kate. Her brothers were now over forty—and Kate would be joining them in that club soon enough—but they still tried to pull rank on a fairly regular basis. Happily, Kate thought, with about the same level of success they had when all three of them were kids. It seems this James was more skilled, or perhaps Eileen threw him a bone for the reunion's sake. Even if she had slept a solid eight the night before—which was unlikely considering the level of anticipation she must have been experiencing—she had to have been thoroughly wiped out from the crossing.

This was the first letter to contain an actual date of arrival, and Kate—the researcher in her desperate for a bit of institutional evidence—wasted no time hopping onto the Castle Garden website to search for Eileen. And there she was: her ship, the *Mary*, arrived from Dublin at 16:00 on a Tuesday. It had left Ireland a full five weeks earlier, stopped in Liverpool for three days, and then sailed straight to lower Manhattan.

Chanting, from the direction of the stairwell, interrupted her train of thought.

She followed the incantations toward the door, and the scent of sage grew stronger with each step. She put her ear up to the door and, through the crack where it met the frame, asked, "can I open the door?"

"Of course you can," came the Vogelmanns in unison. Kate opened the door.

"You're the final stop, Kate. And Mike will kill for a cup of tea." She turned to her smudge pot-carrying other half, "won't you?"

"I'm technically a pacifist, but, yes, at this moment, I do think I would do some damage for tea. Love your Santa sign," he added. "Our stairwell has a sign too: it says *Danger: Hollow Sidewalk. Will Not Support the Weight of Vehicles*."

"Isn't that great?," asked Anne. "We've decided it was in honor of the Steinway, but we'll have to check with Anya tonight at the lobby recital. I take it from your floor's *Santa* sign that your niece is a little one. How old is she?"

"Two and a half. Come in, come in. The kettle is full, but I need to turn on the stove."

The Vogelmanns oohed and aahed at the floors, the windows, and Molly's bedroom. But they practically passed out when they saw the fireplace.

"Give me a minute," Anne said, with her hand at her chest. "It's too fantastic. Anya told us ours will look wonderful when the work is done, but, I have to admit, we assumed it was wishful exaggeration on her part. The two she showed us were done ages ago, when she brought the building. We figured she would have run out of steam or interest by now; you know, when it came to things like this."

"And it works, right?"

"Look, Mike, there's ashes. Of course it works!" She grabbed his hand, "I cannot wait to move in. Kate, how long did it take for your place to be ready?"

"Mine was mostly done when I came to look at it. And then it took a week or so before it was totally finished. But when Anya says *finished*, she means down to every detail. The floors didn't even need sweeping. All I had to do was hang curtains. Did she give you an estimate on when things would be done?" The kettle whistled from the kitchen.

"Go get that, we'll join you in a minute. I want to finish snooping, if you don't mind."

"Snoop away. Tea will be ready when you are."

The tea was steeping when the Vogelmanns joined Kate at the table for what turned into a full hour of chat and more than one cookie each. Kate took them down in the elevator, so they could get a sense of how to work it once they moved in. They were decades older than Molly, but just as enchanted by the cage and its squeaky progression to lower floors.

"We'll see you tonight. Don't forget: six o'clock sharp! Bring as many people as you can fit in that lobby!"

And with that, the new pied pipers of Water Street left the building.

Kate cleaned the table and turned her attention back to a

winter Tuesday in 1882. Her head was clouded with all the movies she had seen over the years that contained pretty much the same iconic shot of immigrants sailing into New York harbor: folks on deck, chins tilted upward, hands holding hats firmly on heads, wide-eyed stares at the Statue of Liberty, music swelling…she hit her mental *delete*. There was real iconography in Eileen's letter—what else to consider a winter night's rooftop chat with a brother in a foreign country?— there was no need for help from Hollywood here. More realistic was the probability of Eileen being on deck with others, surely bundled up considering the month it was, but scared out of her wits. As for Lady Liberty, she wouldn't be raising her torch in the Harbor for another four years.

James is working long hours and has recently been promoted. He will have a ticket for their father "very soon." The Doyle Bible listed his death as May 25, 1883, and this was backed-up by the *Brooklyn Eagle* obituary: so he arrived sometime within six months of Eileen. Why didn't they travel together? And what's wrong with his leg?

Kate had hoped to end this afternoon with some degree of resolution, not with more unanswered questions than when it began. For now, the letters were a dead end. She decided to turn her attention to the table. She walked in its direction and sized it up like a worthy opponent.

"What is *your* story?," she asked, carrying it toward the kitchen window, where there was the most space and natural light. She took a page from Sunday's *Times*, laid it out on the kitchen floor, and placed St. Brigid upon it.

She ran her hand across the top, which was now clean, and the carvings and inlays were clearer to the eye. There was one thin layer of old varnish bubbling up a little in places, but it did not diminish the intricacy and beauty of what rested just below its surface. The top was fifteen inches square, according to the measurements Finn took to send his uncle Ciaran. It was solid oak, and there were leaf clusters, connected with lovely swirls, on all four sides; they circled the top just a little bit in from the edges. And there in the middle, holding pride of place, was St.

Brigid's Cross. The leaf clusters and cross were both inlaid with a darker wood that Kitty thought was bog wood. Bog wood? Kate didn't have a clue.

The front pulls—one for the secretary and one for the drawer just below it—were recessed, with hands surrounding them, like in a *claddagh* ring. She had never seen anything like it, and according to Finn, neither had his uncle. The space where a crown would be in the ring was simply the pull, giving the appearance of all loyalty and warmth being contained in the little table. Thanks to Finn's expert cleaning, both of the pulls now served their purposes.

The table was only three feet high, with four simple spindle legs that had little harps carved here and there. As unusual as it was for such plain legs to be carrying ornate designs and to have intricately carved harps scattered about—even in the fourth leg that seemed uneven with the others—it was seemed perfectly in keeping with the table's mystery. The letters carved on each leg, always next to a harp, were clearer now: D, L, O for sure, and, on the shorter leg, she saw what she had originally thought was MM was actually MN.

Kate went online searching for Irish furniture dealers. She found one on the Upper East Side, and the one in Chelsea that Finn's Uncle Ciaran suggested she try. Nothing on their websites looked remotely like what she was standing next to, but she took a few pictures and sent them off attached to an email asking if they had any information on tables like this. She hoped to hear back from them with some tidbit of information. She also wanted to see if the Historical Society could shed light on the missing Roebling House and her photo of the Egan Pharmacy on Flatbush Avenue.

The Historical Society was located in a spectacular old building on Pierrepont Street, smack in the middle of the Heights historical district, and just a few short blocks from Number 22. Kate knew it well. She had worked part-time in its Gift Shop all through high school. One was expected to contact them in advance with research queries, but she hoped somebody might remember her and allow her to cut that corner. She lucked out. The desk was staffed with new young faces, but the Society archivist was passing through when Kate entered. She recognized George immediately.

"Do you remember me? I'm Kate Doyle. You used to catch me daydreaming when I worked here in high school."

George squinted over his glasses, trying to place her. Then he smiled, "Kate, of course. Kitty's daughter, right?"

"Forever and always. How are you?"

"Never better. How's your mother? And what brings you around after all these years?"

"Mom's doing well, thanks. And I recently moved back, so you might be seeing more of me. But today I was hoping to find a photo of the old Roebling house that stood on Columbia Heights and see what you knew about it being torn down. And I have a photo here of an old pharmacy on Flatbush Avenue," she dug it out of her tote, "and I want to find out its address. See, the street number is blocked by the people standing in front of the door."

George took the photo from Kate. "I have somebody here who can look into this for you. But not today. Do you mind leaving it with me?"

"Not at all."

"Good. Email the General Info address here, so I have your contact details. I'll get back to you as soon as we have something."

"And the Roebling house?"

"That's easy. Come with me."

Kate followed him up the hallowed stairs and into the magical kingdom that was the BHS library. Except for a handful of computers, it hadn't changed a bit. Gleaming wood, green-globed banker lamps, stained glass windows. Still stunning.

"That's 110 Columbia Heights, if memory serves. Yes?"

"That's the one. It was between Orange and Pineapple streets, I think. On the Manhattan side of block. All that's there now is that ugly apartment building. It has a cornerstone dated 1949. I was surprised that the Roebling house was pulled down. Wouldn't it have been considered worth saving from developers?"

"Not when Robert Moses was around. His plans for the construction of the Brooklyn-Queens Expressway called for a lot more demolition than the old houses on Columbia Heights, I can promise you that. His plans—and the BQE—caused more problems and heartbreak than you can imagine. If it weren't for the intervention of some very prominent folks— including Eleanor Roosevelt by the way—things would have been far worse. Poor Williamsburg got the brunt of it. Compared to that neighborhood, the Heights got off easy indeed. No, Heights powerbrokers saved as many houses as they could by forcing pressure on Moses by going over his head. There were some very well connected folks here and they knew the mayor well enough to quell even the all-powerful Moses. The BQE plans were altered so that it would run below that side of the Heights rather than through it. That's why we have the promenade today."

"Amazing. Are there any photos of what the block looked like before the BQE?"

"Yes. And we have them digitized." He went into a database and quickly found a file on the Roebling address. Kate was surprised to see that the house was a fairly standard Heights brownstone. Nothing fancy. The photo, dated 1922, showed a simple, three-window-across home much like the houses that stood on either side of it. Judging from the top dormer windows, the fourth floor may not have been part of the original structure. It was considerably more ornate than the rest of the front façade.

"And here's the deed. It was purchased from a Mr. and Mrs. Clark on April 26, 1871. Probably the same Clarks after whom Clark Street is named. I could look into that further, if you want. Now, this is interesting: it wasn't bought by the Roeblings together; Emily alone is listed as the Grantee. That's a curiosity: not entirely unheard of for a wife to be the named owner back in that time, but unusual."

"Could it be because of his illness? I read he never fully

recovered from the bends."

"Caisson disease. Right. That affected him for many years." George called Roebling up in the database. "It says here that his injury happened in 1872, so, no, that wouldn't have been a factor. It was a prudent move though considering his illness. Funny thing is, he wound up outliving Emily by twenty some odd years. They sold the house after the Bridge opened, and moved back to New Jersey. Emily died there in 1903."

"What can you tell me about the BQE protest?"

"Keep in mind that the City was not remotely protective of its historical treasures in the 1940s. It took the destruction of old Penn Station in 1963 for the City to get its act together. The BQE protests were organized. And mostly successful. Some houses—like the Roebling's—were lost, but more were saved. And once the Heights was designated a New York City Historic District, the big problems were largely laid to rest...until very recently." He removed his glasses. "You no doubt noticed the building going up on Furman Street?"

"I sure did. It's as big—maybe bigger—than the old building where I lived on Collins Avenue in Miami. It must have 500 apartments in it."

"The Association blinked. And we're stuck with it. There's a few in DUMBO that are blocking our views too. Heartbreakers. On the plus side, all this development has us back on guard. There'll be no more, if we can help it." He stood up. "I hate to send you off with the echo of over-building in your ears, but I have to get ready for a meeting."

"I can't thank you enough, George. I'll send that email about the Flatbush Avenue pharmacy before the day is over. Thanks for everything."

"It was good to see you, Kate. Give my best to Kitty. And don't be a stranger."

Kate headed to Number 22 with spring in her step: there was a kid to collect and a piano recital to attend. She wanted hugs from the former and a glass of wine at the latter.

CHAPTER 22

For the second Tuesday in a row, Kate and Molly woke up to Sean and Kevin sitting at opposite ends of the Table for Ten. Each had a mug of coffee in one hand and a pen in the other: crossword puzzles were a family habit. Sean took the *Post*, and Kevin the *Daily News*. If their sister and niece failed to appear by the time they were done, they took on the Sudoku. If that number puzzle got finished, then they went ahead and made breakfast, knowing the smell of melting butter would infiltrate the dreams of the soundest sleeper. This particular menu featured tomato-swiss-chive omelets for the grown-ups and oats with berries for the little one. And blue juice.

"Are you almost done upstairs?," Kate asked between bites.

Kevin assured her that the work would be wrapped up Thursday. "It has to be, the Vogelmanns told Anya that they are moving in on Friday no matter what. They have to be out of their place before the closing, which is scheduled for Monday morning."

"Their building," Sean interrupted, "doesn't allow people to move on weekends...will you pass the pepper, Kate?"

"Do you know anything about the piano going upstairs? I love the lobby recitals, but the weather's been so gorgeous. Are there plans to take advantage of that?"

"There sure are. Hey, Molly," Kevin turned to his niece, who was closely examining a blueberry. She had a habit of sizing each one up very carefully before popping it in her mouth. "Do you want to see a piano fly?"

Molly looked at her uncle with befuddlement. Her face processed the improbability and elected to find it all doable. "Birds fly," she said, with the soundness of a judge.

"Indeed they do. And today, a piano will fly. Your uncles are in charge."

"Silly."

"What did you call me?"

Giggles began to percolate. "Silly," she said with her head beginning to bow. She sensed tickles were coming. Her predicament was not knowing when Kevin would pounce. And now she had Sean on the other side of her, so anything was possible. She looked back and forth from under long black lashes—first at one then at the other—who would tickle her?

They both exploded from the table at the same time, swooping Molly out of her chair, into the air, and onto the couch for a ticklefest. And so began another day at Water Street.

Kate had the table cleared, dishwasher running, and a shower in before her brothers and Molly began losing interest in Penguin Pete and his fuzzy buddies.

"The glaziers will be here in twenty minutes, Kev. We gotta' go. Bye small person," he said to Molly, bending down to place a kiss on her nose.

Sean crouched down. "Bye tall person named Molly."

Molly kissed Sean on the nose and ran to her room for games of her own.

"So much for me."

"Don't take it personally, Sean."

"Don't you wonder what goes on in her head when she just bolts off like that?," Kate asked. "Or, have you ever looked up and found her staring at you like she's never seen you before? I'd give anything to read her mind."

"She's doing well, Kate. But I was wondering if we should

drive her up to Vermont to see Casey and Joe…and the house. You know, before it starts being shown. Go see Eric's parents too. Is that a good idea?"

"I think it is, yes. And I have a call into the therapist to update him on how she's doing, so I'll check with him too."

"Anya said that now the estate is settled, the house can go on the market. I just need to go up and clean out the gutters first. Margot and I thought we might do that soon." He hugged Kate. "You're doing great with her, you know."

"Thanks. You are too. Now, go to work."

"Yup. It's piano and bathroom day. We've got plumbers coming in two hours and the piano movers are late. I'll call you before the piano flies, so Molly can watch. And let me know what the therapist says."

The brothers Doyle headed to the stairs, and Kate headed to the couch with their discarded newspapers. Her horoscope, Libra, said not to undertake new projects. Seriously? Every single day was a new project. She decided to take it as a sign to focus her energies on solving the mystery of St. Brigid before working further on her book. Then, just as suddenly as she had disappeared into her room earlier, Molly came and sat down next to Kate and announced that she wanted to plant the parsley that had been sitting in the kitchen since the day they moved in. Where in her little head did that come from?

Getting the plant out of its starter pot and into a proper planter with room to spread its roots was a fairly uncomplicated job, and everything went smoothly. They even had enough potting soil. The clay pot and its glossy red tray looked at home on the kitchen sill. Molly sprayed it with the mister until her hand began to cramp, which was just about when they saw two ropes appear on the other side of the window. Molly looked at Kate, "piano?"

"Piano! Let's get dressed. Hurry."

Molly was ripping her pajamas off and dropping them on

the floor as she ran in her tippy toed way toward her bedroom for the play clothes laid out on her pink rocking chair. Both dressed quickly and then ran to the door. Kate stuck the keys in her pocket, picked Molly up and tucked her under her left arm, and bolted down the stairs. Molly usually insisted on taking the stairs herself, but this kid with absolutely no sense of time (and why should she at her age?), seemed to intuitively understand that there wasn't a minute to spare. Not if she wanted to see her silly uncles make a piano fly. She said nothing but "wheee!," as they made their way to the sidewalk. If Kate could listen to Molly's inner thoughts, like she wished to earlier, she would discover what a smile sounded like.

The glaziers were in the process of removing a window from the Vogelmann's apartment, while the crew from the Philharmonic was busy wrapping the already padded piano with ropes. None of the workers appeared remotely aware that an audience was forming, until a big yellow lab ran up the sidewalk with its leash—and frustrated human—trailing behind.

The screams—"Elvis! Get back here! Elvis!"—were undercut by some award-winning language that would have done the once busy ports of the neighborhood proud. Kate gave the guy points for elevating adverb usage to a high art so early in the day. He stopped when he saw Molly.

"I am so sorry," he said to Kate, thoroughly embarrassed. He turned to Molly. "I said bad words."

"Bad words! Doggy doo," Molly wiggled out of Kate's arms and began skipping toward Elvis, who had stopped to sniff the front of the crane.

"Doggy doo?," he asked Kate, looking around to see where Elvis had left a present on the sidewalk.

Kate laughed. "No, no, it's what she calls dogs. Actual dog doo is doggy poo. Don't worry about the cursing, she's too young to notice it."

"That's what you think. Just wait until the first family dinner when she says 'please pass the fucking carrots.'"

Kate got brain freeze. She wasn't a particularly big curser, but she made a mental note anyway: no cursing in front of the k-i-d.

Molly enjoyed every minute of watching the piano fly, and so did Elvis, who barked and ran around in circles. Kate agreed to Molly's request that they invite Elvis upstairs for ice cream. Even though it was, technically speaking, not the ice cream hour of the day, Kate had no rebuttal for Molly's simple reasoning that "dogs like ice cream." Elvis's owner, whose name they now knew to be Todd, came along too.

Elvis pulled away from Todd as soon as they entered the lobby, thrilled at the new smells. But the elevator was another story. Elvis was not having it. After watching Todd trying to talk the dog into the cage (dog owners are funny), Kate intervened.

"Is he okay with stairwells, Todd? How do you get him to your apartment?"

"Elvis is actually a she—long story—and, yes, she's fine with stairs. My wife and I are on the sixth floor and Elvis's love of stairs keeps us from needing to join a gym. Lead the way."

Elvis ran ahead and was all the way up to Four by the time Todd caught up with her, busy sniffing the tools that Kevin and Sean had left in the stairwell there. At the sight of her human, she sat down and refused to move. Kate and Molly coaxed her out, and the three people traipsed down to Three, with the tail-wagging lab in the lead.

Once ice cream was served, including a little vanilla for Elvis, talk turned to what do you do and where do you do it. Todd was a dentist, recently relocated to DUMBO from Inwood, where he and his wife had lived since she was a law student at Fordham. They just moved in at the start of the year, but were already in love with the neighborhood. He bought into a group practice nearby and was also covering the occasional shift at the hospital.

"Most people are surprised that I take on extra part-time work, with my wife being a lawyer, but you can't imagine the student loans we're paying back. And my wife is an immigration attorney: not exactly billing at corporate rates."

"You have my sympathy about student loans. I talk about them with my students on a regular basis."

"You're a professor?"

"Sort of. I'm taking a year off to get settled with Molly. To be honest, I'm not sure I want to go back to teaching. At least not in the States. I've even been thinking of applying for some visiting professorships in Ireland or the U.K. while Molly is small…you know, that's the first time I said that out loud. It's a little fantasy that helps get me to sleep some nights."

"Go for it! My parents never let me and my sister keep them from travel. They dragged us everywhere, and we loved it. In fact, my wife and I plan on doing the same thing once we have kids. It was great."

"Really? And for long stretches?"

"Absolutely. Doctors, both of them. They volunteered and took visiting lectureships in every corner of Europe. Our family adventures were seldom less than six months."

"And what about school?"

"Oh, this was all before I started kindergarten. But we still took off for a month every summer after that."

"I'll keep that in mind. More ice cream?," she asked, noticing his empty bowl.

"I can't. It's my only day off for at least a week, and I have a lot of errands to get done. Dry cleaning, post office, groceries, library, dog food, laundry…it's endless."

"I understand. She eyed the overflowing hamper by her bedroom door. But you and your wife have to come to my spaghetti party. It's a week from Saturday, to celebrate new neighbors moving in upstairs. And bring Elvis."

"That sounds great. Once you meet Ruth, you'll see I can mingle with more sophisticated company than Elvis here. Bye, Molly," he was watching her flick Elvis's floppy ears up and down. "It was so very nice to meet you. And thank you for taking care of Elvis while I talked to your aunt. We'll see you soon."

They exchanged numbers, and Molly insisted on walking Elvis down the stairs.

On the way back up, Molly reached for Kate to carry her. Playing with her silly uncles, watching a piano fly, and running after Elvis had all been a bit much. She was asleep by the second floor.

With Molly tucked in for a nap, Kate turned to her laptop. Anya's open wifi channel was still working. Great. Both of the antique shops she had emailed about St. Brigid replied. Yes, they wanted to see the table and would come by her place if that was easier than her bringing it to them.

"They're pretty keen," she said to Penguin Pete, who had recently taken up residency on her desk. "What do you make of that?"

The first one also offered interesting background information on campaign furniture, which they believed it resembled. Score one for Ciaran. The second, from the manager of the shop in Chelsea, had a proposition. She said the owner was *very* interested in seeing it: "might you consider parting with it temporarily? The owner also has a shop on Francis Street in Dublin, and he is based there. If he arranged the packing, insurance, and shipping, would you allow him to examine it in Dublin?"

CHAPTER 23

The Vogelmann's Friday move-in was, Kate thought, very un-Vogelmannlike.

"What did you expect?," Anya asked, as they waited in line at the butcher.

"I don't know, some sort of quirky pageantry. Not the run-of-the-mill steady stream of boxes anyway. Even Molly lost interest after a while, and she adores them. Those lobby recitals were a real hit with her. But Anne and Mike did promise her she can play the piano upstairs whenever she wants."

"I'm hoping she'll take an interest in the cello. I love the cello."

"Why don't you ask Mike if you can take lessons from him? He told me he'll be picking up students in the summer."

"Zero talent. My parents let me try every single band instrument when I was in school, and I was a disaster at all of them." She gave her number to the butcher, "two pounds of meatball mix, and," she pointed to the Italian sausage in the case, "half a tray of those."

"What are you doing?," Kate asked.

"My contribution to your dinner. Let me do this...it takes a village, right? And you can cross the liquor store off your list, Kevin already took care of that. The box is in my office, and the white wine is already in your fridge. Kevin loves having a key to your place." Her phone pinged.

Kate appreciated having one less stop to make. "Okay then. Thank you. Let's hit the Deli. I'm splurging for a salad platter this time. I just can't bring myself to chop that many vegetables or clean that much lettuce. Also, have you given any thought to what I mentioned earlier—you know, about that antique dealer in Dublin?"

"I have. And I don't think you should send St. Brigid off on her own. I'm sure the man on Francis Street is perfectly reliable, but you'd lose it if anything happened. I think you should bring her there yourself. Get away and sort that out at the same time. Do you good."

"Huh. I hadn't considered that."

"Well, consider it. You go get the salad, and I'll see you later at your place."

She thanked the woman handing her the meatball mix and sausage, and she was off, somehow making it to the check-out without ever once looking up from her phone. She was the queen of the ping and the diva of blind navigation.

Finn called while Kate was on her way to order the salad. "And how are you, stranger?"

"All good. I'm wondering if I can bring my former castmate, Pauline, to dinner tonight. I'll be working with her all afternoon—she has an audition tomorrow—and she's on her own tonight. Is there room for one more?"

Kate was disappointed, but didn't miss a beat.

"Always. Bring her along. We're starting early, don't forget. The doors open at six o'clock. Why 'former'? Has she left the show?"

"No, we closed last night."

"Of course you did. I'm sorry I forgot. Busy days. Good house at the end?"

"As good as it was at the start. Sold out most matinees and every evening performance. I can't wait to do another show with Gillian. We're talking about Ibsen, but need to decide which one. She's close though to convincing me that the time is right for *The Wild Duck*, and she wants to direct. Listen, Pauline and I will be wrapping up in midtown at five. What can we bring?"

"Yourselves. All bases are covered. Oh, and a dog is coming too. Make sure Pauline doesn't have dog issues, or allergies, or whatever."

"She has a dog of her own, so there's no worries there. See you around six."

Oh, good for her, she has a dog, Kate thought, as she hung up. But then she checked herself: she knew little about Pauline, and, besides, Gillian raved about what a funny, talented woman Pauline was. Kate relegated being petty to her mental trash can. Kate and Finn both led busy lives, and, she reminded herself, the fact that they had been playing phone tag all week was not worth getting worked up—or petty—about. Finn had left several sweet gifts at her door since they saw each other last, including a bag of rags and furniture cleaner; a small, glass penguin; a St. Brigid's cross made of papier-maché; and an English-Irish dictionary. If Pauline was a date, so be it. Kate shrugged off whatever tinge of disappointment she felt and went hunting for her salad at the Deli, Montague Street's oldest grocery and catering shop.

Molly was in a favorite dress and patent leather Mary Janes at six on the dot, Gillian's crew were at the door five minutes later, and all the kids were making a fort in Molly's room five minutes after that, with Glen, Margot, and Kitty on supervisor duties.

Grown-ups huddled in the kitchen and around the Table for Ten, everybody with a job to do and a glass of wine to sip. With each new arrival, more wine was poured. But when Todd and Elvis appeared at the door, everything came to a momentary standstill. Kids came pouring out of the bedroom, and every single person gushed over the pooch. In the nick of time, Kate saw the happy lab's head tilt toward the Table for

Ten. She grabbed one platter, and instructed those closest to grab whatever they could.

"Nice move, Kate! But my wife and I came prepared to Elvis-proof your dinner."

"We sure did," the voice belonged to a tall blonde standing in the doorway. She was carrying an armful of plastic platter lids. "As soon as Elvis was big enough to reach the table, we invested in these. And they come to every dinner invitation that includes a plus dog. Great reflexes. You must be Kate," she offered her right hand after piling the lids on the table. "I'm Ruth. Wife of Todd and servant of Elvis."

Kate was happy to welcome Ruth to the fold, and relieved to see she had enough lids to cover everything on the table. "Look, we even have tags to stick on the lids. Maybe there's a kid or two here who might want to do this?"

"We do have one of those, and she loves to write and draw." Gillian and Kate yelled "Sarah!" in unison, and she got to work.

Kate saw Finn in the doorway and went over to say hello. She kissed him on the check, "Oh, is that it?," he laughed, steering her into the stairwell. "Time has not made the heart fonder then?," he looked at her with the same curiosity he displayed whenever they were together: a face that said, "I really cannot figure this one out."

"Fond as ever, I promise," she gave him a kiss, licked her lips, and went back for seconds. "Where's Pauline?"

"Took the lift. Couldn't wait to give it a go after I told her about it. More please."

"No time. I wonder who buzzed the elevator up."

Kate and Finn peeked into the apartment. Across the living room, eagerly awaiting the arrival of the cage, stood Gillian and Glen's boys. And then, between them, Kate caught her first glimpse of Pauline. Stunning legs that went all the way up to her ears, and carrying an enormous shopping bag. She opened the gate, said hello to the boys, took one step, and fell over sideways. Everybody inhaled, even Elvis.

But Finn just shook his head.

"She has the motor skills of a drunk goat. They're legend."

Pauline was up in a flash. Spit the hair out of her eyes, straightened her skirt, and said, "I'm good! And I have ice cream, which I hear is pretty popular in this place. Will you kind gentlemen deliver this to a grown up with kitchen privileges for me?"

The boys nodded, mouths agape, then, on their way to the kitchen, fell into fits of that glorious kind of rib-wracking, totally uncontained laughter afforded only to those trying desperately to keep it together. It was contagious, and Finn led the charge on his way to greet Pauline, who stood in front of the cage, hands on hips.

"Oh, will you just shut up, Finn? Leave me alone. Sorry for the dramatic entrance," she said looking away from Finn and toward the amused gathering, "I cannot walk in heels, but I keep trying. Where's Kate and Molly?"

Kate stepped forward, holding hands with her niece.

"It's so nice to meet you, Pauline. Welcome. And this is Molly."

Molly was remarkably un-shy. She seemed to consider Pauline a very tall kid. Some grown-ups were like that.

"Play?," she asked Pauline.

"It would be my pleasure. Where's the toys?" She waved hello to the party, and, with a quick "save me some food!," let Molly take her by the hand and lead her to her bedroom. The rest of the kids came along, with Elvis bringing up the rear.

Kate looked at Finn. "She might be the most charming person to ever roam the planet."

"Oh, she's gas, alright. I adore her, and I hope we're friends well after this play ends, but I want you to know that we are strictly friends and work colleagues."

"Honestly, Finn, I'd have been disappointed for myself, but I think I'd also have applauded your good judgment." She winked at him in reassurance, "now, let's get you a drink."

✦ ✦ ✦

The Vogelmanns arrived with two enormous sketchpads and easels, and possibly the largest box of crayons ever manufactured. It was the good kind, with a built-in sharpener.

"The guests of honor have arrived! And," Anne added as they put down their goodies to reach back out into the stairwell, "we come bearing the tools of our trade!" And, sure enough, they brought in her violin, his cello, and two bows.

"Mind if I put these in your bedroom until after dinner, Kate?," Mike asked. "The easels and crayons are for the kids...big and small."

"Let me help you," Kitty offered. It was her first time meeting the Vogelmanns, and she was thoroughly beguiled. Between Elvis, Pauline, and the building's new musicians-in-residence, it was shaping up to be one enchanted evening.

"Now, this," Kate whispered to Anya, "is Vogelmannlike."

"I take your point. But, come on, we need to check on the sauce."

The food was delicious, and there was plenty of it. Elvis was relegated to the office, but she did not hold it against any of the partygoers when they piled in there to sit around an unlit fireplace sharing pints of ice cream, songs, and selfies. The kids entertained themselves in Molly's room, where Sean, Kevin and Glen had organized the Vogelmann goodies for the kids, who were busy coloring up a storm, taking just enough breaks to help polish off the ice cream next door, where Kate was filling everybody in on St. Brigid and her letters.

Pauline asked to see it. Her "would you mind very much?" was seconded by everybody in the room who was not licking a spoon. And those who were nodded and mmmm'd.

"Not at all."

But Kitty waved Kate off. "Let me. I need to put the kettle on."

Kitty brought St. Brigid into the office, placing her right in the middle of the group. "She should have joined the party hours ago. And," she added, looking at Kate, "you should book a ticket to Dublin and get to the bottom of this so you can move on to other things, including that new book of yours. What do you say?"

All eyes were on Kate, who looked straight at Anya. "Did you put her up to this?"

Anya looked at some imagined imperfection on her manicured hand.

"I don't know." She looked at Finn, who was sitting to her right.

"You should go." It dawned on them simultaneously that her going could put them both in Ireland at the same time. Intriguing.

"Go, Kate. Molly is due for a proper Pineapple Street vacation," Kevin added.

"And if she gets homesick for her room, then we'll have sleepovers here," Sean chimed in. "Go."

A chant of "go, go, go," raised the curiosity of the kids, who scrambled into the room, wondering what the commotion was. Without a clue what they were encouraging, they picked up the rallying cry and the room was filled with an increasingly loud "go, Kate, go! Go, Kate, go!!"

Kate looked at the table then around the room then back at the table. "All right, all right. I'll book a flight."

Half a dozen smartphones were thrust in her direction. But Anya, with the speed of an Old West gunslinger, won. Kate grabbed it.

"Here's my contribution," Finn said, handing her a credit card. "The flight's on me. And book an open return. You're not coming back empty handed just because of a schedule. You'll come back when you're done."

His gesture sent a little current of curiosity through the room. Kitty nodded her head, leaned over to Kevin, and whispered, "told you so" out of the corner of her mouth.

Kevin slipped $5 out of his wallet and handed it to his mother, who slipped it up her sleeve before stepping out to answer the kettle's whistle.

Kate was overwhelmed by all the good cheer, and a few

tears ran down her cheek.

"Boo-boo auntie Kate?," Molly climbed onto her lap, the very picture of concern. Which set off Alice, Gillian and Glen's youngest, who climbed into her father's lap. The chain reaction turned into farce—and the kids were calmed—when Mike sat on his wife's lap and she shooed him away.

"Seriously, Kate. Book it. Now."

Kate handed a reassured Molly to her godfather and picked the phone back up. "Okay, Kevin. I'm on it."

"And I'm on kitchen duty," Pauline said, "but I'm too full to stand up." She reached her arms in the air and wiggled her fingers like a little kid.

Margot and Anya each took an arm and hauled her upright. "Thank you, ladies." And she was off to the kitchen. This official the-party-is-winding-down signal was an opportunity for Gillian to have a little alone time with Kate, and she took it. She sensed her old friend was in need of reassurance, and she wanted to buck her up. Kitty, Ruth, and Todd followed Mike and Anne into Molly's room, when they offered to play a concert beneath the glowing stars. Margot and Anya stayed to clean up the office, and everybody else headed out to deal with the kitchen and the Table for Ten. The opening notes of a familiar jazz standard flowed through the air. Elvis climbed up on the sofa without bothering to ask first, and promptly began to snore.

"Remember when we went to Ireland that summer?"

"Of course I do, Gillian. You met Glen."

"I sure did, but you met Dublin. You always said you would go back when you were a real grown-up, but you never do."

"What are you talking about? I go back all the time. Every two years, easily."

"Yeah, but that's for work: research, a conference, to give a talk. You never go just to unwind and walk around. You even scheduled a talk when you went over for the funeral of that former professor of yours. That's pathetic."

"Point taken." She rubbed Elvis's head. The dog did not so much as twitch. "I want to be this dog in my next life."

"Do this, Kate. Bring Brigid, your letters, and that family Bible, and anything else you've gathered. But do not bring one item unrelated to the family history." She gave Kate a big hug, and then looked Kate in the eye. "You're not going back to Miami, are you? I think your sabbatical is a sabbatical in name only. Am I right?"

"I think you might be. But please don't say anything to anybody. I'm still sorting it all out."

"Everybody already knows."

"Story of my life."

"It really is. You know I love you, but you are hopelessly clueless about the world around you. Except," she smiled warmly, "where Molly and Sarah are concerned. You have an uncanny connection with each of them."

"I do, don't I? I was born to be a godmother."

"You were. And a bookworm too. But there must be work you can do that doesn't require the politics of academia—which I know you hate—and the 24/7 that you devote to the job. Hell, you barely stop even in summers. Do you realize that these three months since Eileen and Eric passed are the most time you've spent with all of us in years? Years, Kate. That's a long time to devote to what looks from the cheap seats to be a dubious profession."

They stared at each other, letting that float between them.

"Do I have to remind you of those reprobates in Philly that you spent five years—five years!—working yourself sick for? Or the visits here that you canceled at the last minute since you took the job in Florida? I love you to pieces, but you need to hear something: the perpetual projects, deadlines, and planning that have comprised your adulthood may well add up to a nifty stack of scholarship at the end, but I don't see that being much consolation to Molly as she's growing up, or Kitty as she's slowing down. If you need a push to get off the fence—really, I 'might be' right that you're not going back?—let it be this: your friends and family need you just as much as Molly does. And you need us. So, please, go to Dublin. Sort out this family mystery. Get your research itch scratched, and come back here and get settled. Enough already."

Elvis got up off the couch, stretched, and then laid down on the floor belly up, and went back to sleep.

"And I know Finn's on his way to Dublin for his friend's wedding, by the way." She smirked. "One more thing…you shouldn't book your flight online before calling the airline. You need to find out how to buy a seat for a table."

Kate phoned. Then she went online and booked two seats leaving Thursday, and hit the *Confirm* button just as Kitty walked in.

"We're close to done out there. And Todd and Ruth look exhausted. I get the sense those two work way too many hours. Will you release Elvis to them?"

At the sound of her name, the yellow lab opened her eyes, stood up, and trotted out to the living room.

"Mom, have I been an absent Doyle?"

Kitty considered her daughter for a minute. "Gillian give you the talk?"

"She did."

"Well, let's just say you take after your father's side in more ways than one. Bit of a loner clan that bunch."

They looked at each other for a minute, nodded their heads, and followed Elvis out into the living room.

The Vogelmanns wrapped up their bedroom concert and Anne thanked everybody for "making us so welcome and giving our instruments their first public breaths in our new home." She and Mike bowed to applause and hoots and hollers before taking their leave.

The rest of the party filed out in pairs and groups. Pauline squeezed into the elevator with Glen and Gillian's kids so they had a chaperone to race their parents to the lobby. Glen and Gillian could be heard yelling encouragement to each other all the way down the stairs, with Elvis, Todd and Ruth chasing after them. Margot, Sean, and Kitty headed back to Pineapple Street, after tucking Molly into bed. Kevin and Anya took the elevator up to Anya's place with some leftovers, leaving Finn and Kate drying and putting away the last of the pots and pans.

"Penny for your thoughts?"

"Gillian and my mom said I have to join the human race. Are you and your family close?"

"I never thought of us as closer-than-average, but as I get older and hear friends talk about their families, I think maybe we are. I ditched my agent and manager when I decided to grow up: hired a lawyer and kept the accountant mind you. Now when things come up that I don't have the time for, one family member or another usually steps up. I'm lucky."

"I remember you saying one of your sisters was looking into a house in Greystones for you. What ever became of that?"

"Funny you should ask. There's a chance it'll come through next week. When I go over for the wedding. Do you know Greystones?"

"I do, yes. I made a good friend, Alan, when I was in graduate school. He's from Scotland, but he's lived in Dublin for years. Anyway, I had a rule to always take Sunday off from all things academic, and he and I used to take these long walks. We'd have breakfast at my place—always a full Irish—and then pick a direction and walk. And then at four o'clock, wherever we were, we had to turn around and walk back. It was great. But every once in a while we rode the DART out to Bray and walked the cliffs out to Greystones. It was spectacular."

"I'm hoping everything goes to plan while I'm there. Buying a place in Ireland is a little complicated. You have to make a sealed bid, and it can drag on." He put the dish towel down, "We're all done here, Kate. Do you have the time to sit for a while?"

"I have a list to make."

"Well grab what you need to do that, and meet me on the couch. And take off the socks. I'm going to give you the foot rub of foot rubs. Back in a flash." She heard him mumble something about "obstacles" on his way to the bathroom.

PART THREE: LOVE

CHAPTER 24

Kate lifted the plastic window shade as the plane descended into Dublin. She was just in time to admire the green fields that surrounded the airport. How many times had she made this landing over the years? Thirty? More probably.

Memories of the first trip were clear as a bell. It was with Gillian between junior and senior year of high school: the summer Kate decided on academia and Gillian decided on a life in the theater. They saw shows from one end of the island to the other: amateur theater, youth theater, prison theater, Druid in Galway, the Abbey and Gate in Dublin, the Lyric in Belfast: as they became aware of a show, they saw it. They both fell in love with Irish drama, and Gillian fell in love with Glen. He was in Dublin to devote a summer to reading Yeats—whose poetry still made him cry—before starting medical school in Chicago. But that trip to Ireland gave him the travel bug and the perspective to see that years of school, severely limited free time, and probably decades of repaying student loans all added up to a future that was not for him. He opted to follow his heart professionally, withdrawing his med school acceptance and enrolling at a culinary school in France; and personally, encouraging Gillian to study acting in Europe rather than New York, so they could be near each other. She was accepted at The Royal Academy of Dramatic Art the winter of senior year, and was on her way to London the day after graduation.

This was Kate's first time flying in first class. It was a novelty for St. Brigid too, she thought, looking at her traveling companion to the left. Brigid was cocooned in a blanket and twine. Her outer layer was a shell of shrink-wrapped bubbles, with a customs label stuck on top. The flight attendant barely batted an eye when she helped Kate secure it with seat belt extenders at boarding.

"Not a first then?," Kate had asked.

"No, not a first. We see it all, especially on the flights from New York."

Getting St. Brigid off the plane was as easy as getting her on. There was a luggage cart waiting, and a man from the airline helped get her settled on it. The slog through customs was tricky to navigate due only to the hour. Kate never adjusted easily to early arrivals or time differences. The afternoon flight from New York to Dublin delivered a double whammy that always made the first day more than a bit fuzzy. She adjusted her watch to 5:30am local time, while waiting her turn in line. She wheeled the cart to Customs and Immigration, and handed the paperwork for the table and her passport to a white haired gentleman. He looked at her sympathetically.

"Slept on the plane did you?"

"How could you tell?"

"You have a pillow line running all the way down the side of your face there. Welcome to Dublin, Ms. Doyle. And I see from this passport that it's not your first time. Business or pleasure this trip?"

"I suppose I'd call it personal business. I'm taking this table," she nodded to her cargo, "to a shop on Francis Street to be appraised. And then I'm off to Westmeath to do a little family research...genealogy research."

"The family search is always popular. Where are you staying, and how long will you be with us?"

"The Gresham, and I don't know for certain. But I'm guessing a week."

"Very good then. I'll stamp you for two, just in case." He matched the code on the form to the label on the table, stamped her well-worn passport, and wished her success in her efforts. "Enjoy yourself now."

Kate made her way to the luggage carousel and saw a man there holding a sign with her name on it. A gift from Sean and Margot, who wanted her trip to the Gresham in the early Irish hours to be uncomplicated. It was the first time that she didn't have to haul a suitcase and an overstuffed carry-on onto the AirCoach and then drag everything to the hotel or, in earlier days, her apartment on Ormond Quay.

The driver got her things settled in the van, put the radio on low, and left her to her thoughts for the drive to O'Connell Street. He took it down to the Bridge and made a tidy U-turn at the statue, placing them on the northbound side so he could pull up directly in front of the hotel. She admired its familiar façade while a porter took her things inside.

"Welcome back, Dr. Doyle. One week I see."

"That's the plan."

She handed over a form for Kate's signature.

Kate turned to get her things, and discovered the porter, her suitcase, and Brigid were gone. She looked back at the desk clerk.

"Already upstairs waiting for you. And," she leaned over the counter to Kate, "so is a beautiful bunch of lavender. I've never seen anything like it. Oh, and this arrived last night."

She handed Kate a white box, with a Butlers ribbon tied across its middle. Kate smiled. Finn, no doubt. He would be here soon enough, but she liked that he sent an advance team.

She walked past the café, where coffee and tea were already being set up for the day, and past the marble table and its elegant orchids. She admired the sparkle of an overhead chandelier while waiting for the elevator. God she loved this place. You can keep the chains in South Dublin and the boutique hotels in and around Temple Bar, this was more her speed. "Old school," as Finn would have it. A bit swanky to be sure, but the small rooms were always manageable on her teaching salary. Her budget was more generous now, and she could have afforded a larger room. But she craved the familiarity her little room, with its long entryway, deep tub, and back-facing window. Most of all, she craved the luxurious Gresham bed.

Her room was at the far end of the hallway, nearly the length of a full city block from the elevator. She barely made it to the door, she was so tired. But once opened, she saw it was worth every tired step. There on the bed was an armful of fresh lavender, wrapped with two ribbons: one a twirl of red, white, and blue; the other of orange, green and white. The intermingled American flag and Tricolor may have held the stems together, but they couldn't contain the fragrance. The room smelled like heaven. The envelope beside it had a card that read, *Remove obstacles, I arrive tomorrow night.*

She looked around the room and saw there were several vases, each filled halfway with water. She could break up the bouquet however she wanted. There was even a small vase in the bathroom. When she lifted the lavender to drink it in, she laughed long and loud. Sitting there on the bed was a CD, its case covered in little bits of purple dust: *London Calling*. She laughed while she filled the vases. She laughed while she washed up and changed into a favorite nightshirt. And her laughter was the last sound in her head as she drifted off to sleep.

✦ ✦ ✦

Kate woke up to a ringing house phone. She looked at her watch: three o'clock. Shit. She knew who it would be before picking up the receiver. "Hello?"

"Hello, Dr. Doyle. There's a Mr. Martin here who says he has an appointment with you."

"Yes, he does. But I'm afraid I overslept. Will you ask him, can he give me half an hour or so and I'll meet him downstairs?"

She could hear a muffled conversation that ended with "that's grand" before footsteps on the marble floor wandered out of hearing range.

"Mr. Martin will be waiting for you in the restaurant. He said not to hurry, he's free the rest of the day."

"Thank you so much. I'll be down soon." Kate managed to return the receiver to its stand on the third try. She was running on Dublin time already. It was a city where three o'clock meant sometime between three o'clock and dinner. She gave the bubble-wrapped Brigid a pat on the head on her way to the shower. "It's show time, girlfriend."

Halfway down the long carpeted hallway, wheeling St. Brigid in the little cart the porter had left for her use, Kate saw an older couple waiting for the elevator. She was fussing with his tie in what appeared to be a well-honed routine. O'Vogelmanns, Kate thought, smiling. There was room for all of them, and they rode down exchanging the pleasantries of an afternoon.

When Kate got to the restaurant, she saw a man sitting with a file on the table in front of him, next to a pot of tea. He was fussing with his phone. There was a plate of fruit and cheese on the table, and two cups and saucers before the empty seats across from his. That looked nearly right, so she took her chances.

"Mr. Martin?" she asked, stopping next to him. When she looked down she saw that she was interrupting what appeared to be a marathon session of Candy Crush.

He stood up. "You caught me. It's my nephew. He keeps putting these games on my phone. Call me Jack, please. You must be Kate Doyle…and this," he closed his phone and gave the bubbled form a glance, "must be your St. Brigid."

"That she is. So nice to meet you," she shook his outstretched hand and sat in the chair he had pulled out for her.

"The pleasure is mine. I have been thinking a lot about

your table since you agreed to come over. I've looked at the photos you sent me last week, and I spoke with Ciaran Murphy. He told me about the letters you found in it. I hope you don't mind, but I asked him to join us. He's going to bring the translations his niece sent along." He opened the folder. "Tea?"

"Yes to tea, and I love the idea of meeting Ciaran. Go ahead with the file, I'll pour."

She saw a man over Jack's shoulder. He came in to the lobby and was halfway to the restaurant entrance when he stopped to answer his phone. This had to be Ciaran. If it weren't for Finn, she might give the uncle a run for his money. Tall, dark haired, scarf tied in the manner few American men can pull off, no coat, and nice boots clearly not afraid of a polish. He finished his call and looked around. Kate raised her hand hesitantly. As he walked toward her, she saw Finn's eyes ran in the family. They were the same greyish blue.

"I think you might be Kate," he bent down and kissed her on the cheek. "You were checking me out when I walked in. Don't try to deny it now. Shameless," he added with a pleased grin.

"Caught me."

"I thought so. Watch yourself now. Jack," he reached out to shake the antique dealer's hand, "howiya?" He shared more than the eyes with Finn.

The two men caught up on trade gossip, while Kate poured out for Ciaran, who helped himself to a strawberry before offering one to Kate, who accepted it with a fond memory of a certain night in Queens. The apple didn't fall far from the tree here.

Jack sipped his tea and looked up to Kate, "I don't have pictures here of the underneaths. Did you look beneath the drawer or the bottom of the legs by any chance?"

"No...I don't remember doing that. What would you expect to find there?"

"You never know. But there could be a date or a name carved in. Or initials, like on the legs."

"I didn't hear about leg initials," Ciaran said between chunks of melon. "What are the letters?"

"D, O, and L," Kate replied. "At first I thought Doyle, but of course that can't be right. We didn't come along until much later. And one leg has MN on it."

Ciaran pulled his copies of the letters and the translations out of his back pocket, and took the glasses down from their perch atop his head.

"Tell me the letters again?"

"D, O, L, and MN."

"What if I said I might know what some of those letters match up with?" He paused for dramatic effect, the ham. Yup, apples and trees, apples and trees.

"Well?"

He picked up Jack's pen. "Watch me now," he leaned over the first letter and circled the name Delany.

"Holy shit," Kate said, wide eyed and impressed.

He slid the second letter on top of the first.

"And L is for Lawless," Kate said, and Ciaran circled that name.

"And O for O'More," Ciaran said, smacking his hand on top of the third letter. The sound alarmed two waiters, who quickly sauntered over.

"We're okay, gentleman, thank you," Jack said, "sorry about that. Enthusiastic antiquing. But I think something more than tea might be in order. What's your pleasure, Kate?"

"Jameson. One ice cube."

Ciaran glanced at her approvingly. "The same."

"Three," Jack said. By the time the first waiter had the table cleared, the second was there with the drinks and a plate of apple slices. It all happened in less than two minutes.

"Love the Gresham," Kate said lifting her glass. Jack and Ciaran seconded.

"So," Jack said, "we have one mystery solved. Each leg has an initial of a family friend who emigrated to Brooklyn."

"And one, O'More, who was an actual member of the family. He was my great, great grandfather."

"Finn told me it was a second marriage. Is that right?"

"Yes. He came to America with his first wife, but she died somewhere between Newfoundland and Brooklyn. I don't know the particulars."

"Well it looks like they knew each other when he was married to the other one." He looked at Kate with raised eyebrows. "You can save that for the next book, as they say. Jack, would you agree this could be campaign furniture? That it could have been taken over in pieces?"

Jack shook his head thoughtfully. "Might Delany, Lawless and O'More—and this MN, whoever that is—have each taken part of the table with them on the ship?"

"It is possible. If it's campaign furniture, which it might be judging from the photos. Then, yes, it would have come apart and been reassembled fairly easily. That's what campaign furniture was designed for: mobility. I'll know better when I actually touch the thing." All three of them looked over to St. Brigid, standing there on her cart, holding her secrets close.

"In their pockets?," Kate asked.

Jack looked at her. "What's that, Kate?"

"Delany, Lawless, and O'More all traveled in winter. What kind of coat would a working-class man wear back in the day?"

Ciaran knew. "Longish. You know, a duster. Bit of oilcloth in parts to keep out the damp. Going across like that, they'd have worn as much clothing as possible, so they could carry less. The coats were long, with deep pockets to stow things. Food, mostly, as I understand it. But sure, I think a leg of no more than three feet—that's the measure, right, Kate?" she nodded, yes—"would fit fine. Might come in handy when they got to Brooklyn too," he winked at Kate. "Mean streets of New York and all that."

"I need another drink." She spoke into her hands, which were covering her face. Jet-lag, getting slagged, and too much information all at once.

"And I need to see this table," Jack said, collecting the letters and translations and adding them to his file.

"I'll take care of the tab here, Jack. Get the Saint to Francis

Street. Kate can catch up with you there tomorrow."

He turned his attention to Kate.

"Come on, we're going down the Quays. You'll love it. But don't get any ideas. I'm married, and she fights by Ringsend rules. You wouldn't stand a chance."

CHAPTER 25

Kate woke up to a ringing house phone for the second time in as many days. It was Finn calling from London.

"My auntie says Ciaran showed you a good time last night. How's the head?"

"It's not too bad, all things considered. You happen to be phoning in my—let's see—thirteenth hour of uninterrupted sleep. That'll cure anything. And don't tell Ciaran, but I was watering down my drinks from the second round."

"Smart move. I heard about the initials too. Well done, and on the first day. You'll have all your mysteries solved in no time at all."

"I hope so. I'm going over to Francis Street as soon as I get dressed. Did you notice any markings under the drawer? Or on the bottom of the legs? You know, where they actually hit the ground?"

Finn was quiet for a moment.

"I did turn it upside down when I was cleaning it, and I cleaned the bottoms, I'm sure of that. But, no, I don't remember noticing anything. Why? What's there?"

"I don't know yet. Maybe something, maybe nothing. It's just that Jack Martin, the man from Francis Street, asked me if I had, and I hadn't. I'm sure he's looked it over by now and settled his curiosity. What are you up to?"

"Getting ready for my meeting. It's a good part, and I've wanted to work with this director forever. But the timing's shit. It would mean I'm on the road the rest of the year, except for that short break in the summer. I could do with some real down time."

"Timing is seldom good, you know that. And forever is a long time to want to work with a director. If the meeting goes well, and you like what you hear, do it."

"Listen to you, all *carpe diem*. Trying to get rid of me?"

"Not at all. I just know from Gillian how fickle your profession can be. I'd hate to see you regret a passed opportunity."

"Me too. We'll see how it goes. I need to pack soon. It's to Dublin and Nick's bachelor party right from the meeting. And then I'll meet you at the Gresham after?"

"I'll be here. And I want details from the bachelor party."

"We'll see about that." And he hung up before she could thank him for the flowers. She'd take care of that in person.

Much as Kate was dying to get to Jack's antique shop, a little detour was required. Crossing O'Connell Bridge, she took a left down the Quays and then a quick right. There in the shadow of the Tara Street DART Station, no natural light anywhere, was Alan's pub. She pushed on the door and opened it slowly. She seldom caught him by surprise and wanted to have the upper hand today. But it was late morning, so there was a chance the surprise would be on her if he wasn't in yet.

Any potential for an upper hand was obliterated while her eyes adjusted to the dark. She couldn't see him, but she heard his voice from across the room, "Darlin'! What are you doing here? I've told you, you're to let me know when you're coming. Get over here, there's a Scottish hug waiting."

And an American hug in return. Every time Kate saw Alan, she was filled with gratitude. She never would have made it through graduate school without him and worried she had never thanked him sufficiently for his friendship and support. He was the kindest man she knew.

"So what brings you over? Giving a talk? Snooping in a library somewhere?"

"Not the first and sort of the second. There's some changes, Alan. Do you have time for me to catch you up this morning? I have an appointment in the Liberties in an hour or so."

"Always time, darlin'. I'll get us some tea."

Kate showed him pictures of Molly and told him about the table and the letters. He was swiping through the pictures on her tablet, oohing and aahing, and then he stopped.

"Is your man there who I think he is?"

Kate looked over. "Yup. Your man is one Finn Murphy."

"You're not leaving this pub until you tell me everything. You'll go to the Liberties when I say you're going to the Liberties. Or when my delivery arrives. Whichever comes first."

In the end, the delivery came first. But they had a nice visit.

Kate practically skipped up the Quays. It was the Alan Effect. And she discovered that she liked talking about Finn. Gillian was the only person she ever talked with about her relationships, and they hadn't had two minutes together since the Vogelmann party. Gillian knew, of course, but still, it would have been nice to say out loud that her old friend was right: Finn was good for her, and she seemed to be good for him.

Talking with Alan gave her the chance to articulate why she liked Finn's company. She got to make a list, much to her relief. He was smart, funny, and understanding of the limitations on her time. He gave her room and appreciated that she gave him space in return. And he made Molly smile. He respected her work. He had bought a copy of her first book and emailed questions and comments about it every now and then. Kitty had a crush on him. Kevin and Sean liked him. Margot and Anya too. And he laughed easily; he was an anti-brooder, which took the edge off of her predisposition to stew.

Kate took a left at the old Smock Alley and stopped to see what was playing. They were doing a revival of *The Beggar's Opera*, in honor of the anniversary of its Dublin premiere some 250 years earlier. Beautiful old theater. The Alan Effect carried her around the corner and inside St. Patrick's Cathedral to pay a quick respect to Dean Swift. The she crossed at the light for the last stretch to Francis Street. It was lined with treasure-filled antique shops, one right after another. She took Jack's business card out of her tote to check the address. Two more down on the left. Kate peeked in the window and there he was, behind a row of black figurines, slowly circling St. Brigid, examining her carefully from every angle. She went inside.

"How's it going, Jack?"

"Oh, it's going, Kate. This is something special. See the darker wood on the top?," he traced the leaves and cross with his finger. "That's definitely bog wood…so are these figures there," he pointed to the owl, hawk, and two Celtic crosses in the front window. "I have been collecting bog pieces for years, but I have never seen anything like your St. Brigid."

"My mother said it was bog wood, but I didn't know that bog wood was particularly special."

"Oh, it is. And I have another surprise for you." He lifted the table and placed it upside down on a cloth on the floor. "These would have been hard for you to see even if you had flipped the table over and looked for them. They are worn down from the table being slid here and there. But I applied some solution to take off another layer of grime, then poured on a little water-based ink—don't worry, Ciaran will get that off for you—and look what I found." He stepped aside so Kate could get a closer look. "Start here," he touched the leg closest to her, "and go clockwise."

There, carved on the bottom of the first leg, was the letter L, the next held an O, then a V, and then an E.

"What in the world…" she turned to Jack. "Love?"

"I know. This table is a letter too, just like those you found between Eileen, James, and their father. Made of wood, the source of paper. Poetic really. Would you have any idea who the table might be, for lack of a better word, addressed to?"

"MN maybe? I don't know."

"That's as good a guess as any, Kate. There's no MN in the file, but we can't presume the correspondence you found inside the table contains the whole story here. Do you have any ancestors with those initials?"

"There's one M that I know of, Marcella Stanley. She was Sean's wife, Eileen and James's mother. I have no idea what her middle name or maiden name might have been. Maybe one of those begin with N?"

"Is there any way for you to find out?"

"Westmeath. I'm driving out Monday. Sean and Marcella are buried in a church cemetery there."

"Well I can't wait until Monday. What's the name of the church?" He sat at his desk and opened the laptop.

"St. Patrick's."

"Seriously?"

Kate nodded. He punched a number into his phone and handed it to her: "ask them."

She stared at the phone like it was a foreign object. A woman's voice said, "Hello. Hello?"

Kate put it up to her ear. "Hello. My name is Kate Doyle. I have an appointment Monday to see the Stanley parish records. But I wonder if you can tell me now, do you have a middle or maiden name for Marcella Stanley?"

"Hello, Kate. I do. I was pulling your file together today to get ready for your visit. Give me a second."

Jack was forehead-to-forehead with Kate and heard every word.

"Hello, Kate? Are you there?"

"Yes, I'm here."

"Her full name is the same on the marriage and death certificates. Nolan. Marcella Nolan Stanley. No middle name.

Can I tell you anything else?"

"No. Thank you. Thank you, I'll see you Monday."

"See you then. Safe trip." The church lady hung up. Kate handed the phone to Jack, who slipped it into the pocket of his sweater. He took her hand in his.

"Kate, this is all too lovely. I won't lie, I was going to try to talk you into selling Brigid to me. But I wouldn't dream of it now. How can I help you while you're here?"

"I don't know. I guess...can you tell me anything about the last leg...the shorter one with Marcella's initials on it? Might it be older—or maybe newer—than the others? I'm a little stuck on it not matching up."

"It's quite a good match actually. It's oak, like the rest of the table. The color is slightly lighter, but I think that speaks to wear. Maybe in this case just being cleaned more than the others. Not unheard of. People are funny with their furniture. And it's not shorter. Not really. If you look at where it meets the top, you can see the mismatch is in the fitting. I measured each leg, they are all the same length exactly. It's the same style as the others, definitely made by the same person as the other three. But I think this fitting is newer, I can send it out to be tested if you want, but I would bet that's the case. Not a lot newer, same time period. That's why it wobbles. No big mystery there."

"In that letter to her father, Eileen says," Kate picked the letter up from Jack's desk, "'the secretary is here waiting only for your leg to be set right.' She's telling him the table needs a repair, so that backs you up. But she calls it the secretary, not the table. Does the top come off as easily as the legs would have? Could the secretary, in Brooklyn, have been the actual top to the table?"

"Absolutely. This whole table, I'll say it again, is made to be taken apart and put back together. The British officers were moved around constantly. And there was no time to have the basics—a desk, a table, what have you—remade at every new post. Nor was there any guarantee that officers would be sent to a town or village where the caliber of furniture they required could be manufactured."

"There's no way that Sean Stanley was an officer. That side of my family is working-class to the core. So how would he have gotten his hands on this?"

"Maybe he didn't get his hands on it. Maybe they were the hands that made it."

"Of course," Kate nodded slowly. "And he didn't want to leave it behind when he and his children emigrated."

"It fits. I'll do some digging to see if your Sean shows up on any of the databases I have for military furniture makers. There are lists for everything in this country."

"Yes, well, I had to get my list-making gene from somewhere."

"Do you mind leaving it with me for a while longer? I'd like to finish documenting it. And Ciaran wants to give it a proper cleaning. I can leave it by his place tonight when I'm finished. I'd say he'd have it back to you Monday. Tuesday at the latest."

"Of course. Jack, I can't thank you enough."

Kate walked out into a sneaky Dublin rain. She wrapped her coat tight, popped open her umbrella and took her time walking back to the river, stopping in a few shops along the way. She peeked over the side of Butt Bridge, looking for the mullet that swam up and down the Liffey. Too dark to see much of anything in the brackish water. She went back to the south side, walking east until she got to the Ha'penny Bridge. She stretched up the steps, crossing over to Bachelor's Walk. The entire block was one enormous apartment complex. She knew the place from her school days. A classmate had lived there. The memory made her even more nostalgic. She texted two Trinity friends to see if either was free while she was in town. They had all completed their doctoral theses around the same time—Irish drama all—but Stephen and Leslie stayed on to teach in Dublin while Kate returned to the States.

The old Bachelor's Walk, like the old Gold Street near the Brooklyn Navy Yard, had been erased. Time marched on in Dublin and Brooklyn, just like it did everywhere else. And, she discovered upon seeing a Starbucks at the corner by O'Connell

Bridge, progress in both cities was measured in coffee cups. Must re-read *Prufrock*, she thought. With no Anya around to give her a hard time, she stepped in and ordered a latte. Kate took it to the counter and sat down to people watch the evening rush hour through the window. Her tote vibrated. Finn.

"Where are you? How did your meeting go?"

"I'm in a suite at the Clarence Hotel, and it went great. I'll be playing O'Neill in the fall. And I have to go back to London from here. Before I go to Canada. That puts us in different countries for most of the rest of the year, Kate."

She actually hummed out loud, more than a little intrigued the prospect of a long-distance dance with him.

And he suddenly remembered who he was talking to. "Down girl," he laughed.

"Where are you?"

"At a Starbucks watching the world go by through a plate glass window. Congratulations on the O'Neill, Finn. I'll guess it's Jamie in *Long Day's Journey*?"

"You would be guessing wrong. Although I'd love a crack at that part before I age into playing James. No, it's Mat Burke in *Anna Christie*."

"You'll kill that, Finn. Have they cast Anna yet?"

"No. But they told me their short list. I'd be honored to work with any of the women on it. And I understand they've all cleared me. So, it's just about schedules now."

She could hear a little commotion in the background. "Kate, I have to go. The life of the party just arrived."

"Ciaran?"

"Ciaran."

"Good luck with that. And tell him I said hi. Oh, and thanks for the lavender, Finn. It's beautiful."

"You're welcome. See you tonight."

A reply from Leslie saying she was free tomorrow was quickly followed by Stephen saying the same. She texted them back that Sunday was perfect. She would meet them at Front Arch at noon. She finished her coffee, while she walked across

O'Connell Bridge, down Westmoreland, past Trinity, and around the Provost's House. She was on the way to her decaffeinated habit of choice: Hodges Figgis, a bookstore whose more traditional signage would surely be forgiven by the proprietors of *The Page Turner*. In some respects, the two bookstores could be cousins. She received a warm "hello" upon entering, and was then left marvelously alone to wander. The hard sell under a guise of helpfulness was as unheard of here as it was back on Montague Street. Kate detested being followed. This shop, like *The Page Turner*, respected browsing. The result, at least for a bookworm like Kate, was to facilitate free-range intellectual curiosity leading to titles she never knew she wanted to begin with.

Starting downstairs in the children's section, she picked up a few picture books by Irish authors that she thought would round out Molly's growing library. Her method of selection was simple: she only chose books with dogs on the covers. It was as good a system as any. The clearance racks kept her downstairs long enough to find a few classic plays she thought it smart to read again before getting too far into her new book project. Did she officially have a new book project? In all the excitement preparing for Dublin, she had lost track of that. And she hadn't checked her email since leaving New York. But it dawned on her that the deadline she and Jennifer agreed upon was yesterday. She saw a sign that the shop had wifi, so she took out her tablet to check. True to her word, Jennifer had replied by 5pm New York time the day before:

> May 12 4:45 PM (1 day ago)
> Dear Kate, The press is pleased to offer you a contract (attached) based on the strength of the outline and two chapters you submitted. Please review the contract and contact me with any questions. I do believe the revolution is underway #FarewellAcademicTango, Jennifer.

Kate replied that she would have the contract back to her

by the end of the month. All she had to do was recalibrate things so that she treated it like the "real job" it was. Whoever coined that contemptuous term had never sat down to write a book. She braced herself for a 'whoosh' of panic in her stomach that never materialized. At some point in the recent weeks, the 'whoosh' of worrying that she would soon stop receiving a monthly paycheck had been replaced by a happiness at being untethered from committees, meetings, and department politics. And grading. She definitely did not miss grading.

Once upstairs, she selected some new titles on modern Irish history, including two on emigration to America. Much of the Stanley experience was uniquely its own. But a great deal was shared by families all over the world who left a much loved home because it was disintegrating in the violence of war, occupation, segregation, or institutionalized hunger.

The residents of Pineapple Street were not forgotten. All loved mysteries and had been asking Kate if she knew anything about the Irish detective series that were becoming staples on Best Seller lists. She looked through the Crime Fiction offerings and picked Stuart Neville for Sean and Margot, Declan Hughes for Kevin, and John Connolly for Kitty. She grabbed two books by each, and tossed in the latest Tana French for Anya. It took two bags to contain her loot.

One quick stop for a pint with Alan later, she was back in front of the Gresham. To her surprise, so was Finn. Earlier than expected. He had a black watchman's cap pulled low on his forehead, and he was looking down, reading a magazine. Or at least pretending to read it. Too many years of teaching: she could spot a fake scan from fifty paces.

"Hey there," she called out.

He looked up, smiled, removed his cap, and tossed the magazine into a garbage bin on the sidewalk. "They wouldn't let me upstairs without your okay." This seemed to amuse him. Or he was just a little bit drunk. Maybe both. He gave her a quick peck on the lips and reached for her bags.

"I'll take those for you."

"Cheers." She steered him to the door by his elbow. There was more than one double take as they crossed the lobby. "You're a head-turner here, I see."

"Hometown boy made good. Dublin's like New York, though, when it comes to celebrity. The natives will put you in your place at just the hint of a superior attitude. You haven't been cut down to size until a Dub thinks you're trying to fight above your weight class. Trust me."

"You're taking the elevator?"

"Not likely. Just keeping you company. Third floor, right?"

"That's right. Meet me up there?"

Her O'Vogelmanns appeared from the lobby, gently bickering about the play they had just seen at the Gate. He thought it excellent, she thought it didn't quite reach its potential.

"Like my neckwear?"

"Oh, stop that," she gave him a little swat on the shoulder. Then proceeded to remove some lint and *tsk-tsk* about a loose thread on the seam of his coat sleeve.

"Hello again," Kate said.

"Hello again to you. I see you've exchanged your bubblewrap for a shopping bag…"

"…and a handsome young man," interrupted Mrs. O'V, with approval.

Finn said hello, kissed Kate on the cheek, and whispered something to Mr. O'V that resulted in a nod of approval in Kate's direction. Then he disappeared through the stairwell door.

"Dare I ask what he said to you?," Kate asked as the elevator doors closed.

"He said he was a lucky man. That you were way out of his league in looks and brains."

"And you make sure he never forgets that, love," Mrs. O'Vogelmann winked at Kate conspiratorially.

"I'll do my best," Kate promised. She was laughing as the doors opened on the third floor.

The white-haired gentleman took his wife's arm, and

nodded to Finn, who was flushed from the run upstairs. The two couples went their separate ways, each taking their time on the walk to their respective rooms. The older couple because they had been treading a similar path for decades, Finn and Kate because they wanted to set the pace for a night spent pretending they had all the time in the world.

CHAPTER 26

Kate stretched from nose to toes, belly to back against Finn. She arched her foot and slid it against his calf, liking the muscle there. Her mouth fit perfectly in the dip between his shoulder blades. There was some light through the curtains and more when a little gust blew them in. The breeze carried some street noise too. She enjoyed hearing footsteps and the muffled voices of folks out and about in the magic time before dawn.

"Why is it so few hotel windows open? Can't all be the fear of someone jumping. Any of them can be fixed to stop short, like this one." It only opened about four inches.

"You're awake." She kissed the back of his neck.

"I am." He reached back and stroked her hair.

"Still planning to cut it?"

"Still thinking about it anyway. I like starting it over every few years. And it makes mornings less complicated. What about you? Do you want to clean things up a little before today's big event?"

"I suppose I should. Look smart for the family photos. I'll stop at the barber on my way out to Howth. Sure you don't want to come to the wedding? It's no bother. Nick's all for it. He wants to meet you."

"Thank him for me. But I'll meet him another time. On a

day with just a tad less pressure on him and Emily…and on single folks like me." She smiled. "Weddings make everybody think of marriage."

He kissed her hand and drifted off back to sleep.

She listened to him breathe for a while. Once she was certain he was out for the count, she got up and headed to the bathroom, leaving two fluffy pillows in her place. She was wide awake—her body clock still thrown off by the time difference—and had not enjoyed a quiet bath since leaving Miami. Delicious as the pleasure of Finn's company would be in a luxurious bathtub, Kate wanted some Kate time. With bubbles.

In true Gresham fashion, the shelves were stocked with all the goodies for a deep soak. She mixed the cold and hot to her pleasure and surveyed her options, removing the caps to check out each one before settling on Lavender & Lime. She poured it into the flowing water and watched the bubbles form, shut the door, and climbed in.

She was in free fall, slowly drifting from Molly to Finn, then to St. Brigid and the letters and back to Molly again. She floated blissfully like this until her fingers were raisins and the water was beginning to cool off. She picked her phone up off the towel she left folded on the floor. It was getting late in Brooklyn, but they were night owls there. She dialed Pineapple Street.

"I was just thinking about you, Kate. How's the trip going?"

"Great, Mom. I'm calling from a decadent bath at the Gresham Hotel. How are things there?"

"Quiet. Margot's working late, Glen took Molly for a sleepover with Sarah and Alice, and your brothers are at a Knicks game. I have the run of the place."

"Good for you. I'm having lunch with some old friends today. Then it's off to Westmeath tomorrow. To the church where Sean and Marcella are buried. I can't believe I've been here less than two days. It's been something else. How's Molly?"

"She's fine. She misses you. But," she quickly added, "she knows you're coming back. You can stop worrying about that."

"Alright. Well give her a kiss for me, and tell everybody I say hi."

"Will do. Enjoy the soak."

She pulled the plug from the drain with her big toe and stood up to take a shower. It was an ungodly hour, but she was looking forward to starting her day of leisure. Plus there was the haircut and wedding to get Finn out the door for, and the city to get reacquainted with. But, both could wait until she was done watching him sleep.

She got dressed and watched Finn wake up with the most minor of grumbling.

"Where do you think you're going?"

"To wander aimlessly, have lunch with some old friends, and then wander aimlessly some more."

"No Westmeath today?"

"No, sir. That's tomorrow." She sat on the edge of the bed.

"What do you expect to find there?"

"The gravestones, of course. I want to take a picture of them. And the parish records, so I can maybe fill in some more gaps and learn a little about the life the Stanleys lived here in Ireland. And I know it's a long shot, but I'd love to meet somebody whose own ancestors maybe knew mine. I guess it's my turn to be a cliché."

The Quiet Man redux?"

"Something like that. I don't expect a thatched cottage, but it would be nice to be able to point to a piece of earth and imagine Sean, Marcella, James, and Eileen being there and being happy together."

"Sentimental suits you, Kate."

They shared the morning quiet until Finn's phone rang. Best man duties called.

✦ ✦ ✦

O'Connell Street was still relatively quiet when Kate

stepped outside. She had two hours to kill before meeting Stephen and Les, and she opted for a walk up the Quays. She started at O'Connell Bridge and walked west up the north side of the Liffey, past the Four Courts and right through Smithfield, until her watch read eleven o'clock, at which point she was on the edge of Glasnevin Cemetery, and dangerously close to The Gravediggers, also known as Kavanagh's Pub. She walked up to the window and peeked inside. Not open yet. But the barman setting up noticed her and waved her toward the door, which was unlocked.

"Mind if I just look around? I'm taking a little walk down memory lane."

"You're more than welcome. American?"

"Guilty as charged. But I lived here in Dublin for a while, and I used to love this place. All the old pubs with snugs to be honest." The snug: a table and chairs partitioned off by old wood and stained glass. Space apart from the crowd to flirt, argue, make-up, hide, or conspire. Hands down, one of Ireland's great traditions.

He nodded his head. "I love the old ones too. Can I get you a glass of water? That's the best I can do until we open."

"No. I'm fine." She looked around at the worn wooden tables and chairs. Even the frames to the snugs were scratched up, from bad times as well as good, no doubt. She flashed back to the hours she spent in Gravediggers and other Dublin pubs just like it, from Kehoe's and The Brazen Head to the Long Hall and the Stag's Head. There had been plenty of pints, but mostly she would go early in a day. She loved to sit and read, sipping a coffee and, depending on the pub, eating a truly horrendous sandwich or a solid fish and chips. Sometimes Stephen joined her, and they played chess on his homemade set. Good memories. She thanked the barman and headed back out into the Sunday. If she walked a New York pace, she would make it to Front Arch in time to meet her friends.

And she did.

Front Arch has been a meeting point for the centuries of Trinity's existence. If the weather is nice, you meet by the wrought iron fence that lines the walkway to the front door. If the weather is soft, then the massive oak door serves as entry way to a musty oval space that contains boards for the student societies to post events, and portals to the security office, a mailroom, and a lecture hall hidden in the front wall to the college. Kate had been around her fair number of American universities and nothing held a candle. She got the same thrill today that she did the first time she wandered into Front Arch that summer with Gillian. A sense of tradition and an overwhelming desire to open a book emanated from the place.

A tap on the shoulder interrupted her reading the schedule for the term's final Hist and Phil Society debates. It would be finals week here soon enough. She turned around to find Leslie and Stephen, arms outstretched, big smiles on their faces.

They all talked on top of each other until settling on the Buttery for brunch. It usually wasn't open on a Sunday, but there were events going on, so in they went for a full Irish: eggs, mushrooms, tomato, sausage, bacon, toast, and coffee. Stephen went so far as to include a black pudding, but Leslie and Kate forgave him that nasty business.

After eating, Stephen and Leslie took turns showing off their cluttered offices before taking Kate on a tour of the campus. She had been back over the years for conferences and to use the library, but she had not taken the time to look around closely. She had not slowed down any more on her visits to Dublin than she had on visits home to Brooklyn, and now here, as there, she was seeing the folly of being in constant motion.

New buildings, and updates to some of the truly ancient ones; beloved trees felled, and ambitious saplings in their places. They sat on a bench in the rose corner and gossiped about the teachers they once had, some of whom were now colleagues of Stephen and Leslie. They enjoyed each other's company until dusk told them it was time to go. Home to his wife and daughter for Stephen, home to her partner for Leslie, and back to the Gresham for Kate.

✦ ✦ ✦

She had left a room key for Finn, and he let himself in well past midnight. Kate woke up at the sound of the door opening.

"Good wedding? You look happy."

"Great wedding," he sat on the edge of the bed, "and you look rested."

"I am. It was a lazy afternoon."

"I have a surprise. My sister says the deed to the Greystones house will be ready tomorrow."

"That's great news. But does this mean you're giving up your place on Water Street?"

"Not at all. I love that apartment. I'll rent it until Anya gets around to turning the building into a co-op. Then I'll buy it. Have both places…New York is as much home to me as Ireland. Might you ever consider both places home?"

"I can see that happening, yes." And she drifted off to sleep with Finn beside her.

CHAPTER 27

By the time her alarm rang on Monday morning, Kate's body clock was on Dublin time, and she was in full research mode: loading her tote with her file, a notebook, and tablet. She and Finn shared coffee and an egg at the hotel before heading their separate ways. Finn was about to sign papers on his new house, and Kate was off to Mullingar in County Westmeath. When she went outside to meet her car, she recognized the same driver that had picked her up from the airport.

"You got stuck with me again?"

"I'm stuck to you for your entire trip, Kate. Somebody named Margot Smith put the fear of God into our office manager when she booked things. Said you were to have the same driver, not be kept waiting, and generally given *carte blanche* if you changed any scheduled routes. We expected some difficult celebrity under a false name to tell you the truth. When I told the office you were a nice woman who was no bother, they were relieved...and maybe a little disappointed that I didn't have a wild story to tell them after I dropped you at the Gresham."

Kate was amused—wait until they get a load of Finn—and a little horrified.

"Well, if you're stuck with me, I should know your name."

"Donal. Good to see you again."

"Good to see you again too. Margot is my brother's partner. She wanted to make sure my trip went smoothly. The last few months have been rocky for our family, I hope you won't hold it against her."

"Not at all. That's good you have people looking out for you. Can I ask what your plans are out there at St. Patrick's?"

She told him about the table and the letters, and then about Eileen. He handed some tissues to her from the front seat.

"Thanks. I'm sorry. It's getting better, but my face still leaks when I say her name."

"Of course it does. No need to apologize."

They drove along in silence for a good half hour, when he exited off the M4 in Mullingar.

"The church is only about ten minutes down the road, but I thought you might want to stop for a minute or two. Maybe have a tea, stretch your legs?"

"You're a mind-reader, Donal. It'll be good to work off some of my nerves. Collect me back here in twenty minutes?"

"Consider it done."

Kate stuck a ten euro note and her phone in the pocket of her jeans, left her tote in the backseat, and walked down the street. A morning here was not much different from a morning in Brooklyn, or Miami for that matter. Parents were herding their kids to school, couples were sharing quick coffees, and uniformed high school girls were busy trying to look sophisticated—free from the constraints of parents and teachers—as they made their way to school.

They reminded her of Gillian, and she reached for her phone. Straight to voicemail. She left a "thinking of you," and stopped in the Spar for a buttered roll and tea. She took it outside to a sidewalk bench for a few minutes of people watching. And to try and organize her thoughts.

What did she know so far about the Stanley family? That Sean and Marcella's was a big love that ended too soon. Marcella died at the age of thirty, leaving Sean, a widower with two young children, seven-year-old James, and five-year-old

Eileen. Marcella died in 1865. This was past the peak famine years and in a place not commonly associated with that devastation and the illnesses that followed, at least not mentioned as frequently as the counties further south and west. She knew Sean and Marcella were married and laid to rest at St. Patrick's, and that Sean might have been a furniture maker. And she thought Marcella could have been an Irish speaker, which suggested she might have been from the west of Ireland. She finished her roll and tea, tossed the wrappings in the trash, and headed back to the car.

Donal was leaning against the front door, enjoying the beautiful weather.

"I saw you go into the Spar, did you get a snack?"

"Yes, and a cup of tea. All I had at the hotel was a coffee and a poached egg. I'm used to more fuel than that in the morning."

"I grabbed two sandwiches, do you want one?"

"No, thanks. I'm good."

"Then let's go," he said, opening the back door to let her in.

They rode in silence for the short drive to the church. It was a more expansive property than she expected. On the far side of the cemetery was a school, a sports field, and, judging from the well-dressed people making their way up the short steps to the front door of the church, a wedding was about to take place. Must be the season for it, Kate thought. The parking lot was entirely full, so Donal dropped Kate at the door to the parish office and went to create a parking space of his own.

"I'll be right over there," he pointed to a picnic table in the shade of an old oak tree, "when you're done. Take your time."

Kate had not walked into a parish office in years, not since graduating high school. Now, here she was paying a call to the second one in as many weeks. She noticed the gold stenciled lettering across the door and wondered if there was some sort of manual about what such front doors should look like.

But unlike St. Charles in Brooklyn, this door had a huge

brass door knob right in the center—on the panel below the glass—and a mail slot beside it. Nobody answered when she knocked, so she gave the knob a little turn. The door opened part way, stopping on a small pile of envelopes. As Kate bent down to collect them, a woman not much older than herself came down the hallway. Even if other people were around, she would have been hard to miss. She had bright pink hair and a face covered in white foundation, bright red lipstick, and one big black arched eyebrow. Kate stopped in her tracks.

"You must be Kate. I know, I know, I'm a sight. You caught me halfway through my transformation…I'll take that from you. I never heard the postman." She took the stack of letters from Kate's outstretched hand. "I'm Celia. Welcome to St. Patrick's."

Kate shook the woman's hand, not sure what to say.

"Come with me. My office is just down the hall. This," she waved a hand in front of herself, "is not my usual work make-up. It's my son's fourth and the clown I booked with the bouncy castle called me sick as a dog. I found the wig at the euro store. Now I'm just doing my best with the face. What do you think?"

Kate assured Celia it was all working.

"But what are you going to wear?"

"My sister-in-law's at the house figuring that out for me. I'm hoping the wedding clears before I leave. Can you imagine?"

The two women laughed together at the prospect of Celia inadvertently photobombing the wedding party, while Celia guided Kate over to a chair by her desk.

"Here's your file. There's not a lot, but I'll take you through it. And you can have this, I kept the originals."

Celia was taking Kate through a wedding certificate, James and Eileen's baptismal records, and the cemetery records, when Kate's eyes fell on a small table in the corner. She couldn't help but stare. Celia turned to see what caught Kate's attention.

"You're ahead of me now. This form," she picked a paper

from near the bottom of the stack, "shows that your Sean Stanley worked at the local woodworks. He was a detail man apparently. He would have been responsible for carving and sanding. But he was something of a frustrated artist I think. The woodworks made furniture for the area garrisons, all pretty straightforward as I understand it. Nothing fancy. But he earned a reputation for intricate carvings that he did on his own time. He made extra money on the side, selling designs to local parishes, including this one. And including that table over there."

Kate was astonished. She got up and walked over to the corner. Standing in front of her was a nearly exact replica of her St. Brigid. The legs looked the same, there was a secretary and a drawer, each with *claddagh*-embraced pulls.

"Do you mind if I move these papers?"

"Not at all. Let me help you."

Kate was disappointed to find the top was not a match. It had the leaf clusters, but no St. Brigid's cross. The cross carried a more traditionally looking religious design.

"What's this?"

"That's a *cross pattée*, it's one of many that can be seen in conjunction with St. Patrick. If you're here when the wedding lets out, you're welcome to visit the church. You'll see quite a few in there, including near the front doors. The list I found of your ancestor's work—I put a copy in your folder—shows he carved quite a few of them as well as other designs and tables. I think the most beautiful work of his though is over by the holy water fonts. He inlaid the designs with bog wood."

"Would that have been common, do you know? I mean using the bog wood?"

"I'm no expert, but I think it was unusual for the area. Apart from a table over at the Dempsey place, I've never seen work like his anywhere else in town. And I've lived here my whole life. Call on Daniel Dempsey. He runs a B&B during trout season. His table is not unlike this one. But it has a St. Brigid's cross on the top. I always remember that because we used to make them in primary school on the feast day."

Kate spun around so fast that she tripped over her own feet. She steadied herself, averting a fall.

"Are you okay?"

"Yup, I'm good. I just didn't eat enough this morning, and it's been a lot of travel."

"I understand. Let me get you a glass of water. I'll be right back."

Kate sat back by Celia's desk and caught her breath. She was flipping through the file when the door opened.

"Hello! I'm looking for Celia."

It was a tall man, easily 250 pounds, and he was in full clown attire, right down to the biggest, floppiest pair of shoes Kate had ever seen. Celia walked in right behind him.

"John! You're up and about!"

"Must have been a touch of food poisoning. I was fine an hour after I called you. Your sister-in-law said you were putting on the gear, so I thought I'd catch you here and we could go to your house together."

Celia gave Kate the water.

"How are you feeling?"

"I'm fine really. Go ahead to your son's party. I want to see the cemetery and then, if the wedding is out, I'll look at the church. Can you give me directions to the Dempsey B&B?"

She wrote them down on a slip of paper and saw Kate to the door. Kate waved to Donal, who was seated on a bench, eating his sandwich.

"Are you ready to head back to Dublin?"

"Almost. I'll be back in a few minutes."

She walked the footpath. It was laid with pieces of slate, surrounded by grey pebbles, and framed by a pair of statuesque oaks. The path opened up into a small thicket that included two palm trees. She checked the chart in the file Celia had given her, and found her way to Markers 17a and 17b. She stood still, honoring the moment before casting her eyes directly at the headstones.

The less ornate of the two read:

Sean James Stanley
Mullingar 1825-Brooklyn 1883
Loving husband of Marcella
Devoted father to James and Eileen

She kissed her fingertips and tapped the stone. "Hello there. I'm your great, great, great, granddaughter. I have your table. I have St. Brigid."

She took pictures from all sides. Then she took out some paper and traced the inscription as best she could. She turned to the second stone, and tears fell:

Marcella Nolan Stanley
Inis Mor 1835-Mullingar 1865
Loving wife of Sean
Devoted mother to Seamus and Eibhlín
ag brionglóideach i nGaeilge

She kissed her fingertips once more, and touched the stone. "You weren't forgotten, Marcella. It just took us all a while to find you."

She photographed and traced this stone too. And she looked around at the landscape, imagining the couple here in this place, attending mass, getting married, and baptizing their children.

Just as she realized it was beginning to rain, Donal walked up beside her, holding an umbrella over her head.

"These are your ancestor's ancestors? Nice names, Sean and Marcella. I have a Marcella in my family too."

"You do? I thought it was unusual for an Irish name."

"Not overly common, but, no, not unusual. Do you want me to take a picture of you here?"

"I'd like that."

He took a few with his phone and promised to email them off when they were in better reception.

"Do you want to see the inside of the church? I hear it's nice, and the wedding is over. People are still leaving, taking pictures on the steps, but it's thinning out."

"I'd like that. I love the outfits women wear to weddings over here."

"There's some nice ones," he said leading her toward the path. "But they've nothing on the two clowns I saw drive off while you were at the cemetery."

CHAPTER 28

The oldest part of the church, including the woodwork Celia said was done by Sean Stanley, dated back to the 1820s. That section had been built when it was still tantamount to treason to be a practicing Catholic. It was built there by the community because it was surrounded by trees and off the well-traveled route from Mullingar. It offered the least chance of detection. As the years moved along and penal laws relaxed, the church grew. The carvings on the wall over the holy water fonts were simple crosses inlaid with bog wood. The fonts themselves were of oak, but the centuries of use had polished them down to a patina as dark as the crosses above them. Kate agreed with Celia: they were magnificent.

When Kate told Donal she wanted to stop at the Dempsey B&B, his eyes lit up. "By the trout stream?"

"You know it?"

"It's legendary. I'm an angler from way back. You?"

"I'm an angler from way back too. If I look you up the next time I'm in Ireland, will you point me to some good places?"

"You don't want me for that. My brother runs an excursion firm for people who like the outdoors. And he guides in trout and salmon seasons. I'll put you in touch with him. There's none better."

"I'll hold you to it. How far is the Dempsey place from here?"

He looked at the directions Celia had written down and punched a few things into his GPS.

"Twenty minutes tops."

"Let's go."

✦ ✦ ✦

They pulled into the graveled driveway that circled the front of the B&B as two boys were running out of the house. They neither shut the front door nor broke stride. Just ran past the car shouting, "somebody'll be right out" as they headed toward the road.

"Sorry about that. Not much of a welcome," said a man left standing in the doorway in their wake.

"Boy energy," Kate said by way of a hello. She was out of the car before Donal had actually brought it to a complete stop.

"You've got that right. I'm Daniel, can I help you?"

"I think you can. I'm Kate Doyle. My ancestor was Sean Stanley, and I think you had an ancestor who was a priest whose life crossed with his."

"Well, well. My grandfather wondered why none of yours had ever showed up. He thought ill of you for your absence." He saw that Kate wasn't sure if he was kidding or not, "come in, come in, I'm putting you on."

Donal rolled down his window. "Mind if I take a walk around the lake while you two visit?"

"Not at all. Enjoy yourself."

Daniel got Kate settled in the front room, and went to get some coffee. He returned with two steaming mugs, and took a seat across from her near the window.

"You're right that our ancestors—how did you put it?— crossed lives. But it was more than that. They were good friends. It's my great, great, great, great uncle Michael I'm talking about. And Sean Stanley is as many greats your grandfather, is that right?"

"One less actually."

"One less then. They grew up next door to each other. Both planned to join the seminary, but your Sean took a job at the woodworks to help his family out. He intended to catch up with Mick later, but then he fell head over heels in love on a trip to Galway to deliver some furniture. She was all of fifteen, sixteen maybe, and basically told him to get lost. But he was older and sure she was the one."

"Marcella."

"That's right, Marcella."

"He made a fool of himself for years. Volunteered for each and every Galway delivery, went back there every chance he could. Wrote the priesthood off altogether. Finally, when she turned eighteen, he actually proposed. She wouldn't have him. Hoped to become a teacher before she settled down, and she had no interest in moving up here to Westmeath. She was from the Islands and liked being near the sea."

"How do you know all of this?"

"It's been passed down." He wore a conspiratorial grin. "I come from a long line of collectors: collectors of gossip, of stories, you name it. And every generation writes a family history, and they're all here. My grandfather organized things that had been passed along over the years, then my father added to it and updated things. He took to the research with a lot of energy after he retired. He scanned everything and plans to submit it to the National Library's Ancestor Database. Loves the genealogy in his retirement."

"He should meet my mother...tell me more."

"Well at some point or another she realized she loved him back. But he couldn't leave here. He had steady work, and that was not easy to find. She thought that if she delayed awhile then maybe he would eventually look for something in Galway and agree to move there. Sean wrote Mick that she said yes. What she actually said was that she'd marry him when they could have a place with their own St. Brigid by the door. She meant a house, of course, knowing full well he wouldn't have that kind of money anytime soon."

"He lived with his parents?"

"Yes, not far from here. There's nothing left of it though. The Stanley family moved along. There were none left here by the time your Sean passed. Marcella lived with a sister and the sister's family in Galway after her own parents passed away."

"He had a brother, didn't he?"

"He did. But they had a falling out. The brother went to Belfast. I expect you'll find him in the parish records here at least through his early adulthood. His story—whatever it might be—doesn't appear in my family's archives. Just Sean and his Marcella. No, for him you'd have to track things up in Belfast. Have you been to our county's St. Patrick's? It's just over in Mullingar."

"I have. I just haven't had time to read through the file yet. I'll check it when I get back to Dublin. Go on."

"Well, she was ready to agree to a date, but he didn't know that. And she didn't know that he had spent about a year getting the upper hand on her. Mick wrote his parents about these two tables Sean was working on every night and day off he had. A matched set with a St. Brigid's cross on the top. He said Sean planned to bring them to her and say he held up his end of the bargain. It was sort of a game, but with a lot on the line. She could have gotten angry. But she didn't mind this trick of his. She was biting at the quick to marry him too at this point. Mick wrote that Marcella admired Sean's ingenuity and loved him all the more for it."

"And how did you wind up with this table? I have the other one in Brooklyn. It led me to you."

"You have it? How 'bout that? Well, this one never left Ireland. After Marcella died, Sean had a rough time. He got sick and couldn't work as much. Some sort of eye infection that made the intricacy of carving—that was his bread and butter—close to impossible. He started selling off what he had; it dragged on for years. When he asked Mick's parents if they would buy this table, they said they would borrow it, and gave him the money to send his son to America and to get him and his daughter to Dublin. She found some work there to tide them over until they got to the States themselves."

"Jesus."

"I know. It's a heartbreaker. Mick was assigned to a parish in Brooklyn and looked after James. Helped get him a job. Then arranged for Eileen to have a place to live when she got there. It's an old story: Irish priest looking after his countrymen and countrywomen who come over." He sipped his coffee.

"Dreaming in Irish comes up in the letters that I found in my table. And I saw it on Marcella's gravestone too. Do you know anything about that?"

"It was what Marcella said to the children when she put them to bed at night. She grew up in an Irish-speaking family, but they had to learn English too once they moved to the mainland. There were Irish speakers in Galway too of course, but her father and the family wanted to get ahead, and that meant English. As Marcella got older, she tried holding onto the language, but, as you can imagine, it does fade with time. The saying became a sort of touchstone for her. A way of keeping the memory of her family alive and encouraging the new generation to keep the ones who came before in their memory. Sean kept it up when Marcella was gone."

Kate looked out the window.

"It seems to me that you're reconnecting with a past yourself. Your Marcella must be smiling down on this. Things have come full circle."

Kate looked at Daniel, and put down her coffee. "I need a hug."

Daniel helped her to her feet. "It's been a long road for you, has it?"

"It has been at that." She eased herself out of his embrace and thanked him. "Everything *has* come full circle. I have one last question. Do you know how my table made its way to Brooklyn?"

"It was the Stanleys way of keeping the home they all shared with Marcella, however briefly, with them. He trusted people he knew to send pieces with them when they sailed to

New York. And he brought the last piece over himself."

"The top?"

"Exactly. St. Brigid's cross: the saint Marcella insisted be with them when they began their lives together. Will you send me some pictures of it?"

"Of course I will. And I'll send pictures of the family too."

"That would be nice. Do you want to take this table with you? It's rightly yours, you know. Or I can have it sent, if you like."

"No. Keep it here. It's just as rightly yours. Your many-greats Uncle Michael took my many-greats Grandfather Sean home. That's a big gift. I would like to take some pictures though. Do you mind?"

"Not at all." The boys, Daniel's sons it turned out, came running back in just as Kate was getting her camera ready.

"Would you two mind helping us out here?"

They harnessed their boy energy and took pictures of Kate and their father in front of the table. Then Kate took pictures of them with their dad. They all said their goodbyes with a promise to stay in touch. It was a promise Kate intended to keep, and it was clear Daniel did too.

Kate fell into a restless sleep on the ride back to Dublin, pictures of Eileen behind her eyes. She arrived at the Gresham tired, a little sad, and a lot hungry. And aching to see the Doyles. She connected to the lobby wifi, and saw there were plenty of seats on the next day's flight to JFK. She'd take care of that later. She emailed Kitty all the pictures from her day, before finding a table in the restaurant, which was already filling up with the dinner crowd.

Dinner done, she asked the waiter to send up a bottle of wine. It was at the door to her room, with two glasses, before she was. Wine, a soak, and no answer when she Skyped Pineapple Street. So she videoed herself telling the highlights of the day and promising the full story when she returned. She would be flying back tomorrow afternoon. Not quite a week's stay, but long enough to get all the answers she needed to move past the family mystery.

Finn let himself in just as Kate was sending her video. They sat up all night, looking at the pictures while Kate told him the story of Marcella and Sean, and the table and the Dempsey family.

"You realize, Kate, that you've done what Marcella wanted most. You've found a way to reconnect with the past. And you can share it with Molly, so she holds on to it herself. You've brought everything full circle."

She smiled. "Daniel said the same thing."

CHAPTER 29

Kate woke with Finn asleep beside her, and the curtains dancing their little dance. She got up and closed the window, it was a chilly breeze egging her on to jump into a day she would prefer to approach slowly. She brushed her teeth, threw some warm water on her face, and climbed back beneath the covers. She lay down on her side, propped up on an elbow and watched Finn sleep, listened to him breathe. She undid the few connected buttons and watched his chest rise and fall.

"Admiring the view?"

"Yes, very much. Good morning." She kissed his belly button.

"You can do better than that."

She helped him out of the rest of his clothes. And she did better than that for the better part of an hour before he helped her out of hers and showed her a few tricks of his own. They shared a soak and a shower, got dressed and went downstairs to face the public part of the day, which included a late breakfast with Ciaran.

Finn turned heads as they walked through the lobby. When a couple stopped to ask for a selfie, Kate went ahead to Ciaran, who was already seated at a table in the corner.

Ciaran stood to greet Kate. "He's good about that sort of

thing, don't you think?"

"Yes, he is. Do you remember the time when he wasn't so good about it?"

"It's no secret that he was the ass of asses for a time. Running around with a fast crowd there in California; drinking too much and carrying on. He was young, and it all went to his head. We figured he would settle into it all eventually, but the bad years were truly awful. His sisters dote on him, they'd forgive him anything. But his father—that's my brother—and sure his mother too, well they wouldn't have it. They finally told him to stay away until he grew up. It took a while, but he did. He's back in their good graces now. Has been for some time. He's happy. Happier even for the past month or so. That's due to you and that niece of yours, I think."

"He makes me happy too. Your brother and your sister-in-law…were they at the wedding?"

"No. Broke their hearts to miss it. Nick is like a second son to them. Nick and Finn grew up together, but he probably told you that. No, they're in Australia visiting my niece and her kids…she's got three. Can't disrupt grandparent travel you know."

"No, I don't suppose you can. Is that the sister who did the translations?"

"It is. She's the older one, he has two. She moved over there right after university…Trinity, like yourself. She and her husband have been there more than ten years. Plan to move back before their kids start school. This summer, if her husband can get a transfer. He works for one of those pharmaceutical firms that are all over Ireland. So how did Westmeath go?"

She was filling him in on what she learned at the church, the cemetery, and the B&B, when Finn finally peeled himself away from the lobby.

"What'd I miss?"

"I was just telling her what a nightmare you've been to your poor family since Day 1. She'll fill you in. I left Brigid in the office behind the front desk. Let me go get her. I have everything I need to wrap her up for the trip home, but I wanted you to see her first. She's shining, she is."

"Speaking of flights home…we need to book our travel."

"Already taken care of. I asked the concierge to get us on flights out of Dublin as close together as possible…and as late as possible. I was hoping to show you the house before we go to the airport. Interested?"

"Very much."

He squeezed her hand. "Good. We'll have less than an hour, but I want to walk in for the first time knowing it's mine. And I want you there with me when I do."

"You're such a romantic. I like that you wear it on your sleeve."

"You're a romantic too, Kate. And I like that you do everything possible to cover it up." He kissed her.

"None of that now. This is a family restaurant."

It was Ciaran. And Brigid. And she positively glowed. Kate stood up and circled her, astonished at the brilliance of the bog wood in particular. It shone as brightly as the pieces in the Martin Antique Shop and the fonts at the church in Westmeath. It looked like rare ebony.

"Have you shown it to Jack?"

"Of course. He came over this morning, and took a video. And pictures of course. It's really something, Kate. Do you want to take any pictures before I wrap her up?"

"Just one."

"Give me your camera, I'll do it."

"No, Ciaran. You're going to be in it. I want the three of us with her."

They enlisted the help of a waiter, who took a dozen pictures before Ciaran approved of how he looked. Then the three of them took a few group selfies until Ciaran instructed Kate and Finn to get upstairs and pack.

"I'll have her wrapped up for you in an hour. Will that give you enough time to pack?"

They assured him it would and excused themselves to head upstairs. It was perfect timing really, Kate and Finn agreed on their way to the stairs. Because the only packing they had left to do required depositing toiletry bags into their suitcases. They raced up the stairwell and down the hallway to say goodbye to their Gresham hideaway, agreeing—as they gave their night in Queens a run for its money—that they would find a way to get back here again as often as possible, house in Greystones or no house in Greystones. And that they would always stay in this very room.

When they returned downstairs two hours later, Ciaran was nowhere to be found. But Brigid was waiting with the front desk staff, all bundled up.

"Mr. Murphy asked me to give you a message," the clerk blushed. She leaned over the counter, while the porter took Brigid and their suitcases out to the car. Kate and Finn leaned over to meet her halfway. "He said you two were shameless."

Kate and Finn laughed their way to the car. Finn gave Donal the address in Greystones, and settled in with Kate. Donal looked at them in his rearview mirror and realized privacy might be in order. He raised the divider and left them to themselves.

"Collect yourself, Kate. We're almost there. Jesus, your hair's a mess."

"I had a busy morning mess or I had a semi-quickie in the backseat of a car mess?"

"The latter. It's always the latter with you."

He managed to get his shirt tucked halfway in when they pulled into the driveway of his new house. "And I'm beginning to think it always will be." He shook his head. "Come on." He opened the door without waiting for Donal, took Kate's hand, and helped her out of the car.

They stood in front for a few minutes, giving it a good look. It was impressive, but not ornate: a family home rather than a party palace. The three-story limestone Georgian possessed large, welcoming windows, and the previous owner clearly appreciated gardening. There were boxes affixed to each window, and raised beds lined the path to the front door. They turned around to admire the view its windows would afford. The sea. Right there, out in front of them, just across the road. Kate gave Finn a one-armed hug.

"It's wonderful. I'm so happy for you." She rubbed his back.

He stood there looking out to the sea, and then back to the house.

"I've loved this house for as long as I can remember. Nick and I used to fish just out there," he pointed to a sand bar that extended off the beach. "That was our spot. I came close to buying this place in my crazy days, but it's just as well I didn't. Probably would have lost it in the end."

"Do you want me to wait outside while you take your first steps into Chez Murphy?"

"No, that's where we're different, Kate. I don't keep myself to myself quite like you do. I admire that you can though, it's not a complaint. No, I'd like you to walk through that door with me. A way for the house to know you're welcome anytime." He took her hand. "Come on."

He took a key out of his pocket and walked up the front path, opened the door, and guided Kate ahead of him, "after you."

The front foyer was narrow, but with an incredibly high ceiling and simple moldings at the top. Kate dropped Finn's hand and went wandering in and out of the main floor rooms. Including the kitchen in the back, she could see it was a renovation of which Anya would instantly approve. Lots of old detail, but thoroughly modern. And bright. The late morning sunlight poured through a series of enormous windows, one right after another across the length of the kitchen. The windows opened out to a well-tended back garden, complete with a gazebo that had a table to easily sit as many friends and family as one would want to share a meal. And it was framed, to her delight, by two palm trees. She felt Finn's presence behind her, and turned to see that his often bemused face had taken on a look of complete serenity. She took his hand and kissed it.

"You have the look of a man who's come home."

He kissed the back of her hand in return, dropped it by her side, and draped an arm around her shoulder.

"I think you're right. This will be with me for the long haul. Keys for everyone though. My sister and her family will need a place when they move back to Ireland. Just temporary until they get settled, but I'm happy to know I can offer them this while they sort things out. Do you want a key, Kate?"

She went into an immediate brain freeze. Flashing back to the times—not many, but a few—that the man in her life pressed her for some form of commitment or another. Her unwillingness to make one always led to an ending. Sometimes right away, the reaction of a wounded pride. Other times, it became an elephant in the room that led to awkward silences and a drifting apart: a failed regrouping after Kate said 'not now' rather than the 'no' she lacked the courage to utter. In both scenarios, she came to understand later, she was wildly disrespectful to the men who dared to put their hearts on the line like that. She had been unkind. Of course, there were some instances where the man asked simply because he thought that was what he was supposed to do. She was of an age that placed the men in her life in the last row of a generation where such thinking was in play until only recently.

"No, Finn, you hold onto that. I want to be here again. But I want it to be with you, and I expect you'll have a spare key handy."

He smiled at her and rubbed her shoulder, the way he did when he thoroughly approved but didn't necessarily agree. And the way he often did when he was just about to run his fingers through her hair, rest his hand on the back of her head, and pull her in for a quiet kiss. And this he did.

"Have you ever been in love, Kate?"

"Many times. I've been lucky that way."

"Good. I'll need your help with this."

Finn showed her the rest of the house. They admired the furniture that came with it: just a few pieces here and there. And they admired the water views from the upstairs windows until Donal honked the horn. Their signal that it was time to head to the airport. Finn to London, and Kate to New York.

They were a tangle of arms and legs from the minute they piled into the car. Kate began to drift off to sleep as the car turned onto the N11 roadway.

"None of that, Kate. You can sleep on the plane. Talk to me."

She kept her eyes closed. "Ask me anything."

"Who taught you that thing you do on my thighs?"

"A fly fishing instructor in the Bahamas. He did wonders for my cast."

"I'd like to send him my thanks. What is it about the back of my neck that you find so intriguing? You're often up to something back there."

"Are you complaining?"

"Not at all."

"Does it make you nervous...my snooping around back there?"

"None of that. You're not allowed to ask. Just answers from you."

"You have a little cluster of freckles back there. If I squint just right, they look like a happy face."

"You're back there squinting at me?"

"Among other things."

"Now it's your turn."

She thought about it for a minute, and looked out the window at the passing landscape.

"Do you miss living in Ireland?"

"Sometimes. But when I'm here for any stretch, I miss New York. It's been twenty years since my first film. I've grown accustomed to the back-and-forth. It suits me now."

Then he drifted off, and Kate did too. Donal woke them up at the airport, loaded their bags and St. Brigid onto a trolley, and wished them well.

They went as far together as possible, then faced the point at which they would have to split directions to board their separate flights. Kate through the American security area, Finn to a less complicated process for his short flight to London. They held onto each other as long as they could.

"See you in July?"

"See me in July."

Kate looked back just as she approached the elevator with her trolley of treasure. Finn was there, across the way. He raised his hand and smiled. She waved back. He was grinning, with his head at that same crooked angle of bemusement that was becoming familiar to her.

'July,' she mouthed silently. And she turned around to guide Brigid ahead.

✦ ✦ ✦

She saw Kevin, holding Molly—and a tutu-wearing Penguin Pete—in his arms. The two of them were waving frantically, Molly bouncing up and down in her godfather's arms. When Kate was close enough, Molly leaped out of Kevin's arms. Kate caught her, and the two of them held onto each other with everything they had.

"Kiss nose, Molly?"

Molly pulled back just enough to honor the request.

"Did you get bigger while I was away? Did you grow in just a few days?"

Molly nodded enthusiastically. "I bigger. Pete bigger."

They made their way to the car. Kevin put Brigid in the trunk along with Kate's suitcase, while Kate got Molly settled in her car seat.

"What do you have in this thing?," Kevin shouted from the rear of the car.

"Books. Always books. Couldn't help myself." Kate climbed in the backseat next to Molly, and the two of them smiled at each other all the way to Water Street.

✦ ✦ ✦

"There's a welcome committee waiting up there…and supper too," Kevin announced as they packed into the elevator.

"Spaghetti?"

"Sgetti?"

"Yup, sgetti, meatballs, the works."

When the cage opened into the apartment, the entire extended Doyle clan was there to greet it. There was a banner stretched across the living room, with multicolored handprints—Molly's contribution—interspersed through *Welcome Home Kate and Brigid.*

Everybody began talking at once, and Kitty came out of the kitchen to hug her daughter, while Sean grabbed the suitcase and brought it into Kate's bedroom, and Margot helped Anya lift the bubbled Brigid onto the Table for Ten so they could begin unwrapping her.

"You look tired, honey, but I want to hear every single detail."

And so did the rest of the clan. But first they wanted to see Brigid, who, once Margot and Anya had her padding removed, did not disappoint. If anything, the flight seemed to make it shine even brighter. With glasses full, she was toasted by the group, and Kate placed her back by the cage, so she could resume her job of protecting Kate and Molly's home.

The entire family fit around the Table for Ten. The Doyles were at their most quiet around a meal, but this time they were hyper-attentive. Nobody interrupted Kate—a first!—as she relayed her Dublin adventure, judiciously editing out a few private details. They took ice cream into the office, where Kate held court from the sofa, with everybody standing around to get a look at the pictures she narrated. Kate began to run out of steam at about the moment the last pictures—of Ciaran, Finn, Kate, and Brigid—were swiped into view.

"Whoa. That Ciaran looks like trouble walking," Margot said in blatant admiration. She couldn't help herself. All of the women nodded their heads in agreement, while Sean and Kevin squinted to get a closer look at what had the women in their lives swooning.

"You got that right," Kate replied. "And you don't know the half of it."

"You need to turn in, don't you?" It was Kitty. Ever the voice of reason.

"I do. And from the look of Molly's eyes, so does she. Do you all mind if I throw you out? I was there just long enough to get on Dublin time, and now I'm wrecked. And leave the dishes. I'll load the dishwasher. The rest can wait until the morning."

There was some minor protest, but they eventually acquiesced and filed up to Anya's for coffee.

Kate and Molly got ready for bed. Hands and faces washed, teeth brushed, jammies on, Kate helped Molly under the covers, tucking the blanket right up under her chin.

"Night night, Molly."

"Night night, Katie." She kissed Molly's nose and Pete's too. Then she added a little something to their ritual before turning off the light. The last thing Molly heard as she drifted off to sleep, cuddling Penguin Pete, was her Auntie Kate, whispering "bí ag brionglóideach I nGaeilge" into her ear.

ACKNOWLEDGMENTS

I was fortunate to have friends and family in Ireland and the States who were willing to read drafts, share their wisdom, and encourage this project along. Special thanks to my mom, Carol, Chip, the Goose, Robin, and Terry. To editor Jane Murray, who misses nothing (any errors are entirely my own); Caoimhe Ni Bhraonain, for the translations; David Blinken, who provided the cover photo of the Brooklyn Bridge (visit www.davidblinken.com to request permission for further use); and Daniel Beddow, who designed the cover. My thanks also to the numerous proprietors on Dublin's Francis Street, who let me roam their antique shops in search of a table that could stand for this tale's St. Brigid. I owe a particular debt of gratitude to Martin Fennelly Antiques, where I was introduced to the history of campaign furniture.

Like this story's Kate, I turned to The Brooklyn Historical Society to answer questions about the house where Washington and Emily Roebling lived and worked during their years spent supervising the building of the Brooklyn Bridge. I am grateful for the Society's archives and encourage readers interested in the history of the area to pay them a visit. Other invaluable resources included Robert Furman's *Brooklyn Heights: The Rise, Fall and Rebirth of America's First Suburb* and, of course, David McCullough's *The Great Bridge*.

This is a work of fiction, but there are three characters very much based on real folks. Alan represents a great friend with whom I shared many a pint during my years living in Dublin. Cheers, Alan. The real Vogelmanns, while musical and fabulous and very much in love, do not live in Brooklyn.

ABOUT THE AUTHOR

When not lecturing and publishing in the fields of drama and Irish Studies, the author writes fiction under the name Sarah-Jane McKenna. She is also a dedicated reader of history, collector of fancy pens, and better athlete in her mind than she will ever be in reality. This is her first novel.

Kevin and Kitty arrived first, and they came with enough bagels to feed an army.

"Hello? Hello! Where are you?"

The sound of her grandmother's voice brought Molly racing into the living room. She was wrapped in a yellow towel that had a hood with duck ears on it, and she was scooped up by Kevin before Kate managed to catch up. Kevin grabbed Penguin Pete from St. Brigid and put him nose-to-nose with Molly.

"How are you this beautiful Saturday, Molly?"

She beamed at her godfather. "Tickles!"

"Oh, I'll give you tickles," he said as she wiggled out of his arms. "And I'm a big scary monster too!" He chased her into her bedroom.

Kate kissed Kitty, and peeked into the bag.

"Yum. Bagels."

"That's right. And Margot said she would bring juice and a salad. Do you have cream cheese?"

"I sure do. Come on, let's make some coffee. And, tell me, do all little kids like being scared? She can't get enough of the big scary monster routine. Between that and tickle sessions, I barely make it to lunch every day without needing a nap. I'm exhausted."

Kitty put the coffee on while Kate grabbed a platter and

cleared off the table.

"Well, she's about the right age for it. You were just a little older—maybe three and change—when you were enchanted by monsters. Eileen too. The boys never went through that phase though. I think they were too busy scaring each other. Where's a table cloth? I'll help you set the table."

"It'll be more like cloths than cloth. I still haven't gotten around to finding one that fits this beast of a table."

"Beast it may be, but you were right to buy it."

"No regrets on my part. I love it."

"Me too. Oh, those are perfect," she said admiring the first two table cloths that Kate grabbed from the drawer. "Hand them over, and grab the plates and things."

They managed to finish setting the table before Kevin appeared with a dressed Molly. Her hair was wet, but combed, and she opened wide to show Kate that she had brushed her teeth.

"No socks, Auntie Katie." She stuck out her tongue and said, "Ah."

"Very good, Molly. Nice breath, and it's good that your teeth aren't wearing socks."

"No socks, no socks," she chirped, shaking her wet hair, and eying the bagels. Kevin grabbed her, as she was about to climb in a chair.

"Not just yet. We have to wait until the company gets here."

"Sean and Auntie Gogo?"

"Yes, and a special guest." *Special guest*. Two words guaranteed to get Molly bouncing on the soles of her feet.

"Speaking of which," Kevin turned to Kate, "when does his majesty arrive? I didn't know there were morning flights from Dublin."

"There aren't. He was supposed to get in yesterday afternoon, but his flight was delayed. He got into JFK in the middle of the night, and then there was a snag at customs. Something about his passport. It apparently took hours to get sorted out. Neither jet lag nor Customs seem to have spoiled his disposition though. He's texted me every half hour to double-check his directions. He's chipper as ever."

"I'm going to freshen up," Kitty said, strolling toward the bathroom.

Kevin pushed his glasses up his nose and rolled his eyes. "What is it about this guy? I mean, I saw the pictures too, but, you all behave…well, you all behave. You should have heard Anya when I told her he was coming over. She was a little pissed not to be the one to meet him with a key to Finn's place."

"Bad word," Molly whispered to no one in particular.

Kate laughed. "You're right, Molly. Kevin said a bad word." She turned to her brother, "we surely do behave. But then all the Doyle women have excellent taste. You'll just have to trust that. And wait until they actually meet him, we'll need smelling salts."

And with that, the elevator opened.

"Perfect timing," Kate said, welcoming Sean and Margot. "What did you bring?"

"Hello would be nice," Sean said, handing her two grocery bags and kissing her cheek. "Where's my niece?"

"Here, Uncle Sean, here I am. Tickles?"

"Tickles it is," he replied, bending at the waist to charge after her. She squealed and raced to her bedroom. Sean would let her win.

"Kate, do you might if I leave you and Mom to the getting ready?," Kevin asked. "I want in on that tickle fight."

"Not a problem. We have about fifteen minutes, if Ciaran's last text is accurate. He should be close to High Street about now."

"Do you think I should go look for him?"

"I offered to, but he said not to bother. No, let's give him a few more"—she was interrupted by the buzzer from the lobby—"and there he is."

Kate buzzed him in, and gave him directions for the elevator through the intercom. Along with the working fireplace in Kate's office, the elevator was part of what made the apartment so unique. The old cage, with accordion door and period buttons, opened directly into the living room. There was also a door from the stairwell, but most visitors took the elevator. The only exception was Finn, whose claustrophobia made the stairs a more practical choice.

The apartment occupied a full floor and there were enormous windows, but neither was particularly unusual in old DUMBO buildings. No, what made this special was that Anya had purchased the building from a man who was only its third owner. Three owners in well over one hundred years, and none had made major changes. What was done was primarily in the name of convenience: popcorn ceilings in the stairwell, cheap carpeting in the lobby, that sort of thing.

Getting rid of those was Anya's first order of business when she began working on the place. Where moldings had been torn out, or fireplaces boarded up, Anya turned to photos at the Brooklyn Historical Society to replicate the originals. It was a labor of love that she expected to fund an early retirement, and she was sinking every cent she earned into maximizing its marketability, particularly regarding sustainability. Hardly a month passed without some green advancement or another being considered. This summer's project was a rooftop deck and garden. She hoped to have it ready in time for everybody to watch the Fourth of July fireworks from the roof.

"Come on, everybody! Get out here." Kate stuck her head into Molly's bedroom, where the entire group was entertaining Molly and she, in turn, was charming them. "Come on, come on," she waved them out.

Kitty and Margot each took a quick glance in the mirror that hung over Molly's dresser before filing out to the living room. Molly adjusted the sparkly tiara that was now sitting atop her head, and clapped her hands. Sean and Kevin shook their heads.

The entire group was lined up to greet Ciaran by the time the elevator ground to a halt. They could hear his voice through the door before it opened, "well, this is something."

And when he came into view through the accordion door, there was a collective sigh from a select few.

Kate reached out to open the grate. "Welcome to Brooklyn. Give me that bag."

He handed over his suitcase, slid an oversized duffle bag from his shoulder, and set it on the floor.

"You're a sight for sore eyes, Kate. Come here." He drew her in to a bear hug and kissed her forehead. "You're looking good," he said, releasing her.

He scanned the welcoming committee. His eyes stopped at Kitty, "and you would be Mrs. Doyle, I think. How do you do?" His took her hand and raised it to his lips. "This is a distinct pleasure."

Kitty gave him a seasoned side eye: "and you're all the trouble I expected."

"Will you introduce me this good-looking brood of yours?"

"I sure will. This is Sean, my oldest, and his partner, Margot." They nodded at him, and stepped forward to shake his hand. "And this is Kevin."

"Kevin. Good to meet you," Cairan said, shaking his hand. Cairan held the handshake a bit and slapped Kevin on the shoulder.

Molly peaked out from behind her grandmother.

"And this is Molly."

Cairan fell to his knees, put his right hand over his chest, and bowed his head. "Well, now that I've met a real Brooklyn princess, I can say the trip to America was perfect. Howiya little one?"

Molly giggled, delighted that he noticed her tiara, and looked up to Kate.

"Old Finn?," she asked her aunt. The adults held their collective breath, unsure just how Cairan would respond. But he laughed.

"Old? Old you say? Well, would an old fella have known to bring this?" He reached into the duffle bag, and pulled out a little bundle wrapped in tissue paper. He unfolded the paper and held out a plush doll. It had orange yarn for hair, blue blinky eyes, and was wearing a dress, socks and shoes made of every color of the rainbow.

"This, my Molly, is Rainbow Brite. And she's come all the way from Ireland just to play with you."

She reached out for the doll, her eyes big as saucers. When she looked back up at Cairan, he was holding his hand out for a shake. Molly took his hand—her first time shaking hands with a big person—and it was clear these two would be fast friends.

"Thank you."

"You're very welcome. And there's more in this bag. A little something for everybody. But, first, if you don't mind, Kate, where's the gents? I could do with a wash up before I go upstairs to drop my things off at Finn's. Oh, I see you've laid out a feast there," he said, glancing towards the table. "So then, maybe a nibble before I head upstairs. But I can't stay long, I'm knackered."

Kate led him to the bathroom, while everybody else made their way to the table. Molly placed Rainbow Brite on the window sill, so this exotic creature could be part of the party too. Cairan lasted all of an hour, devouring a plateful and handing out goodies from Dublin. There was a bottle of whiskey each for Sean and Kevin; another for Kate, along with a box of chocolates for her and one for Kitty; and there was a coffee table book for Kitty that featured window boxes of Dublin, many containing geraniums that would rival her own on Pineapple Street.

"And this," he said, reaching in to the bag one last time, "is also for Kate. Special delivery." It was a manila envelope with her name on it. "Your man in Westmeath—Daniel Dempsey—called me to go look at his table. You know, the sister to your St. Brigid. He had your address, but didn't want to trust these to the post." He slid the envelope across the table to Kate. "His father gave these to Daniel when he heard you'd paid a visit last month. Said you would be interested in them."

Kate eyed the envelope with a mix of suspicion and

curiosity. She was a researcher at heart, and when her hand touched the envelope, it buzzed like a metal detector on an abandoned beach. Mysterious envelopes were her particular brand of treasure.

"I'll leave that with you and fill you in with what I know after I get some rest. Everybody," he looked around the table, "I can't thank you enough for the welcome. But this old Finn," he winked at Molly, "has been up for two days."

He slowly raised himself from his chair, and looked to Kevin. "Would you give me a hand getting into Finn's apartment? I have a key and a code, but I think I'll fall asleep in the lift, if left to my own devices."

Kevin got up, grabbed the suitcase and reached for the duffle bag. "This is still heavy, what do you have in here?"

"Just a few provisions. Comforts of home. I'll carry that." The two men disappeared into the elevator, leaving Kate staring at the envelope, and the rest of the family staring at her.

69233169R00156

Made in the USA
Middletown, DE
19 September 2019